"*Feminist on Fire* by Coleen Kearon (Fomite Press) is a raw, taut fictionalization of the life of Pamela Kearon, the author's aunt and a founding member of the radical group The Feminists, active in New York City in the 1960s and 70s. Shifting forward and back in time and written in the first person, the writing is as disarmingly beautiful as the subject matter is harrowing."
—Susan Rukeyser, Necessary Fiction

"Coleen Kearon's bravely imagined family story tore me up. Her aunt's life, in all its energy and pain and contradictions, broke my heart while her novel stands as a powerful reminder: how often, how easily we dismiss someone — too angry, too crazy — when what we need to do is pay attention, listen with compassion, hear the truth. "
— Diane Lefer, award winning author of *California Transit*

"*Feminist on Fire* is a slim, fractured, and hauntingly visceral first novel. Kearon's prose is as muscular as the sun, illuminating the dark reaches of femininity and sexuality and strength from angles too often unseen. Structurally innovative, like life itself, Kearon's first novel is a powerhouse, a small miracle."
— Jessica Hendry Nelson, author of *If Only You People Could Follow Directions*

#triggerwarning

Coleen Kearon

Fomite

Burlington, VT

Author's Note:
This is a work of fiction, and its characters and events are the products of my imagination. In its writing, I have drawn inspiration from the many colleges and schools I have attended, visited, and read about over many years; the various occupations in which I've worked; and the untold number of people I've known well, just a little, and have read about in my lifetime.

ISBN-13: 978-1-944388-10-2
Library of Congress Control Number: 2017939667

Cover Art
"Paper Home" © Dominique Gustin

Fomite
58 Peru Street
Burlington, VT 05401
www.fomitepress.com

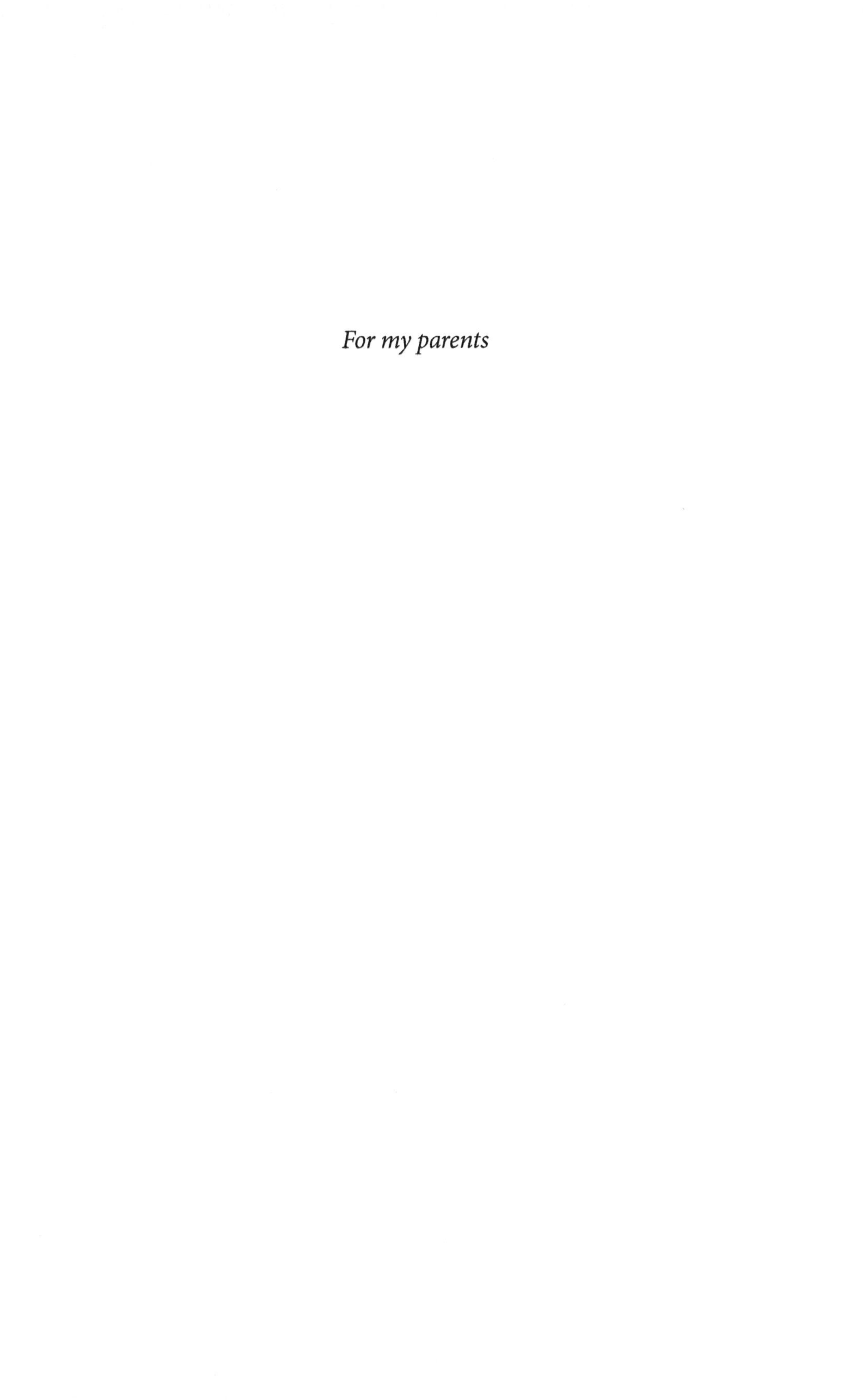

For my parents

"There is a gentrification that is happening to cities, and there is a gentrification that is happening to the emotions too, with a similarly homogenising, whitening, deadening effect. Amidst the glossiness, of late capitalism, we are fed the notion that all difficult feeling - depression, anxiety, loneliness, rage - are simply a consequence of unsettled chemistry, a problem to be fixed, rather than a response to structural injustice or, on the other hand, to the native texture of embodiment, of doing time, as David Wojnarowicz memorably put it, in a rented body, with all the attendant grief and frustration that entails."
—Olivia Laing, *The Lonely City: Adventures in the Art of Being Alone*

"Madness, in its wild, untamable words, proclaims its own meaning; in its chimeras, it utters its secret truth."
—Michel Foucault, *Madness & Civilization*

Clutter

I am an old room. I spend most of my days nostalgic for daybreak, for the quiet, undisturbed blue-gray air with its layers of nearly invisible floaters, shifting in five-, ten-minute increments and according to the light. I also take pleasure in the empty table and chairs. The heavyset table is like something from Henry VIII's Whitehall. It took a small army of faculty and students to bring it through the entrance twenty years ago now. Facing south, the French doors. West, a stone fireplace that was built by a Vermont stonemason in 1950. The fire pit looks like the mouth of a cave. Sometimes during faculty meeting, someone's eye will drift over to this portal, imagining a way out.

It is getting on half past twelve. The front door of the building swooshes shut as the faculty makes its way back from the cafeteria for Monday Meeting, which has been held in my room, the Manor Lounge, since the late 1960s. From year to year, the punctual faculty members can usually be found in their offices by twelve-thirty. I believe that like me they enjoy the relative quiet and perhaps they also like to imagine the building and its many rooms vacant and unused. Free of human clutter. Others, also present in any random semester, rush in at the last moment: alfalfa sprouts twist from their long hair or cling to their beards like pinworms, and a smudge of tahini dressing dries on an upper lip or in their cuticles.

My sense is that people have become more irritating over the years, and that this is the origin of my and the early-arrival faculty's craving for deep silence. Or perhaps with age I've grown weary of their complaints, impatient with their inability to sit quietly. Too many let it all hang out, and seem to have found a means of doing so without misgiving. They are "taking care of themselves," they say, with a barb of self importance, when what they are really asking is for others to take care of them. "Could people not talk in the hallways, play the radio in their offices, let doors slam, bring in baked goods with fat, sugar, or salt to holiday celebrations?"

Big and small issues alike seem to have become conflated. Unwanted ambient noise and unwanted sexual advances and rape are argued over with the same urgency. Dissatisfaction hangs in the air, smog-like.

Community Meeting is another famous Baines gathering. It happens right after lunch on Wednesdays in the cafeteria. Here, students, staff, and faculty try to beat back student drug use and the allure of cutting and suicide. Date rape and incest and molestation and violence and neglect are also dredged up, picked over. People yell, sometimes there are tears. I know this because whatever happens at Community Meeting gets talked about within my walls, at Monday staff meeting. You could almost say that Monday meeting is a meeting about Wednesday meeting, though it's not as upsetting because it excludes the students and staff. But it's not not upsetting. There's always one or two faculty who want to carry on where Community Meeting left off. They turn their steady gaze to the school; accuse it of cultural and institutional insensitivity. The school is entitled and ignorant, they say. It is the white male and the dominant paradigm all rolled up into one. The sound of their wronged voices natters on long after the last faculty member has straggled out from between the French doors, sometimes well into the night. I look backward and forward to the early morning, before the cars and the footsteps, before the light begins to bleed from the sky, when I am filled with darkness, and the distinction between the mouth of the cave that is the fireplace and the black air between my walls is negligible.

The Tours

Buffy Campbell had visited Baines College only once before she moved to Vermont from North Carolina with her husband Ash, for a full-time teaching position. That was for her interview, back in late June. Some of her adjunct teaching colleagues in and around Durham, North Carolina, were vaguely impressed when she said the college's name, though it was clear they were uncertain what they knew about the small, liberal arts college in Plainfield, Vermont. They didn't know much, nor did Buffy, but that didn't stop her from feeling proud when she told them about the full-time, salaried position she'd been asked to interview for, and later, the job she was offered and had accepted.

Baines College's business office had sent her plane tickets and a letter explaining that she would be picked up from the airport in the Baines van by a student. She'd stay at one of the campus dorms, and be reimbursed for meals. Repeatedly, she'd read the tickets and the letter and touched them, as if they were invitations to the beginning of a real, and not provisional adjunct-teaching-and-living-exactly-where-you-finished-your-graduate-degree-two-years-ago, life.

A mundane failure: that's how Buffy had felt toward the end of her time in Durham, when she kept running into all the same adjuncts at the community and junior colleges where they taught a section or two of English and Introduction to Composition. At first they'd all smiled and talked about their applications for real teaching jobs. But they'd left off that sort of optimism after the first year. As the second year past graduate school got underway, their greetings were reduced to silent nods. But with her plane tickets, Buffy felt saved from her outsized sense of failure. She'd been in Durham too long, and felt like everyone saw how stuck she was, as if she were a giant sore thumb announcing her disappointment in herself—or mirroring others' disappointment in her. It was hard to tell where self-hatred began and ended. What she really needed was to cast herself in some other story altogether.

Baines College was far away and exotic-sounding, as colleges go. An hour or so online was enough to learn that in the 1960s and 1970s, Baines was a well-known radical, alternative college, without grades or a set curriculum. If you followed the Internet crumbs, and Buffy did, there were descriptions of Baines's past and present notoriety.

In the mid-1960s, poet Allen Ginsberg had declared Baines "the center of the universe" after his poetry reading at the Haybarn Theatre. Nude and smiling students had followed a dancing Ginsberg out of the theater to the path that circled the Village for Learning— its smattering of dorms — and into the surrounding woods, playing bongos, flutes, and guitars. Drugs, famous writers, and naked people were why people had heard of Baines. No one had ever led, nor would ever lead, a bacchanal procession into the woods near the University of North Carolina at Chapel Hill. Buffy didn't much like modern poetry, bongos, or drugs, but it was hard to deny the nostalgic pull of the 1960s, the world turning over a new leaf, or so it was thought at the time.

In the letter that accompanied her plane tickets, Nicola Williams was designated Buffy's "faculty buddy." She would take her to breakfast the morning after her arrival and escort her to her interview. There was no picture of Nicola on the college's Website, just the cardboard cutout of a woman's silhouette and her bio: Originally from Ohio, with a Ph.D. in education from Stanford, a master's in divinity from Yale, two books on gender studies, and a casual mention that she had played in an internationally known gamelan ensemble. Buffy had to look up gamelan, and then she wondered how someone from rural Ohio fell into playing Indonesian music. Not to mention the advanced degrees and books. Buffy had managed to publish only two short stories and an essay since she'd graduated with her master's in English from UNC. When her thoughts drifted to Nicola and her cameo image, Buffy's sense that she rated a full-time teaching job deserted her. As unconventional as Baines sounded on the Internet, it managed to attract the kind of over-accomplished faculty you'd find anywhere. She imagined Nicola Williams eating crackers and drinking a glass of wine, small crumbs showering Buffy's CV as she looked around for a non-existent second page.

A work-study student named Matty picked Buffy up at the airport at four o'clock on a Sunday afternoon. He had lank, reddish brown hair, and he smiled when he saw her recognize her own name on his homemade sign. He wore sunglasses inside and cutoff shorts, and his feet were bare. Reaching down for her bag, Buffy got a whiff of garlic, and also an old pillowcase smell.

"Let me get this," he offered.

"Thanks," Buffy said. She couldn't take her eyes off Matty, wondering if he was representative of the student body.

She followed him out of the small airport, watching his dirty bare feet slap against the pavement. People didn't seem to notice his feet or his smell, as Buffy knew they would have at Raleigh–Durham International. They climbed into the illegally parked van, its blinkers going in the drop-off lane.

Matty pulled out without looking. She noticed a frizzy shock of underarm hair as he turned the steering wheel to the left, oblivious to the taxicab driver glaring at them. The temperature was in the eighties and the air in the van was close, despite the open windows. Waves of nausea ebbed and flowed at the base of her throat, and her heart began a thunderous galloping that made matters worse. If she puked she'd want to die on the spot.

"Music?" he asked.

Buffy nodded, not wanting to open her mouth. She thought music would mean less talking; as it turned out, it just meant music *and* talking. Matty was a talker. Thankfully, he was fully capable of carrying on both sides of the conversation long enough for her nausea and the rising panic to ease off.

His MP3 featured a mix of death metal and jam bands. Leaning in, he turned up the volume on a weed-whacker/guitar sound, shaking his head meaningfully.

"What year are you in at Baines?" she asked.

Matty squinted at the windshield, calculating. "I'm not sure. I've taken time off to work in Nicaragua a couple of times. Moved back to Manhattan a few times. My dad lives there. I can't seem to quit Baines. Or graduate," Matty said happily. "I keep coming back." He nodded and laughed. Buffy found herself nodding back at him.

Matty's right index and middle fingers operated the steering wheel as he spoke excitedly with his left hand, waving it in the air.

"Where else can you do shit like rebuild a VW engine as your semester project? That's the real thing. Learning by doing, John Dewey, you know?"

"So you did that?" Buffy asked, her voice uncertain.

"Ah, no. Jon Fishman did. You know the band *Phish* right?" He nodded his head, anticipating her agreement. "They went to Baines, back in the eighties."

"Yeah, I've heard of them," Buffy replied. "I guess I read they went to Baines."

"Man, they used to play the Baines Springfest. Now you can't see them unless they're like on a hundred acres of land."

They were like the Grateful Dead, Buffy remembered. A jam band that featured the same kind of long guitar and drum solos to which Matty was just this minute bobbing his head. Buffy had read John Dewey somewhere along the way, or maybe she'd just heard about his theories. She understood the general concept of encouraging students to explore things they were naturally drawn to as a way to develop their passion for learning. The rest would follow. But rebuilding a car engine just sounded weird. Vaguely, she wondered if her fellow adjuncts would be so impressed now, seeing and hearing Matty at the wheel. Probably not. Probably they'd smile enthusiastically to conceal their bewilderment, as she was doing now.

After leaving the vicinity of the airport, Vermont was every bit as beautiful as people had told her, even those who'd never visited. They'd heard.

From a distance, the low mountain ranges took on a smoky blue color, and the late-afternoon sun forked through thin, white clouds.

"It's gorgeous," Buffy said.

"Vermont is amazing," Matty said. "Whenever I return from New York or Boston, I love crossing the state line back into Vermont."

"Hum." Buffy took a deep breath and leaned back, the air hitting her face. After putting off her exhaustion until she made it here, she now felt the full force of its pull.

Matty continued to talk, telling her about the time he had to fly into Manchester, New Hampshire during a snowstorm because the Burlington airport was closed, and how he'd hired a limo to drive him back to Plainfield.

"Big-ass American car with no snow tires and rear-wheel drive, and this guy cruises past everyone like it's the middle of summer. Tells me he usually delivers human organs from Dartmouth Hitchcock Medical Center to Boston and New York."

There was another time on his way back from Boston in the fog: he hit a deer. And another time. Matty kept on talking, and Buffy nodded, the whole forty miles from Burlington to Vermont's capital city.

"I'll drive through town," Matty said, as he took the Montpelier exit.

Buffy moved to the edge of her seat, not quite understanding the meaning of "the smallest state capital in the country." She was prepared for the 40 thousand souls of Burlington rather than the eight thousand residents of Montpelier. Downtown consisted of two streets, which on this Sunday afternoon at five p.m. were almost empty.

"Pretty," she said, when they stopped at the one intersection in town.

Matty pointed out a bar and a couple of restaurants that she would not be visiting on her one-day trip, his underarm hair now damp, less springy.

Plainfield must be bigger, Buffy thought. She hadn't really read that much about it, but she assumed it was like any other college town. In the letter that outlined her visit, the human resources person had told her she could walk downtown from the campus. She imagined herself free of Matty and the requirement to talk, settling into her room and walking to the café where the college had an account, Happy Valley.

The eight or so miles out to Plainfield found them driving alongside cornfields and cow pastures. Off the main road, dirt ones, like small riven arteries, trickled past corner-lot homes with GARAGE SALE signs at the bottoms of their driveways, but no people, only closed front doors. Meaning you'd have to bring your prospective purchase and ring a doorbell or knock until, she imagined, an older, stony person answered the door, only after looking through the curtains or shades drawn against the light. The farther they drove, the fewer homes they passed, until they reached the town, with its small grouping of old peeling-paint Victorians and dour saltboxes. The kind of town you drove through on your way somewhere else and wondered what all of these people did for work. Or what they did at all.

"Would you like a tour of the town?" Matty asked.

Buffy shook her head and swallowed the lump in her throat. With stark determination, she held her tears. She just wanted to make it to her room without crying.

When Matty gestured to Happy Valley, with its homemade CLOSED sign, Buffy's heart dropped, a small stone into a bottomless well. Plainfield was not a typical college town. Just one small main street, which intersected with Route 2 at a blinking light strung above a treacherous hill. Besides Happy Valley, there was a closed breakfast place, an empty laundromat, and a pizza place, whose large fan was audible from the passenger seat, blowing the warm air onto an empty sidewalk.

She'd packed a nutrition bar and cashews, and she considered that they'd have to do, rather than a fancy reimbursable meal. It was either her snacks or a slice from the empty restaurant that hadn't bothered naming itself beyond an old discolored PIZZA sign.

"Okay," he said, pulling into the Baines College campus a moment later.

Buffy felt Matty looking at her. He surprised her by saying, "I know, it's small, but it's a great place." He nodded and smiled. "Once you get to know people at Baines, it's its own little universe. It really is a special place."

Buffy nodded back at him. It was nice of him to say. Smiling, she replied, "I'm just tired. It doesn't seem like it should take a whole day to get from Durham to Vermont, but I've been up since five this morning."

"It's brutal, I know. I just drive whenever I can," Matty said, as he pulled up beside a brown-shingled dorm called the Garden Building. The kids had gone home for the summer. A skeleton staff was here only during business hours, Matty explained.

"But a friend and I are staying in the president's cottage while he's away." Matty pointed back at a small, similarly shingled cottage, its gingerbread trim and trellis making it look not quite real, but fanciful and something you might pay to tour.

"Just call me if you need anything. I help out in the summer in exchange for staying here. Do you need my number again?"

"Let me double-check, but I think I wrote it on my ticket information." She riffled through her book bag. "Here it is, thanks," she said, peering into her purse.

As she climbed from the van, Buffy's legs felt stiff from sitting all day. She blinked at the pretty campus: at its leafy trees and the pebble footpaths, toward the stone fences like parentheses enclosing the upper gardens, a profusion of bleeding heart bushes, bachelor buttons, and day lilies. Matty grabbed her luggage from the back seat.

"This was one of the original seminary buildings," he said, as she followed him inside. The hallways were long and dark and in permanent shadow, as the light from the half dozen or so small rectangle windows failed to reach very far. Buffy steeled herself against the nautical, cold pocket air, wrapping herself in her arms, the lump surfacing at the base of her throat again, lodged there.

"The campus is not that big, but it's spread out. There are some great trails between buildings."

She nodded at the back of Matty's head on the way up a short set of steps.

Buffy's room faced the second-floor stairwell. She closed her eyes and listened as the set of keys jangled uneasily, and one after the other clicked, refusing entry.

Finally, under his breath, Matty said, "Bingo."

Relieved by the unexpected light and warmth in the room, Buffy smiled, walking toward the large picture window with a view of the grounds, its gentle hills and trees, and the shingled cottages and dorms. On the mural facing two single beds, an old woman in a worn housedress and low pumps swept snow from a rooftop, seeming to dance above a small town. There was a small closet and a handcrafted Shaker desk and chair. No mirror or radio or television.

"The bathroom is at the end of the hallway," Matty said, placing her luggage at the foot of the bed closest to the window. "And there's a refrigerator and a microwave in the kitchen downstairs."

"It's very nice," she said of the room.

"Yeah, you can think here, if that's what you like to do. Some people don't." He smiled at her. "Those are the ones who go back to whichever exit they came from in New Jersey."

Buffy laughed a little, and Matty smiled at her.

"Like I said, call if you need anything," Matty repeated.

"Thanks, I will," Buffy replied.

When he left, she sank into the too-soft mattress and noticed four chickens at the bottom of the mural taking a leisurely walk down the main street over which the woman swept the snow. The suggestion of the chickens' movement was strong, vivid, and she followed their small steps as she nodded off. When she woke at seven-thirty that night, the June daylight confused and disappointed her, forcing her to wait for the lowered expectations of night. Always, she felt easier at night, more like a dissolving dot in a black sky, rather than an adult with responsibilities who had to wake up and go to work every day.

For a moment, Buffy couldn't remember where she was. Through

the window, guitar music, drums, and a lackadaisical vocal faintly drifted and she remembered Matty and *Phish*. As she woke up more fully, she
realized the stomach cramp jammed into her side meant she had to pee
so bad that she might not make it down a hallway.

Outside her door, she tripped over a large Tupperware container
and a bottle of water; a fork and knife clattered to the ground. She ran,
relieved to reach the toilet on time. Yanking her jeans to her thighs, her
body relaxed. The sound of urine splashed so urgently she was glad no
one else was in the building to hear.

Closing the bathroom door behind her, with its little man-woman
Unisex sign, something she'd heard of but had not seen inside of North Carolina, she walked back toward her room, considering the Tupperware dish.
Reaching for the opaque plastic lid, she noticed sweat beaded on the inside
of the container. Buffy leaned over and plucked off the Post-It with her
fingers. It was signed, "Matty and Ami. Ami's famous Eggplant Parmi-
giana!" There was also a salad and warm bread, and a tiny cursive invite:
"Join us for a glass of wine if you like!" For a moment, Buffy wished she
were the kind of easy person who would join them. But no. She closed
the door, ate the still-warm meal in a few urgent bites, and called her
husband, Ash.

Lying down again, the pull of gravity too strong to resist, she held
her cell phone close to her ear and tried not to sound like she was yelling.
The reception was about what you'd expect in a town of a few hundred,
surrounded by mountains.

She led with, "It's beautiful here." A safe bet. She couldn't quite bring
herself to tell him about what she thought of the college and its probable
Matty-like student body. He was pulling for her to get this job. After all,

she'd complained loudly and relentlessly for the past two years about how much she needed that first break.

Ash was also a jobless IT person, going on a year. She knew he had good reasons for wanting her to get a full-time position. Buffy couldn't decide which was worse: the ordeal of him looking for a job and all the waiting and rejection for the first six months, or his seeming to have given up altogether over the past six months. Both sucked.

Trying to sound happy, she said, "The kid who picked me up and his girlfriend just left me this amazing meal. It was really sweet of them. I would've called earlier, but I fell asleep. I was so tired."

He asked her questions, and she supplied the answers. A review of the salient details as she stared at the blank ceiling. The filling toilet came to an abrupt stop at the same time she'd begun to hear it, and wonder if she needed to go check on the tank.

"My interview is at ten tomorrow. My faculty buddy picks me up for breakfast at eight-thirty," she said.

She mentioned how small the towns were in Vermont, knowing that most people living in the triangle of Raleigh-Durham-Chapel Hill, as they were, couldn't quite imagine Vermont's scale, and the lack of malls and mini-malls and McDonald's flanking either side of any given road. Just cornfields and cows, dirt roads and unmanned yard sales.

"That sounds great," Ash said.

"It is, I guess."

Like all of her friends, Buffy eschewed the suburbs, with its cars and four-lane boulevards and the identical Bed Bath and Beyonds and Pier Ones. How to explain how lonely she felt here: the isolation suffocating, the silence buzzing in her ears?

Hearing the slight whine in her voice, Ash said, "You don't like it?"

"No, no. It's not that. It's just, I dunno . . . I didn't realize it was so small. Reading about it, I just didn't realize, you know, that there'd be dirt roads and hardly any people."

"You just got there, sweetie. It's different, that's all. Change is good." She sensed his tired, cajoling tone. "Give yourself some time."

"I will. I'm sorry. I'm just really tired. It's fine."

"Knock 'em out tomorrow. I know you'll be great. You're a great teacher, you know that. Call me before and after the interview."

"Hum," she replied, knowing she'd wait until after. "Okay. Talk to you tomorrow."

"Things change, and they'll change again," her mother had said crisply, when Buffy confided that Ash was a different person since losing his job, that things seemed different between them.

"I know," Buffy said, and her mother softened.

"You'll get through this. Everyone hits rough patches in marriage. Totally normal."

"Right," she replied.

Right. Buffy was sick to death of feeling mired in average problems. Money and work and rough patches; she was just beginning to understand that that's mostly what life was—dealing with shit.

She pressed End on the dial pad. The screen briefly flared before it died altogether. Panic fluttered in her chest, as she felt the hallways on the other side of the bedroom darken. Buffy saw herself in the small second-floor room of the former seminary, located at the top of the stairs, where anyone's eyes would be drawn upon entering the building. If someone came to murder her, who would hear her screams? Matty and Ami likely wouldn't hear her cries through the guitar riffs. She decided that if she didn't put her light on, no one entering the building would even know she was here. It helped that she was so tired she fell asleep in her clothes, not washing her face or brushing her teeth until she woke the next morning.

******

At 6:15 the sun rose on the mural, on the chickens' small, gossiping faces, their red feet, and the woman dancing on the rooftop. Buffy could more clearly see the veins on the leaves that hung just outside her window and, in the distance, one of the trails Matty had mentioned.

From the bathroom window, she saw the path from a slightly different perspective. She noticed a sign that read LIBRARY, with a rainbow-colored arrow. The tree canopy formed a fairy-tale arch, the foliage still new enough for the sunlight to pass onto the trail. She and Ash had gone camping last summer, but since then she hadn't been anywhere near the woods. She thought it would be nice to walk and get some air. Back in her room she removed the clothes she'd flown in, which still smelled like the cramped, gray air of the too-close seats and the overhead bins of the plane. She put on the pajamas she'd brought along, which looked enough like a thin gray sweatsuit to pass as one should she run into anyone, although she didn't think it would matter to anyone here if she was out taking a walk in her pj's.

Peace flags were strung between trees at regular intervals to mark the main path. There were other smaller and less worn paths, up hills and down to ravines. She looked into the trees, trying to see the loudly singing birds, but all she caught was a wing, a flash of brown or white out of the side of her eye, and the motion of branches in the birds' wake. The archway continued the length of the trail, about a quarter mile, the sunlight weaving in and out overhead.

The library was a modern, low-lying brick building with alternating long and narrow glass and wood panels. As she got closer, she noticed a large mandala made from colored glass chips, polished stones, and shells near the entrance. It was dedicated to victims of war. MAY THEY LIVE AND REST IN PEACE. Buffy crouched, running her fingers over the swirling pebbles. Glancing up, she saw hundreds of crows watching her from their roost. Buffy's cell phone dinged in her jeans pocket. She stood and the crows burst into the sky in silent agreement, no cawing. A text:

"Hi Buffy, Nic had to fly to New Orleans last night to pick up her new baby! She got the call from her lawyer yesterday morning, and she only had so many hours to get there. I can pick you up for breakfast and take you over to the Manor for your interview after. See you soon. Matty."

Buffy faced a six-person hiring committee: a student couple who lived off campus, two faculty, and two staff. Most had stuck to asking her questions about her educational philosophy, but one, the plump and unfriendly-seeming librarian, asked her which books were on her night stand. Because it was unexpected, the question had the quality of a slap on the hand. She sat there for an uncomfortable moment or two before she remembered: *The Sheltering Sky*. The librarian had simply nodded; the dean smiled; the others looked into space inscrutably.

Afterward Buffy ate lunch with Dean Myers and his wife in the upper gardens. They shared sandwiches from Happy Valley Café, sitting together on limestone benches in the shade of a tall oak tree. Where the abbreviated stone fences left off low hedges continued, creating a private garden. High in the oak the birdsong was loud and clear, the singing sustained.

"From about 1870 until the 1930s, Baines was a Quaker seminary and, as such, part of the Underground Railroad," Dean Myers said. "There's a lot of history here. There's a secret passage in the Manor House where the monks hid the escaped slaves," he added, looking over his shoulder and in the direction of the Manor.

"We'll give you the grand tour after lunch," said the dean's wife, Shelly.

The Manor House was similarly brown shingled. It had more white trim than the other buildings, a deep, elegant porch and an ornate, filigreed veranda on the second floor.

Inside, Buffy blinked away the sunshine as her eyes adjusted to the rich maple wall paneling. A winding staircase came into view at the bottom of which the dean and his wife waited for her.

"We've been here for over ten years, and I still feel a hush when I step into the Manor. Like I've stepped back in time," Shelly said, her hands flourishing through the quiet air.

Dean Myers smiled at Buffy, "After you," he said.

Buffy followed Shelly up the wide steps, craning her neck to take in a large chandelier near the top of the dizzying swirl. Heavy, glass drops were perfectly still, silent, while the weight of Buffy, Dean Myers, and Shelly on their way up the stairs was loud and rude, like bedsprings squeaking rhythmically in a private act.

On the second floor, they passed one locked door after the other, the faculty traveling or gardening, or whatever it was they did over the summer. Buffy noticed evenly spaced florescent strips on the ceiling that neither Shelly nor Dean Myers had thought to turn on. The only light came from the large window on the second story landing, and small, high windows at either end of the long hallway.

Midway down, Shelly depressed a length of wainscoting, the sort of subtle architectural detail that people loved about old homes, as she explained the façade concealed a hidden room that was used as part of the Underground Railroad. The slender length of wood popped open.

"You wouldn't guess it was there just looking." Shelly pointed. "It just looks like a broom closet. The room is way in the back,"

You had to turn sideways to fit in, which each of them did, in turn and in silence.

"I've never seen anything like it," Buffy said, stepping back into the hall, moving from the historical Baines to the existing one.

"I know." The dean nodded. "Some people think the Manor is haunted. I tend to not believe in ghosts. But there's a definite feel to the building, I'd have to agree with that."

"A lot of Baines is that way," Shelly said, widening her eyes. "Things in the air—I've always felt that here."

Shelley moved to close the panel and the dean smiled at Buffy.

"It's mostly the kids who think the Manor is haunted," Dean Myers protested.

Shelly rolled her eyes at Buffy. "He's a true skeptic. That's a good thing, of course, seeing his office is here. Some people claim to have heard cries and banging through the walls."

The dean smiled at his wife. He shook his head. "Onward," he said, turning. Buffy followed him. Behind them the door sealed with a click.

Buffy didn't believe in ghosts, but it was sometimes fun to pretend they existed. In the too quiet hallway with the dean and his wife, and outside, the birds wildly singing, for a couple of seconds time seemed portentous, and as they walked away she had the impression they were leaving someone or something behind.

The hidden room was the first thing she'd told Ash about her visit to Baines when she called him later that day, remembering the cool, dark air and how the sound of the birds' cries carried through the open windows, reaching back into the damp walls, a peaceful, empty space now that it no longer held the burden of concealing escaped slaves. She told him about her walk to the library.

"You sound better," Ash had said.

"I am. I do, I feel better. I took a long walk this morning, before my interview. It really is beautiful here," she said. "And different. I think you'd like it."

"Yeah, me too."

On the flight back, Buffy kept seeing her quiet dorm room, the mural and the view of the footpath to the library, its tree branches reaching overhead. She also replayed her and Matty's talk on her ride back to the airport, like she was eavesdropping on old friends. There was something about Baines, the small campus, and its impassioned credo. Sweet Matty.

Two days later she accepted the job. The day after that, her contract arrived via FedEx. An email from the HR person at Baines gave her the name of someone renting out a small home near the campus. In a weeks' time, Buffy had signed, called, and emailed her makeshift, adjunct life away.

It would be another month before Buffy found out she was pregnant. By that time, she and Ash were just about to leave for Vermont. After weeks of being tired and nauseated, and not just in the morning but all the time, she bought a pregnancy test. Even after she wrapped the plastic test strip in toilet paper, it made a definitive, hollow whap sound in the tin trash can under the bathroom sink. She didn't want a baby was all she thought, as if thoughts had that kind of power.

Fifth of July

The mailman, Perry, has come and gone for the morning. I listened to him, as I do most mornings, wondering what his words mean. He talks to himself. "Yeah, I know," I'll hear him say. Or, "That's the way it goes." Today, he swore, not under his breath, but loudly, when the wind picked up just as he opened the front door, slamming it closed behind him with a force that shook the building. "Fucking hell."

In the summer months, when the students and faculty are gone, he leaves the mail in a covered box on the small counter to the right of my window. It's not an actual window, mind you, but a split door, the top of which unfolds, opens, and is hooked to the back of the wall. If it's during the school year, the window-door is open from 8 a.m. until 4 p.m., and one of the sleepy or high or homesick students stares out. When the kids are gone for the summer, the window remains closed. My desk is dusty and free of clutter, the air in my space cool, dark, and murky, even on bright summer days, save for when Matty, the only student here for the past two summers, stops by to deliver the mail proper.

He removes the box from the counter next to my window, and I hear him going through the keys on the large ring he carries around with him all summer until he finds the correct one.

"Bingo," I always hear him say.

My overhead lights blast on, or that's how it feels, an assault of too much light too soon. The sound of Matty is jarring at first. He places the box on the clear desktop and shoots letters into the cubbyholes that line one of my walls. That large wall fixture was salvaged from a defunct elementary school over twenty years ago now. Its various sections are joined by pegs you pull apart, and it's easy to disassemble and reassemble. It's an old piece, probably around since the early 1900s, and I consider it my defining feature.

I know it is July Fifth because there wasn't any mail yesterday, and I heard fireworks on and off throughout the day.

Matty has turned on the radio. With two days' mail to jam into the overstuffed cubbies, he will be here longer than usual. On WBCR, the Baines College community station. Democracy Now plays; the low voices from the radio are urgent, yet barely audible.

The front, outer door slams shut. It is a couple of hours after Perry has come and gone, and it's still windy. Matty turns at the abrupt sound, a letter in his right hand, poised for delivery. There is a knock on my closed door. He sets the letter on my clean desk, flicks at the hook, and unfolds the top half of the door open toward him, where you can hook it to the interior wall. An unknown figure appears at the window. Brown clad, shorts for this time of year. He is athletic and convincing.

"This requires a signature," the UPS man says, indicating the small package in his right hand.

Casually, he looks at the address again, the name. His square jaw and prominent brow are saved from being strictly Neanderthal-looking by the unlikely addition of high cheekbones and soft blue eyes, out of which he brushes a slick of blond hair.

"It's for Matthew Feldman."

Matty reaches for the package.

"Are you Matthew Feldman?" he asks.

"You're looking at him," Matty says.

The UPS man watches Matty sign the electronic pad, and then he hands the package through the window. He turns and looks out of the bank of cloudy windows next to the front door. He mumbles something under his breath, and a vehicle bottoms out over the washboard drive, traveling so fast my walls vibrate with the force of its speed. Car doors slam shut as the UPS man moves to the side of my window.

"Wait a minute," Matty says. "What's going on?"

The UPS guy raises his arm in time to catch the front door before it is sealed closed in the wind as two men in suits enter the building. The first man has bushy tufts of red-gray hair around his ears and neck, and an otherwise bare head; the second man is so bald his smooth skin shines. The man with hair unhooks the eyelet to the bottom portion of my door. He punches it open with his fist, banging it against my already bruised wall, two large scuffs exactly where the different levels of the door are hooked to the wall. The bald man steps in front of Matty, approaching him.

"You are under arrest for receiving hallucinogenic substances in the mail with the intent to distribute."

"Wait a minute. I work here," Matty says. "I'm the only one here, so people send stuff to me! I don't know what's in there!"

"You'll have plenty of time to tell us all about it," he says, wrenching Matty's arms behind his back. He recites the Miranda rights.

"You're hurting me!" Matty protests.

His partner places one of his hands on the back of Matty's head and pushes it down to his chest, like he's closing a book.

Matty yells, "Get your hands off of me."

"Shut up," the bald man says, as the three of them perp walk Matty out my open door, into the hallway.

The UPS impersonator, who has been leaning against the window this entire time, watching only, props open the outer door with the rubber wedge that resides in the corner dust. He kicks it under the jam as the men try to push Matty, who goes limp, his full weight resting on the men's arms, his feet scraping against the concrete, as they pull, rather than shove him toward the waiting car. I realize he is making the authorities drag him to their vehicle. There used to be a list posted on the wall that now features a fair labor practices flyer about recommended tactics when under arrest that don't amount to resisting. There was an illustration that Matty now mirrors exactly.

"I want a lawyer," Matty yells. "I'm going to sue your asses off."

The air coming through the open doors creates a wind tunnel that ruffles the expired notices on the bulletin board inside of the door, and even down at the other end of the hall. Their fluttering precedes the heavy footsteps that land like kicks on the old Linoleum tiles.

A state trooper arrives, so tall he dwarfs the three other men. He draws out yellow tape the length of my door. CRIME SCENE it says. I hear other vehicles pull up, all of them banging over the washboard drive, their car doors opening, then slamming shut, as though none of this can be done quietly. Ami appears outside the Community Center door asking what is going on here, her question and her confidence blatantly ignored by the three men. It is the UPS guy who addresses her without meeting her eye.

"You need to stay where you are," he says, and Ami freezes.

The four member skeleton staff present on this fifth of July, run down the stairs from the second floor. The urgency of their steps also shakes the building's foundation, its walls. The trooper tells them to please stay back as four other men in uniform file in, one after the other. The letter that Matty was about to shoot into its cubby drifts under the desk in a gust of air.

"Call my dad," Matty yells at Ami, as the men in suits push his crumpled form into the running car.

"Get off of me" are the last words I hear Matty speak.

The trooper approaches the staff.

"Who is in charge here?" he asks

Gretchen Wright, the human resources coordinator, steps forward. Though she is a tall woman she reaches his chin at best. She says her name and extends her hand to shake. He gives her a search warrant instead.

"We'll be searching the mailroom and Matthew Feldman's current residence," he says, then turns away, effectively erasing their concerned faces from his sight lines.

I hear the vehicles speeding away from campus. I can always tell the difference. When cars leave the grounds, they are traveling uphill, and their engines shift, groan a little. It is especially true of box vans, like the one the UPS impersonator arrived in.

In a few moments only, Matty is gone. Ami yells to the staff that she *will follow them to the Montpelier police barracks in the school van, where the man in the brown costume told her they were taking Matty. In the next few hours, the police who are left behind, including the giant state trooper, turn out every drawer and closet and all the cubbies, and they dump boxes full of recycled junk mail over my once clean desktop. The debris eventually lands in heaps on the floor. They search for drugs that aren't here. I overhear the staff in the hallway say that they are "turning the dean's cottage upside down, too." They wonder who tipped the police off, and if the drugs were Matty's or, as he claimed, sent to him by a student due back in the fall who knew he'd sign for the package. The possibility that he didn't know what he was signing for makes everyone quiet. They mention other drug busts on or near campus over the past three or four years, two students and one former student. I know from listening to the kids who've worked here that there have always been rumors that the FBI taps Baines's phones, and Gretchen Wright now repeats this claim. It isn't just the drugs that make Baines a target, she continues. All colleges have those to deal with. It's the school's lefty politics. Long ago visits by people like Allen Ginsberg and Cesar Chavez linger in the imaginations of the local people and the authorities. "They want to punish us," she says. "They fear anything different."*

Many hours pass before the police finally leave. They close but don't lock my door. They don't turn off my lights or the radio. ProPublica, then Quilting Today, play along in the silence. Gretchen Wright stops by at around six p.m. to lock up. She steps around the piles of mail and memos, a small, high-pitched squeal escaping from deep in her throat at regular intervals.

******

*The day after, Saturday, as Perry arrives, I hear him say, "Dumb kid."
He whistles. "Man," he adds. Then he is gone.*

*The following Monday I hear people in the hallway talking about how
Matty's arrest made the local papers and all their Internet counterparts,
and for a day, the News Briefs section in the "Boston Globe". In the "Montpelier Times," the Central Vermont newspaper, there were a few letters to the
editor about how the cultish, drug-worshiping, hippie enclave in Plainfield,
always a blight on the community, the college without grades, has proven
once again not only how useless it is, but how dangerous. Not far away,
there is a high school. Children. The most vitriolic letter is from former faculty member Elmer Boone. Nell, the switchboard operator, mentions this.
She has been at Baines forever. A native Vermonter, she pronounces her
vowels flat and a little hard, and I'd recognize her speech anywhere. Over
the years, she's come to have as much clout with the students, staff, and
faculty as any president. And she has outlasted them all. She says Elmer
Boone's name with a barb of disapproval that everyone I've heard speak of
him shares.*

*Elmer Boone was fired after he'd simply stopped working last Novem-
ber. Word was that student papers and Post-its piled up outside his locked
office door, and that his whole section of the hallway took on the character
of disuse before it dawned on everyone that he had no intention of returning. The rest of the faculty had to assume his duties. Faculty memos and
instructions landed in and were plucked out of my mail slots as the faculty
agreed, or did not, to fill Elmer Boone's absence.*

*He moved to Vermont from Wyoming for the position, and no one can
figure out why he is still around. He's had a punk band named after him.
Warm copies of flyers have curled into perfect O's in my dark cubbyholes*

twice during the spring semester: "The Elmer Boone Experience, Tonight at the Haybarn, 9:00 pm." Baines kids are creative, irreverent. They are easy to love.

Mind-altering substances will always be dangerous, and always they will exist— and be used. Is their sale to college kids on a remote campus, kids sitting around in their dorms listening to Phish, really worth a twelve-year prison sentence?

Each day that Gretchen Wright collects the mail Perry has delivered, turning on the lights and carefully placing letters and envelopes in their corresponding slots, I think of Matty's expert hand, of pieces of mail landing in their boxes, featherlike, and his under-the-breath exclamation, "Score," and the emptiness inside my walls fills with sadness. The days fall away, and we're out of July and into August and then at its end, the fall semester about to begin, the nights cooler already.

Second year Baines student Ally Littleton heard herself howl and was secretly gratified when she noticed people's heads snap to attention, weary flowers, blown upright in her rage. "Breeders!" she bellowed. Assuredly, her chin jutting upward, she stepped from behind the lectern. On each side of the cafeteria stood eight foldout tables about ten feet long, with brown, simulated wood tops. The plastic, ugly to begin with, was now scuffed and had grown a sort of gray matte finish from years of being dirtied and cleaned. Lunch had been crowded today because pizza was on the menu instead of tempeh chili or a marinated slab of tofu. Ally had a large audience because most of the lunch crowd had stayed on for Community Meeting, which was not always the case. She focused her attention on the two tables in the front, where the faculty usually ended up assembling. She turned an especially hard glare on Pablo Ramirez, who sat in the very front row, though she stopped short of singling him out. Next to him was the new teacher, the pregnant Buffy Campbell. Ally let her eyes travel from Pablo's chin, his chest, to Buffy's small, round belly.

Ally knew how offensive she was being, she thought it was hilarious that most people seemed to not understand that she aimed to offend. They thought she was misguided by anger, a blinded feminist cliché. But Ally felt renewed by anger and by feminism. She felt clarity. And anyway, fuck what people thought.

Pablo had been her favorite teacher when she first came to Baines, two years ago. He taught photography, filmmaking, and video. Ally had actually spent her first Christmas at Baines with his large family. She still had pictures of herself with his twin girls and two boys, spaced one year apart and products of hormone treatments, he had once confided in her. At the time, she'd just thought the babies were cute. But now she believed that if you couldn't have kids or it was so difficult that you had to artificially goad your eggs into doing their job, like Pablo's wife, Ruth, why not leave it? People always fuck around with nature, manipulating it in the ugliest ways to meet their needs. It sucked. Maybe there were good reasons why certain people couldn't reproduce; maybe we should listen to what nature has to say for a change, was what Ally now thought. Let it the fuck be.

Along with the baby fat around her face and midriff, Ally had shed her soft, accepting self during the past year. Simultaneously she'd found a cause in zero population growth, or negative population growth, even. Less. Fewer. Of everything. Public policy in support of population con-trol would mean an automatic unshackling of women. And while they were doing the whole excess hormone manufactured-egg-thing, why not test tubes until birth for women who freely chose to mother? Women's role as sex and baby machine would finally die.

As she looked into the cold deep at the centers of Pablo's eyes, she understood that he'd gotten over the acute betrayal he'd felt when she'd first begun to speak out against population growth and heterosexual preference. He'd armed himself against her words, actively ignored their meaning. She could feel him ignoring her. Or trying to. Good, Ally thought. You should be afraid of me.

Ally lowered her voice, making it confidential.

"We need to think hard about the things we value and why. The people we value."

Her voice quavered. They were listening. She smiled at the rows and rows of heads and shoulders, in silhouette almost, given the stone gray November air that always managed to seep into the air inside as well, no matter how many lights were on. Plus there were those overhead fluorescent strips that emitted only the stingiest kind of light, pale white rays like something from a nuclear winter.

"Is it intrinsically good to procreate? Is it even ethical, given the state of the world, to keep mindlessly reproducing, when there are so many people who are already here, suffering? she asked.

As Ally scanned the crowd, she noticed Clyde Drewry and Tristan Krummel leaning against the wall nearest the cafeteria entrance. There were a handful of people she didn't like at Baines, but Clyde and Tristan were scary as shit, too. Every week, there were stories about how they'd terrorized their writing class, interrupting people as they read, using their critiques to annihilate the other students. Someone in the unofficial school weekly had referred to them as a three-dimensional comment section of a right wing paper, in an open letter called "The Matrix Reloaded Twins," that did not use their names. No need. Everyone knew who the letter was about, had seen the two of them bully-walking around campus like one of them, and Tristan in particular, might purposely shoulder you and laugh when you fell. Tristan was the leader, you could tell. He noticed Ally looking at them first, and he pushed his tongue into the side of his cheek, his hand in fist near his lips. Alongside him Clyde laughed. The disgusting motion only lasted a split second. When Ally next looked at him, Tristan stood up straight; he stared at her intently, like he couldn't wait for her to speak again.

Looking away, Ally continued.

"We need to re-imagine and redefine what a family is. It's not all about having babies and buying houses. Our society is so nuclear family focused. It's just not healthy."

Tristan whooped and clapped loudly. "Ally, tell us what it's like to be a late term abortion," he yelled. "Is that what we're talking here, you freak of nature?"

At this the crowd erupted, the word "assholes," moved through the crowd in waves. Ally's best friend, Sarah jumped up, and Gretchen Wright, the HR person also stood, her hand in the air, "That's enough. Tall and loud, she got everyone's attention. "You're leaving now," she said pointedly, to Tristan. Clyde laughed beside him, a burst of glee and she said, "You as well, Clyde."

Sarah smiled and gave a thumbs up to Ally as Tristan and Clyde walked off, backward middle fingers held up to the audience. Students applauded and stamped their feet rhythmically, and the staff and faculty seemed to collectively look around to see if any authority might take hold of the situation. No one did. The Dean of Students, Dean Myers, the one most likely to intervene, wasn't there yet. He usually came in at the tail end of the meeting to make announcements no one listened to.

Ally said into the microphone, "A few more housekeeping details." A big, gratifying laugh from the audience. It was one of Dean Myers lines, and once he said it, he couldn't stop with the housekeeping details.

Community Meeting, a Baines College tradition, along with Meal Team, Community Green up Week, and going nude when you felt like it, was held each Wednesday afternoon at one. On Ally's first day at the college, two boys, Hazelo Cast, or Hazy as he was known, and Du-Pont Mayer, had streaked by her bare-assed, their legs and feet caked in mud, holding aloft a box full of bean sprouts, small green peppers, potatoes, and lettuce that they'd just harvested from the lower garden. About twenty minutes later they were behind the counter serving lunch, clothed, but just barely, in women's lingerie. Ally's instincts about the college when she'd first read about how it was "alternative" and "student-centered," had been right on. She fit in at Baines, loved that it wasn't inert and drab, like her whole experience of school before Baines, had been. It was wild, thrilling. People here were art, they were politics: none of that was separated out, but integrated in who they were, the choices they made. Baines was the most dynamic and globally holistic environment that she'd ever been a part of and she was grateful for its existence. She had felt giddy just being on the periphery of the pervasive buzz on campus that first day, and while at first she had been a little bummed that her parents hadn't bothered to stay and help her set up her room, after the naked lunch episode, she was relieved.

Their faces would have screwed up in shared recoil. Her mom and dad didn't actually like each other anymore, but they did join forces to express dislikes and disapprovals, judge and jury moving closer in proximity to purse their thin lips and frown. Had they stuck around for any amount of time, they would have found a lot to scowl at and eventually their ranks would have closed against her. It's possible their eagerness to get her gone would have been somewhat diluted, and they might have hesitated slightly before leaving their adopted and only child, however wanting she'd turned out to be (the dyslexia and the solid B grades, her innate inwardness, all of it rankled the two of them: not what we ordered!), in a place where, scrawled on the bulletin board in the women's only dorm, in red, gooey lipstick, were the visiting hours for men for the seven days of the week, with a succession of zeros written in the Canadian form, with a slash through their centers.

Ally knew that her parents would have eventually driven off. It was too late to get her in anywhere else, after all, and they were itchy up there in the front seat, couldn't wait to begin the process of easing her from their lives (and the backseat of the car) now that she was finally an adult and they wouldn't be judged as harshly for not really wanting her around that much. But if they'd seen the nude boys and the obscene lipstick scrawls they would have felt obliged to at least go through the motions of expressing concern about leaving her with a bunch of whack jobs. They just might have taunted her with the idea that they would turn around and go back to Tenefuckingfly, New Jersey, with its rich people and tribal brick homes edged in circular driveways, and its green, green grass, courtesy of the landscaping company that everyone used named Chemlawn. Alongside the uniformly robust and verdant yards that Chemlawn manufactured, they left signs warning people not to let their dogs or children play on their poisoned grass. Fucking Chemlawn!

Ally caught Pablo's eye again and she thought she noticed a flicker of recognition. His arms were neatly folded across his chest, his face implacable and in the next moment, she doubted any sort of acknowledgment.

"I'd like to invite my therapist to hold a guided imagery to better educate and sensitize Baines's staff and faculty about the gay, bi, and transgendered community. The overemphasis on the heterosexual paradigm, with its breeding imperative, creates a hostile environment in the world at large, and right here, to sexually fluid people. For our community to truly evolve, that needs to change."

A few students in the back of the cafeteria clapped. Hazy Cast shimmied, saying, "Yeah baby," and people laughed.

Pablo's chair scraped against the linoleum. He stood, slicing his hand through the air in a veiled bit of arrogance.

"This sort of attitude does more to divide the faculty and students by casting everyone as being so different, when really they are all just people struggling to get along, and, essentially, the same."

"But some groups have more advantages than others," she countered. Brandishing her own hand in the air, she stepped from behind the lectern. "As a result, the advantaged groups are collectively more myopic than is healthy or helpful to those who are ignored by their sense of entitlement. Don't you think you can learn from the oppressed, the cultural underclass right here?"

"Actually, no," Pablo said. He walked around to the front of the table, his gaze alternating between Ally and the cafeteria audience. "I've been at Baines a lot longer than you have, Ally, and I've been led in plenty of guided imageries and have participated in all sorts of other consciousness-raising workshops and retreats—you name it," he'd said, checking the workshops off, dismissing them. She noticed that condescension had replaced the cold stare from earlier. "I honestly believe we'd do better to fully realize our similarities than to emphasize our differences, which we have a tendency to do here at Baines. I've stood by for too many years and let people dictate what I need to learn about them. I want my experience of people to be one of spontaneous discovery, not a proscribed crash-course in the pain they've endured. There's more to people than that, and I think when you start designing workshops around oppression and anger, you're suffering from the very myopic vision you're so critical of."

Ally cut her eyes away from Pablo and looked out at the expectant faces that stretched from the first row to the last. She tried to remember what she was doing up here. Floating a few inches from the ceiling, she watched herself and the others from a distance and above. The walls in the large, cavernous room swelled, and then receded; the floor buckled. Her new therapist, Kayla Freeman, who was her fourth therapist in ten years, called it disassociating. Approvingly, Ally thought, almost like she admired the odd spells. She understood that this technique, if you could call it that, was something she used when her emotional pain receptors reached overload, and like fuses, flipped off. All the intensity drained from her veins, replaced by absence and a vague sense of relief at not being present. The first time she had described this sensation to her therapist, Kayla had asked her if she'd ever been sexually abused. Incest and molestation survivors often disassociated, she'd said as she leaned forward in her chair. But Ally had never been touched inappropriately, or otherwise, come to think of it. Her parents and their families were not at all touchy-feely. Instead, she thought this tendency of hers might have more to do with how she felt inanimate while growing up, a mirror or a table positioned in a box-shaped room at the end of the second-floor hallway.

"I think Ally's disassociating, guys," she heard her best friend, Sarah Moore say. Sarah rose from her seat in the front row, throwing this line over her shoulder.

"Can you hear me Al?" Sarah asked. "Let's take deep belly breaths together." A deep exhalation, followed by a little cough, escaped from high in Sarah's throat.

Ally couldn't manage a deep breath, only a small shallow one, like she'd had the wind knocked from her.

"I can hear you," she replied from somewhere muzzy and far off.

Sarah was an obese woman, 5'9 or '10 and 250 pounds. Ally came up to her large breasts, which now shuffled toward her like amiable town-folk in a shared, hemp tunic. Her bare feet were pitch-black with dirt thick as tar. Taking Ally's hand she squeezed it, smiled, and bowed her head slightly. Sarah had lived in Japan and China until she was fifteen, and she liked to bow. Her father was a foreign diplomat or something. Not that long ago she'd been a willowy beauty, a Queen at a fucking Aza-lea Festival in Virginia or D. C. Ally had seen pictures of her on a float, luminous, skinny, and perfect.

Turning to the audience, Ally announced, "I check out sometimes, it's a past-trauma thing."

Ally was vaguely aware that people would assume some sort of aw-ful physical or sexual abuse, which wasn't the case. Ally's was psychic in nature. She was an unwanted child, and adopted child, neglected and feared. The list was fucking endless.

She hugged Sarah and scanned the many rows, her eyes moving from left to right, trying to focus. The people appeared small and awed, as if she'd been up here speaking in tongues. And maybe she had. It wasn't that much of a stretch to think that the ability to leave your body was holy.

"You're at Community Meeting, Al. 'Member, you wanted to set up a time for Kayla to come in and—" Sarah whispered into her ear.

Ally nodded her head. In the periphery of her vision she saw the salad bar and the cash register, the long bank of windows on the side wall of the cafeteria, looking out at the empty picnic table. On her first day she'd sat there with her parents and waited for the Resident Assistant to arrive with her room key. There'd been no talking, like they were waiting for a prison sentence or some other sort of bad news. After about twenty minutes Summer Stroymeyer had breezed down from the dorms, her blond dreads and loose halter top inviting not stares from her parents, but two sets of hastily averted eyes. Something clicked in Ally as she recalled this scene. Sensation returned to her limbs, and a slow smile spread across her face.

"Okay, I'm back." Ally laughed, raising her fist in the air.

There was loud applause, and a smattering of fists rose among the audience. In the front row, students from the women-only dorm stomped their feet like they were at a concert, demanding an encore.

Pablo was back in his seat. He said something to Buffy Campbell. One word only, whatever it was. Buffy raised her hand to shield her stomach, and caught Ally looking at her, which she continued to do long enough to make the new teacher glance away.

"Listen, all I'm saying is that it's important to have a dialogue about

these issues. You don't have to come if you don't want to, Pablo, or whoever else thinks they totally understand what it's like to live outside the
dominant paradigm. But for those of you who have even a little doubt
and would like to open up your minds, I would like to set up some workshops. Can I see a show of hands—maybe we could start like that—instead of like bam! rejecting the idea?"

Hands shot up all around the room. Colin, Ruby, and Shane, three
students in the very last row, and members of the Elmer Boone Experience, raised both hands and waved in tandem, singing the chorus from
their song, "731 Princess Anne Ave". *"You'd really have to be in in love, to
want to touch another person naked in this heat."*

Ally noticed Dean Myers arrive, and lean against the same section of
wall that Clyde and Tristan had vacated. Smiling, he nodded at Ally. Dean
Myers was one of the few people who really cared about other people.
He'd been in the Peace Corps and had worked for Habitat for Humanity.
He was kind of old and out of it, but Ally had always liked him.

"All right, then," Ally said. "Very cool! I'll arrange things and check
in next Wednesday, or, if I find out something anything before then,
I'll post it on the Community Board. Maybe we could get something
together by Christmas."

Ally was totally energized. Her body actually felt light. The ragged
hole in her chest that managed to feel heavy and empty at the same time,
closed just a little. Sarah squeezed her knee. It was hard to keep still.
She texted her therapist: We're on! Talk later." Everything she and Pablo
had said to one another, Ally replayed in her mind, carefully reliving the
applause that followed her statements. A couple of times during the next
hour, she looked over at the faculty table, convinced that they looked

cowed. Buffy Campbell's healthy glow at the beginning of the meeting, her tawny skin, the flushed cheeks an appealing dusky rose color, had taken on a green hue. Ally thought that the rest of the faculty looked similarly peaked, and she imagined that they were too frightened to confront the students publicly, but that that wouldn't stop them from holding some emergency session to rag on them in private. They were out of control, she imagined Pablo saying. Young people needed boundaries, parameters. He had shitloads of psychobabble to draw on from his gazillion years of being single. Judging from his bookshelves, he'd read every self-help book ever written. His wife, Ruth, had come from a personal ad in the local paper. To the relationship she brought her own brand of self-help vocabulary from her divorce, and she was always talking about how people had chosen all these really bad lives for themselves. Ruth liked to wonder aloud, idly and stupidly, what addicts and other unhappy people were learning from all their awful decisions. They learned nothing, Ally was certain, or not soon enough to be spared or to spare others a lot of useless pain.

The last person on the agenda was Dean Myers. He asked if any of the new faculty or students would like to volunteer for the Sensitive Issues Committee for the spring semester. Nobody said a word or even moved. Ally was already on SIC, and had been since its inception. With Dean Myers, she looked around at the crowd as he encouraged people to get back to him. "Anyone? Don't all raise your hands at once," he said smiling.

No one would volunteer. Eventually one of the students, staff, or faculty who hadn't signed up for their community service hours in time to get on the gardening, party planning, or meal team committee would get stuck on SIC. It was a committee that had been born after two date rapes and a suicide attempt on campus, all within three weeks of each other.

Dean Myers stopped trying to be jovial. His voice lowered a register, so that it became confidential.

"Sitting on committees is the best and fastest way to get educated about the inner workings of Baines, its guts and its glory," the Dean continued. "Next Monday afternoon at five, I'm offering an information session about the various committees, all comers welcome and we can talk about getting folks signed up then."

Ally noticed Pablo leaning in toward Buffy Campbell, whispering. This irritated her. She'd noticed before how they were together a lot. She wondered if he ever thought about having sex with her, even pregnant. Ally often imagined men she knew fucking. It was all they thought about, right? Or that's what she'd always heard. Every seven seconds. How could you not think about them fucking everything in sight? Like stupid machines. Kayla said she'd internalized this idea from the male dominant culture that surrounded her every waking moment. It was one of the things Ally was working on in therapy. This, and why she hated Pablo so much.

"There's something to that," Kayla always said. "Whenever you have that strong a reaction to someone, you have to look at that, kiddo."

Ally didn't think he'd come on to her, was what she told her.

"Well, there could be other things. Think about it. Write it out," Kayla had recommended. She hadn't, yet. Every time Ally began to write, she found a reason to do something else.

Her New Jersey therapist (Clinton Tillman—just thinking his name conjured his stooped posture, his bad breath, and his too soft voice) had said she needed to look at how her adoption had informed the anger that took up so much space in her life (his words). Ally now felt certain that her anger encompassed greater wrongs than anything that had happened to her, personally. The universe could be awful. You'd have to be stupid not to see that. Now, Clint not only seemed stupid but mean-spirited, always wanting her to "own' (his word!) her feelings, like they existed outside the crappy world that she lived in. Fuck you, Clint.

The meeting was winding down, though not over. People were restless, gearing up for the mass exodus. A few people had begun to openly talk. Ally looked at the clock behind the cash register, which was ten minutes slow. Three-fifty it said. Pablo moved closer to his briefcase, eyed it but did not yet reach for it.

∗∗∗∗∗

Ally was embarrassed to admit that at first she had really liked Pablo and his wife, Ruth. Even to herself she was embarrassed, and by now most of her friends had no idea that she had spent time at their home. A couple of nights a week sometimes. Ruth made her soothing cups of tea from loose leaves that she pretended to read. Once she'd told Ally that her life would be full of grace. Also she served fresh pesto made with basil from her garden, salads with tomatoes she'd picked earlier in the day.

Pablo took her on walks around their property, pointing at the smoky, blue mountain ranges. But little by little she had begun to think they were like everyone else. They just made it look different, with their pretty sun-catchers and their tapestries from Guatemala. Over time it really began to bother her, the way they insisted that everyone basically got the life they'd asked for and deserved—infants, toddlers, child soldiers the world over, blacks, women—anyone with gripes, or much worse, had made a decision about where they were and what they were learning from their shitty life. Ally hadn't chosen to be born. She hadn't chosen either set of parents. And one day she just started to hate Pablo and Ruth. Or that's what it felt like at the time. That sudden. It wasn't anything specific, but an aggregate response that burst onto the scene one February afternoon, her heart thumping as blood rose into her face and their voices chirped back and forth about personal choice. Who chooses to be fucking unhappy? she wanted to scream. And if someone did, didn't that mean there was something wrong with them to begin with, for making that choice? A sort of a priori unhappiness, bred in the bone, independent of particular decisions?

The dean thanked everyone for their time and walked back to his seat. People shifted in their chairs and began to speak, quietly at first. There was some laughter. Petra Armstrong, the pottery teacher, grabbed the microphone and apologized for not having signed up on the agenda. "I'll take just a minute," she said.

A large woman with a flat, pleasant face, somewhere in her forties and fit, she always looked she'd just come from a few hours of snowshoeing or hiking with her shepherd mix, Ollie. Petra explained how to sign up for the march on Washington, scheduled for the day after Thanksgiving, only two weeks from now, the cost of the bus fare, where they were to meet and at what ungodly early hour. As she spoke, Pablo got up and left through the side door of the cafeteria. He would be on his way to the Design Building to set up for his video production class. This time last year Ally would have walked alongside Pablo, asking him about what it was like to study at CAL Arts and Pratt. When she'd first met Pablo she'd ordered both schools' catalogs from their Web sites. Thick and glossy, they'd gathered dust on her bureau until she thought to throw them out, after deciding that Baines was where she was meant to be. It was now brilliantly sunny outside, and when Pablo opened the door a carefully demarcated yellow beam advanced into the dank, murky cafeteria, and then withdrew as the door slammed shut.

As she watched Pablo become smaller and smaller, moving along the footpath, Ally decided that the bad ending between her and the Ramirezes had been inevitable. That it happened to fall on the twin girls' third birthday, with all of Pablo and Ruth's friends and their friends' kids gathered around the picnic table with all of their names carved in the top, and that they loved so dearly, was something that sometimes she felt ashamed about. But other times, this circumstance pleased her.

Their birthday was on February first, nine months ago now. As Pablo and Ruth had doled out birthday cake, the conversation went like this:

"We're so lucky. It's not lost on me how lucky we are," Ruth had said. She shook her head.

"We're rich," Pablo replied. "In family, friends, and cake!"

"And the cool thing is that everything that's ever happened, the good, bad, the ugly, each moment has led to this exact spot."

"True. That's why we need to cherish each moment," he said, smiling widely so that Ally could see into the dark of his mouth.

Ally didn't think anyone else was even listening to them. Or not closely. It was their routine, so anyone who'd been around them for any length of time had likely heard this dialogue before. The more she listened to them, the more Ally thought they sounded like they were trying to convince themselves about how great the world was, and in the face of evidence of how not great it was, like everywhere you looked. As they spoke, the table was raucous with five-year-old voices, their younger siblings' cries and their parents' soothing sounds, dogs' tags clicking together and their high-pitched yelps when a child stepped on one of their feet, not that she could clearly delineate any of it without really concentrating, but it had a predictable rhythm nonetheless, a generalized roar that Ally wasn't part of; therefore, it was easy for her to focus on Pablo and Ruth's tremendously annoying duet while she made herself think about the puppy that had been cooked alive by two boys in Ohio or Indiana, wherever the fuck it was. One of those awful flat states. It had been in the headlines that morning, along with another about UN fucking peacekeepers who raped twelve-year-old girls living in refugee camps. Was it even twelve? Maybe it was nine. Probably it was.

"Like most people, you're full of shit," she'd begun, looking back and forth and directly into Pablo and Ruth's eyes as they stood, stunned, their arms suspended in midair-cake-serving mode. Her last words as she headed out the door—"everything about you makes me sick. Literally, like I could puke just looking at you"—had had the effect of quieting even the dogs and the youngest of the children.

And that's when Ally had found her voice.

Candy had arranged to meet her advisor, Helen Wallace, at the B-Side, a beloved greasy spoon on the Barre-Montpelier Road, a much smaller version of the strip mall roads you find everywhere, with fast-food yellows and oranges and shiny car dealerships, at ten on a Monday morning.

In her phone message she'd said, "I need to talk to you privately. I'd prefer if we did it somewhere off campus."

A few minutes before ten, Helen texted to say she was sorry, but she needed to move the meeting to 11. The longer Candy waited, the more she wanted to bolt out the door.

She had decided to tell Helen about her affair with the Dean of Students, David Leppert, in time for Monday Meeting. And it wasn't really the affair she was revealing. That was over. But she'd broken up with him, and David wouldn't leave her alone. A grown man with a family and a house and a good job stalking her was more disturbing to her than if he'd been another student. If he'd been a student, she could've told people at least. She could have reported him to the administration, and she wouldn't feel trapped. That was it, exactly: she felt like she couldn't turn around or breathe. Like she had no choice but to wait for his next move, and you never knew with a man when the next move was the one where you became another woman killed by your husband or boyfriend, or ex. Sometimes, she'd read in *Elle*, stalkers murdered the woman they targeted; their behavior escalated and the stalking was just the beginning of the story. If the women weren't killed, their lives were ruined. They were forced to move and change their names. Candy wasn't in the change-her name-category. But she had thought of leaving Baines to get away from David. Then, one cold-as-hell morning last week she'd woken up thinking it was totally unfair that she would have to go; plus, how would she explain such an about turn to her parents; plus, the scholarship money. Both Baines and the federal government had given her enough money to pay all of her tuition. She couldn't afford to walk away.

An hour after she'd gotten there, Candy rubbed her eyes, tired from all the bad coffee she'd drunk. The runny eggs and buttered toast she'd ordered and had only partially eaten, made her stomach roil. She listened to the voices from nearby tables, to the sound of the heavy dishware the diner used—almost the width of her thumb, she'd measured them— being stacked in bus trays by waitresses for the one scrawny bus boy to carry into the kitchen once they were full of dirty maple syrup and egg-streaked plates. Seated at the large booth by the front door, she was in peoples' sightlines as they were herded through the restaurant by the hostess— they couldn't help but look at her—and she was the only non-white person in the diner. For hours and hours it seemed she'd felt people register her. The awful words, nasty and demeaning that they may be saying to themselves, rained down on her, unbidden. She felt inert and on display.

Candy was Native American and Portuguese, her skin dark brown. In the summer, she became black, or close enough, the whites of her eyes, her teeth, and even her fingernails, pearl-colored. As a little girl, she'd watched herself turn darker and darker in the mirror each June, admiring the sharp contrast, the sense that she glowed from within. She still loved her color, thought it was prettier than white skin, with its spots and freckles and too-large pores. But by now, of course, she knew that her skin was not just her skin. It meant things to people. Bad things mostly, though at Baines, which was every bit as white as the rest of Vermont, Candy's status was perversely elevated. She was a moral superior, if nothing else about her was superior, because she was a #poorbrownwoman. Not an oppressor. Wouldn't it be great if that meant something other than people's sidelong glances wondering what *you* thought of *them*—still all about them, right? Sometimes she did her own guided imagery of what it would be like to walk through the world as a happy or just-living-your-life or raging out of control, mostly unconscious and unremarked upon, #bigwhiteman.

Finally, she saw Helen Wallace's pewter-colored Volvo wagon pull in. Helen was in her sixties, with short gray hair, black glasses, and ageless in a weird way. Candy had read her books. Or, mostly. She'd tried to get through her thick, definitive histories of Middle Eastern geopolitics. In her author photographs Helen looked no different at 29 than at 59. It wasn't that she looked young, but that she'd always managed to look the same, anywhere from 35 to 45.

Once inside the diner, Candy watched Helen pause for a moment to let her eyes and her person adjust to the dinginess of the place. The amber-tinted windows and wall-to-wall carpeting gave the diner a basement feel, the air flat, a trap for old, dull smells that you got used to once you were there a while but at first felt like they had plugged your nose with layers of grime.

Their advisee meetings over the past two months were strictly about her classes and assignments. This was unusual for a Baines advisor, most of whom took (or pretended to take) an interest in the whole person. Candy appreciated Helen's focus and distance, the way she took in her thoughts about what she was learning so seriously, as if Candy's mind and the way she learned to work it, were what was most important. Had Helen been a normal advisor, she would have known about Candy and David Leppert's affair already. Candy and David had known that, had congratulated their luck over Helen's singlemindedness, her academic focus, rather than the personal touch so many of the other advisors prided themselves in.

Helen slid into the booth and Candy reached toward the manila folder on the seat beside her.

It was Candy and David's emails, from the first time they'd agreed to meet in a Plattsburgh, NY hotel last spring, to Candy's breaking up with him, and pages and pages of David's desperate begging and pleading and then demanding emails. Worse, he had begun to approach her on campus, waiting for her. About to make a scene. "I love you, my life is nothing without you. I've told my wife," his most recent message claimed. Candy had begun to hate the sight of him. Wanted him to stop.

"Sorry I'm late," Helen said. The booth's heavy vinyl covering sank under her weight, made a farting sound that they both ignored.

Helen looked around for a waitress.

"I need some coffee," she declared. "Busy day, but they all are. It's nice to see you, Candy" she said.

It occurred to Candy that if she did not tell Helen Wallace about David, she might just leave the B-Side, and Baines at the end of the semester. She could feel herself a month from now, climbing into her rusted Honda Civic and driving out of Vermont, hating herself.

A different waitress from an hour ago swooped in. She was young, probably not much older than Candy, twenty, twenty-one maybe, her makeup thick and bright, meant to be noticed.

Helen asked for coffee and the girl said she'd be right back. Loudly, Helen's phone rang.

"Hold on a sec," she said. "I just want to turn this off." Helen fumbled in her briefcase.

Candy suddenly wished she wasn't here. She was so tired and it was all so stupid. She didn't even know why she'd ever liked David Leppert. Last spring her work study placement had been in the financial aid office, just next to his office, and each morning he hovered at her door, flirting; his eyes bright with joy at the unexpected sight of her here on the drab second floor of the Community Center, where all the administrative offices sat, implacable and boring.

She didn't dissuade him. Life in the administrative offices, even for fifteen hours a week of work study, was screamingly dull. They fucked in his office, his administrative assistant down the hall. And a few of the bathrooms, almost getting caught, not on one, but two occasions. It was exciting, at first anyway.

They waitress returned, a coffee decanter and cup hanging from various fingers, the saucer fitting in the crook of her elbow. They were quiet as she set items on the table, watched her deferentially.

David couldn't stay away from Candy, like countless boys and men, most of whom she'd slept with, and many of whom she wished she hadn't, starting with her older cousin, Joey.

It was summertime. Twenty-one, Joey had just graduated from Macalester College. Candy was twelve. He pushed her down in the weeds behind their family's lakeside cabins. He spat out his gum, and laughed in her face when she struggled. "Aren't you a beauty," he said.

Joey was cute. He was older and cool. Candy had a crush on him, like all the girl cousins did, ages six through sixteen, if she remembers everyone who was there. All their mothers joked with Joey about how he must be leaving a trail of broken hearts. And Candy had wanted him as a boyfriend. But he was never that.

Candy had just begun to realize that men, from her cousin to David, scared her. That she did what they wanted, what they insisted on.

Out of the corner of her eye, she saw the waitress was motioning with the coffee and she quickly slid her palm over her cup, shaking her head.

She placed the manila file on the Formica tabletop. It was huge and deep with the months' worth of email, printed and in order, but not very neatly contained.

"This is for me?" Helen said.

Candy nodded.

Candy slid the folder toward Helen.

"It is. I need you to read them. I need your help. Dean Leppert.... we've been seeing each other, for about eight months, I guess. But it's over and he just won't get it, he won't leave me alone."

Helen said, "Oh," the sound and then look of surprise in her o-shaped mouth and wide eyes. She touched the file's edge, smoothing her fingertips around one corner.

"You can read it now if you like," she said.

"Of course." Helen replied. She paused for a moment, looked at Candy. This was serious, she said with her eyes.

"I really hope you know that it is all wrong—that he was having a sexual relationship with you, a student, to begin with—it's not just that he is harassing you after you've told him to leave you alone."

Candy nodded. She had known all of it was wrong. She just hadn't thought about it. Used to being wanted, she liked it, even; the urgency of men's hands, their mouths, familiar and expected.

More tentatively, Helen continued, "I will have to report this to Dean Myers. I will also have to give him your emails. They are evidence."

"I know," Candy replied. "I feel bad, but..." Candy said. Her voice broke; she felt like she might cry, but she stopped herself. If she started crying, she might not stop.

Candy had thought about little else. It would get out, all of it, despite the college's best efforts. Certain people knew or had guessed already. David's need and insistence obvious, as he followed and stopped her on the path to the Manor House once, and again in the Village for Learning, each instance witnessed by other people on those two occasions at least. Perhaps there had been more sightings of them. Maybe they were one of those open secrets? Candy frowned and nodded. She did know. David would have to resign, apply for work at other schools. Move away. He'd already enumerated the ways she could ruin his life. And if he'd already told his wife, as he claimed, the ruining had already begun.

"It's not your fault," Helen said. "Anything that happened, it's his fault," she continued, as if reading Candy's mind.

"I hate this," Helen continued, her usually even voice, bitter. Candy thought she was hearing what Helen sounded like stripped of the teacher role she played so faithfully. The encouraging, even admiring voice, replaced by a less contrived response.

She shook her head, "I heard rumors when he was first hired. Someone at Baines knew someone in the English Department where he'd taught for years. But no one knew the details. I'll bet he's done this before."

Across the street Candy watched a bored-looking middle-aged couple follow a young car salesman from one truck to another. He looked back at the couple, smiling and chatting as they strolled the lot, totally animated in the face of their joint, indifferent expression. At one point the couple stopped, and the salesperson faltered. Turning, as if on an invisible string, he pressed his card into the man's outstretched palm. His mouth slackened as the couple walked away, not looking back. She felt Helen following her stare and turned to meet her eye.

"This time, we'll get him, we'll make it stick," Helen said, as she bowed her head, opened the manila folder before her, and began to read.

Before

It was six-thirty in the morning. Outside the kitchen window, the sky was a soft, buttery color rippled pink. Far off on the horizon it looked three-dimensional, like the gentle whorls that feathered up the side of dunes. Listening to the forecast the night before Buffy had expected the opposite: one of those solid gray, forbidding mornings that made her feel bunched up inside, not expansive or welcoming. This unexpected light made her happy, and where she'd gone to bed thinking she couldn't make it at Baines another day, she now felt smoothed out and able. It helped that it was Thanksgiving week, and the four-day weekend she'd been excited about since September, was about to begin.

It had been such a long two months. A lifetime, as the saying goes, contorted and fun-house style, into this small increment of time. One of the first things she'd noticed when she started at Baines was that there was no Matty, barefoot or otherwise. It turned out that he'd been busted by the FBI not long after her interview in June. Dean Myers had told her. Instead of helping around the college as part of his work study, he lived with friends in Burlington and wore an ankle bracelet. His father's money enabled this circumstance rather than jail, while he waited for his trial. Everyone hoped the money would continue to do its work, and everyone now included Buffy. She'd been sad to find Matty wasn't there. Her touchstone of sorts, had disappeared.

Buffy let Ash sleep a bit longer than usual this morning. More than she'd like to admit, it was irritating to have him around every morning, focused on her because he didn't have anywhere he needed to be. She sipped her tea, watched the chickadees hop around the small trough that encircled the bird feeder just outside the picture window. For a moment she thought of nothing but their fat little bellies, their stick-figure legs and feet, how well they balanced. She envied them their focus, not to mention their ability to lay eggs. Buffy was still pregnant, and now it was too late, though she sometimes thought of abortion as still being an option. In odd moments, she hated herself for not having acted. But she hated her mother even more, who, from the moment Buffy had told her she was pregnant, kept asking why did she want to have a baby now? She had to establish herself in her career, she was still young. Truth was Buffy wasn't sure she wanted to have a child. But Buffy just let the days pile up, time passing until certain, key dates had passed altogether.

Buffy's hand was drawn to the icy window etchings. The little birds, startled, flew off.

She listened to the hum of the boiler, felt the warm air struggling through the dirty grate in the kitchen floor, exhaling a burnt dust smell.

It barely competed with the chill coming through the window seams. The pink sky quickly faded.

By all accounts, and there were plenty of women and even a few men giving them, she was having an unusually tough pregnancy. At last week's faculty meeting, she'd fainted. The nauseated beginning of her pregnancy had continued into what everyone assured her would be the more trouble-free middle part. She walked around feeling as if she were stuck inside one of those horrible mummy bags, unable to turn from the cloying air. The faculty meeting that day had been similarly constricting, airless, and down she'd gone, with a thud, it was said.

Buffy had fainted into Hal Wentworth, the Social Ecology teacher. When she came to a few seconds later his tall wiry frame, the starfish of frazzled hair standing on end, filled her line of vision. He called out to people, directing them. "Water," he'd said, and "Stand back, everyone."

Pablo had told her that Hal Wentworth was a former Green Beret who'd been struck by lightning twice, and had almost drowned in a rafting accident. They'd laughed at this because he looked like someone who'd suffered multiple lightning strikes, something stony in the set of his face, not to mention the hair.

Beyond Hal Wentworth, she could see the faculty, many of whom she disliked from afar, hovering around her in the dusk. It had been a very long meeting that was scheduled to end at four, when there was scant enough light in the November sky, and just before she'd hit the ground, it was nearing 6:30 and pitch black outside the windows. Twice, she'd texted to Ash about being late. She was in the process of thinking about whether she should message him again, or wait until seven.

At least her loss of consciousness had ended up with a strategic purpose. She'd been spared a seat on the infamous Sensitive Issues Committee, which just last week had taken up the unenviable task of addressing an incendiary issue involving the Dean of Admissions, David Leppert, and a freshman girl named Candy Johnson. They'd evidently been meeting in Plattsburgh, Boston, and Montreal on a regular basis to have sex while the dean conducted his fundraising and recruiting efforts. So there was the issue not only of an inappropriate relationship with a student, but of his having been on the college's dime while carrying on his assignation. There was a paper trail: emails and text messages and letters, leading all the way to the online Women's Magazine, *Jezebel,* and their "Another Horny Old Man Caught with His Pants Down" column. They printed this email from the Dean to Candy Johnson: "Your ample ass in my face is all that I see," under the pictures they'd been furnished—by Candy? No one knew for sure. Candy was half Chippewa Indian, grew up on a reservation in Michigan. She was poor and young and brown, the news items liked to point out. The one of her in the sexy squaw costume went semi-viral in certain online circles: a short suede, fringed dress, beads, hair plaits and a headband with her thumb in her mouth, and right alongside of that, a candid shot of Dean Leppert and his wife leaving St. Augustine's Catholic Church in Montpelier on a Sunday morning, shielding his wife with a scowl at the photographer. The thought of the Dean's ugly pear-shaped old body laboring over a teenager was difficult for Buffy to think of. This vision, almost exactly, was one of the reasons she'd been happy to have met Ash during her first semester of grad school, so as not to find herself married to a male college professor. Most of the men she worked with saw the female students as new crops of fruit, ripe for the picking each semester. One of them had said as much to her once, something to the effect of, "Well, they're there, who else am I going to date?"

The racism implied in the squaw costume made the already titillating story a media darling on not only *Jezebel,* but *Gawker,* and the UK's *Daily Mail,* where pages of comments appeared below the brief stories, sometimes only a couple of sentences long. People were wittier and more creative in their one-offs than Buffy ever would have guessed. On the ground, at Baines, there was considerably less levity perceived in the affair, and for weeks now, the campus had been infused with a dangerous, pulsating anger. Stepping out of her VW Golf each morning since the story went public, Buffy almost expected to see the Community Center, the Village for Learning, the Manor, and the upper gardens burst into flames. The therapist that disassociating Ally had enlisted to lead guided imageries about heterosexual oppression, Kayla something, of the shapeless hemp dresses and clicking beads, saw the scandal as a opportunity for her practice. Buffy kept seeing her around campus, leaning into groups of students and taking them into her arms. She had a sign up in the cafeteria saying she was ensconced at the Yellow Brick Road, a dirty coffee shop in downtown Plainfield, for anyone who needed to process the recent events, the word ensconced bringing to Buffy's mind a queen bee, feeding on her drones.

Candy had turned over the evidence of her affair with Dean Leppert to her faculty advisor, Helen Wallace, who Buffy felt sorry for more than anything else. Physically, she looked like Velma in Scooby Doo. She was neither young nor hip, and in two days' time she'd gone from being a blank and anonymous presence at Baines, the history teacher with two celebrated, but largely unread, books about the Middle East, to a haunted-looking soul very near the center of a scandal and pursued by SIC members, students, and Ally's therapist.

Buffy set her mug down. Its definitive sound echoed in the morning silence, and sharply, she inhaled. There but for the grace of God go I.

*****

Buffy knew that Ash was awake when she heard Sally plaintively make her strange, Siamese mew. Some people thought she sounded like a human baby, but Buffy thought her yowl was creepier, like a broken doll with a needling mechanical cry, becoming louder, more prodding, the more Ash woke up. She'd been waiting for him to feed her, and hadn't moved from where she been all night, at the top of Ash's head. She never begged from Buffy, or even much acknowledged her. The two of them sounded more like a herd, than a single man and a cat, on their way down the narrow staircase and into the kitchen.

"Hey babe," Ash said. He kissed the top of Buffy's head.

Buffy watched the cat wind herself in and out of his legs, as he opened a can of food and put her bowl on the placemat with bits of dried, moist cat food and gravy stuck to the cloudy plastic. It was one of those things she thought about cleaning but never did.

"You know it's because you're home all day with her that she expects you to jump through her hoops." Buffy said.

Ash put the water on and stood with his back to Buffy as he waited for it to boil. The cat ate her food quietly and with focus.

"Yeah, well. I gotta talk to someone out here. I think we both have a little cabin fever."

61

"Hum," Buffy said.

"Have you seen my fleece?" he asked, turning to face her. "I don't know how it could've just disappeared, but I can't find it anywhere."

"No, I haven't," she said, glancing over at him.

It was probably under what resembled a small hill of clothing next to his side of the bed, but here he stood, puzzling it out, again.

Ash had been to a few interviews with the State of Vermont for IT positions, but hadn't yet heard back. At this point, she kind of wished he'd take anything, just to get a move on, but she couldn't say that.

"So tonight, when you get home, I'd like to read you the sixth chapter. I want to go back over it today, but it's just about there, I think," he said.

Ash had decided to write a novel. To use this time to his advantage, he liked to say. This embarrassed Buffy when he repeated it to anyone besides her. He'd never written anything beyond computer code. The adage that "everyone had a novel in them," had become frighteningly real. Everyone was writing a novel. Buffy was one of the only English teachers she knew who wasn't penning a book at night or on weekends, fighting for a place on the world stage, or at least the state you lived in—on that— much smaller stage. That, she was glad of. One less potential for humiliation to tuck into on bad days. So far, Ash's novel wasn't great or awful. It brought the reader from one plot point to the next. The language was basic, not beautiful or original. Fortunately, most of what he asked her about was whether or not she understood what was going on, and to that, she could truthfully answer "yes."

"We have another emergency Community Meeting today, so I won't be home until after six. But yeah, after that I'm all yours for four days."

"Oh God, that's right. The squaw thing. Of all the times not to be able to drink," he said, grabbing the kettle as it began to scream. She heard the water trickling through the coffee cone. The smell made her momentarily nostalgic. Quickly, she brought her lemon-ginger tea to her lips, the mug covering her nostrils.

"I know. It's so…fucked up. I don't even know how Baines ended up like this…attracting these kinds of students…they seem to like these sorts of meeting, the longer and more brutal, the better…I don't get it."

Ash sat down and reached across the table for the sugar. The tiniest oil drops flecked the surface of his coffee.

"You know, they're not bad kids. They're very creative," she continued, nodding her head. "Very talented, most of them. Just, so hurt."

"Right," Ash replied.

Buffy paused. Even the kids who acted out, like Ally and Sarah, seemed hurt more than anything else. Baines students were like all teens when you gave them too much freedom. That was the problem, not these particular students. She set her teacup down more forcefully than she'd intended, so that the tea water sloshed against the sides of the mug.

"It's just not a healthy place." Buffy shrugged.

"I just wonder sometimes if kids so young should be there—the way the college does everything is, it's—anarchy. Most of these kids are very angry. All the time. It's exhausting. They need the adults in their lives to rein them in a bit, not, like, give them more license to go wild. You know?"

"What are they so angry about do you think?" he asked.

Shaking her head, she smiled sadly. "Everything. They really leave no stone unturned. It's not enough to hate bigots and sexists, they go looking for other offenses—breeders, that's a big one right now. Like you and me, Ash. We're having a kid, breeding, you know?"

Ash narrowed his eyes. "So they're abolitionists of the human race?"

"Yeah," Buffy laughed. "Exactly! You know, Pablo, the film teacher I told you about? He's offered to bring in some of his kids' baby clothes for us, but we whisper about it, and then joke, wondering where he could possibly hand them off —in the upper parking lot, down by the Red Store? Isn't that crazy?"

"It's perverse," he said. Sally, finished with her meal, leaped into his lap. She bumped her head against his chin.

"I never dreamed that my pregnancy would be a problem in quite this way. I thought of how it would be difficult for me. But some of the kids actually avert their eyes when I walk by, like I'm a criminal."

At a little over twenty-five weeks, Buffy had just begun to show. Also, she had begun to dread being on the small campus unmistakably pregnant, a bigger and bigger target.

"I'm sorry, Buffy," Ash said, holding Sally close. She closed her eyes, trilling. Ash leaned back in the kitchen chair, tipping its front legs in the air.

"What time does the emergency meeting start?"

"Oh, well, afternoon classes have been canceled," she replied. "So at one, we're on. The only blessing is that some of the kids will already have left for the holiday, but not enough of them are going home."

"I'll be thinking of you. Me and Sally. We're your team baby, don't you forget it."

Ash set the chair back on the floor. The heavy wooden legs thudded and Sally leapt from his arms.

Buffy stood. Her eyes filled with tears, and for a moment she felt lost in the middle of the kitchen.

Out the kitchen window, the gray and reddish browns of dead and dying flowers and shrubs predominated. The plant remnants felt like hollow stalks to the touch, but they'd been tenacious when Buffy had tried to tear them out of the ground the weekend before. She'd given up before looking around in the basement or the garage for a shovel, and the Black-Eyed Susans she'd attempted to uproot manually looked disheveled, trampled, listing to one side as they did.

Buffy turned to face Ash, away from the window, her tears no longer hot or imminent.

"Hum, thanks. Are you going to call that guy who said to give him a call in couple of weeks? The one at the Mac place?"

She knew it was a cliché, and who didn't hate becoming one of those? But Buffy felt so fucking alone. More alone than she'd feel if Ash wasn't here at all. Part of her had come to believe that with the arrival of the baby, she'd be taking care of two children. One with a college degree and a resume.

"Oh, I will. I've been meaning to do that."

He didn't look irritated with her for nudging him, but unruffled as he sat there at the small kitchen table. Instead, he smiled.

"Come here and give me a kiss," he, turned slightly toward her in the chair.

Buffy stepped toward him and he wrapped his arm around her waist. Sally jumped from his lap. The chickadees hadn't returned. The view out the window was empty.

"It'll get better. I promise. I'll find a job," he said.

"I know," she said, not knowing. She wondered if it was her hormones that had made her lose faith in Ash. In herself and Ash. If it was her hormones that made her feel so alone.

Buffy pulled away without giving or getting a kiss.

"I gotta go," she said.

"Okay. Don't worry about dinner tonight, I'll get that."

"Thanks," Buffy said.

Just under the sound of her rifling for her car keys, Ash said, "Good luck today," and she tried to soften herself.

"Thanks, buddy," she smiled a little.

Outside she leaned against the rotting clapboards, puking. Buffy glanced up to see her hand, the ugly, already cold and mottled skin, repugnant. She wished the day were over. The semester. The year. A faint thunk against the window sill. Sally, glancing at her from inside. Even more than her baby-like Siamese meow, there was something about Sally's eyes that reminded Buffy of a doll. Unblinking, knowing and intent. They followed her as she strained to look over her shoulder, the distance of the long driveway, and then as she drove off.

The first floor bathroom is to my right. *The girls forget to turn off the combination light and fan a lot. The sound can drive me buggy, especially if it's during the day when no one is around and the possibility of someone turning the damn thing off is not a possibility. Sometimes they also leave the kitchen fan on, and the two fans drone on for hours and hours.*

Buzzing flies are another sound I can't stand. They don't just get trapped in the summer, but into the late fall, when the slow, dull ones bump against the windows together, sounding like electrical shorts just before they die.

There is a lot of crying, too. Girls—which is how I think of them—they are so young, even though I live in the "Women's Only" dorm—cry in me and in the bathroom, which just like in here, has a tile floor and cheap plaster walls, but because it is the next room over, they sound like they are crying at the bottom of a well and totally lost.

Sarah, the girl who lives here now, is totally lost, but usually sounds like she's on top of a mountain screaming down at the bad people and the bad world, and not at the bottom of a well.

Sarah is hurt and angry and scared, and lost in those feelings. If she were in a play or a novel or a movie, the writing teacher would say she was too one-dimensional. Sarah would need to be fleshed out, the teacher would say. People aren't just one thing. But I think that sometimes they can be, or so close to being just one thing that they can fool you. Young people especially.

Tonight, though, Sarah fools no one. Very quietly she cries and cries to her friend, Ally. I hear Ally tearing off paper towels, Sarah blowing her nose.

Her voice is soft and thick. It catches like it is being pulled back inside her with each word.

"How could nothing happen to him? Nothing ever happened to him."

Ally is silent, but the sense that she is listening has a sound. Her breath moves high in her chest, thin and shallow. The nothing that happened to him is the everything that happened to Sarah, and Ally gets that.

I've heard Sarah recite her poems. Her top of the mountain performances, her voice loud and ragged. They revolve around her grandfather. The basement. And a ruby birthstone ring in 14k gold that her Nan gave her when she was six. How she would look at it as the washer lurched from the wall in its spin cycle. Or worse. When the washer was still. No sound but her grandfather's heavy breathing. Disgusting.

"I used to pray

for the washing machine to

the washing machine

Be on."

The last few lines of a Sarah's poem, "Underwater."

Finally, Ally says, "I don't know why. What he did was wrong. It was criminal. That nothing ever happened to him..."

Here she pauses and everything goes silent.

In the stillness between the two young women there are no words to fill the air between my walls. There is nothing to say or to hear, no real promise but the secret, unspoken, about the way stories are supposed to end. With the grandfather punished and not moving on to an endless supply of young girls. A school principal, he was moved from school to school, went from girl to girl—and like with one of those Russian nesting dolls, the littlest and most carefully hidden, always within reach. He liked them at nine and younger.

I'm paraphrasing from another of Sarah's poems. Sometimes she reads it out loud to herself. Her voice is always strong and clear until the last line: the always within reach one.

Tonight, I listen as Sarah tells her friend Ally that she couldn't remember when the heavily shellacked, loudly colored dolls had begun to remind her of all the girls and their older sisters and their mothers, when they were girls, that her grandfather had told her he loved. Sarah thought he liked telling her about the others; he liked that together they held these secrets that no one else was supposed to know.

Ghosts

Moonlight tunnels through the octagonal-shaped hole at my crown, creating a spotlight effect on the ground below. Tiny specs of stone catch and reflect the light. A few minutes after the clock on the town green strikes twelve, I hear a busy exchange among three great horned owls that have perched in the treetops nearby. They are the size of toddlers, which is something I've never quite gotten used to. Odd and powerful, their glossy reptilian eyes slither over the air's surface. Their conversation is probably not a friendly one. Unlike crows and ravens, owls are unsociable. They hunt alone and in the dark. Likely, they are fighting for position. Over who stays and who returns for scraps. Guttural-sounding, their voices overlap and interrupt each other in layers of screamed assertion and a cacophony of self-interest in the moments before they grow absolutely still.

I came to Vermont in 1973. A California tipi maker sold me to a

Baines student named Drew Halloran for $325. His senior study was a learning-by-doing semester living without running water or electricity. An interesting kid. He was from a wealthy and well-connected family in Tennessee he wanted nothing to do with. He spent about six months up here. He hunted small game, grew potatoes, lettuce, and squash in the college's community garden, and successfully lived off the land. He meditated each morning for two hours and read Leaves of Grass each night.

In 1973 the actress Stella Stiles' father was researching a book on utopian communities, and he had heard through a friend that someone needed a tipi delivered to Vermont. It was the sort of thing that people had the time to do then, and that they do not have the time for now, as if the very nature of time has changed and narrowed. He visited a number of communes on his way from California. In the acknowledgments page of his book he mentions me, the twenty-five-foot Blackfoot tipi he delivered to Baines College and Drew Halloran, nature boy extraordinaire. The two-year-old Stella spent three nights under my newly constructed roof; her small, pounding feet against the dirt is one of my earliest memories.

In the evenings Stella's parents and Drew talked until the light died. They told him about their stops at communes in Wyoming, Minnesota, and New York, how they bumped over dirt roads that eventually brought them to a scattering of yurts or small cabins with vegetable gardens and free range chickens pecking the ground. The young couple clearly loved the white and yellow VW bus with bad shocks and no air conditioning parked near Drew's garden, cutting a sort of romantic figure in silhouette and at night. You could tell they were happy, that the trip cross-country had opened in them wonder at the land.

My poles and heavy canvas were tied to the roof rack and wrapped in a deep blue, heavy tarp that rippled and snapped in the highway winds. We didn't encounter much rain, and what little we did was heavy but short-lived. The Stiles started driving at sundown each day, to avoid local traffic. To travel at night, under the stars of big sky country and then on through to the East Coast, with its mountain ranges that fit around the various states in small, snug circles and half circles, blue-gray in dusk, ink black by night, was like moving through another world. Quieter and more reflective, the mountain ranges like hands joined together in prayer. It took them over four weeks. If the now famous Stella Stiles remembers anything of the journey it's probably the confusion of batik prints and dirty bare feet, women with long, plain hair, and men with beards and sharp ruts in their face, despite their relative youth who greeted them at each stop, their baskets full of freshly harvested corn, kale, and tomatoes.

Over the past thirty-five years my poles and canvas have been replaced four times by other students who decided to take a semester to live here without modern conveniences gumming up their brains. Thought and action are integrated and become pretty simple when your aim is to eat, stay warm, and keep a lookout for what goes on in your immediate surroundings. The four have been three guys and one girl. I've watched each of them change, explicitly at first, as they learn to live without noise and manufactured images, and then subtly. Their faces actually transform once they get used to the silence that precedes the animals' early awakening, the sense of peace that is the prelude to the noisy bids for food and space. They take a sense of expansiveness and possibility back to the world.

Of course students come up here to get high and have sex a lot, and there's a story that the kids seem to love to tell each other about, morbid pillow talk that serves to heighten their experience.

In 1987 a student with spiky black hair almost bled to death on the floor near my entrance. It was December the thirteenth, around nine o'clock. It had long been dark. The crows looked on in silence, their neat shapes blending with the branches reaching above my head. Another kid followed behind him. They both screamed and their sounds and words were indistinguishable, not like they came from separate people, but from one gaping mouth. I had no idea at first what was happening or had happened, if these boys had been fighting or had been attacked or in an accident. And I wouldn't know the particulars for a few days, until other students started to gather to decompress from the whole thing that next weekend. I learned that the first kid had cut both of his wrists and had walked from his dorm up into the woods. The resident assistant had followed him, shining his flashlight on his footsteps and the drops of blood that pocked the snow.

As I've listened to different students repeat the details of this story over the years, I can tell they are each shaken to the core. The possibility of death being so near hadn't been on their radar. For hours after they leave, their awe-inspired voices circle my space, as their words describe the course of events from that night: how the RA had applied pressure to the kid's wounds, blood staining his clothes, and how the two boys awkwardly linked up and walked back to the community center to call an ambulance. The boy survived, but he didn't return for the spring semester. There's more. What happened to the two boys after this night makes this first story all the more portentous. The students' tones grow hushed, full, triumphant almost, as they report how the attempted suicide was killed in a car accident on the New Jersey Turnpike almost a year later, when the tractor-trailer in front of him jackknifed and caught on fire. He was DOA, the paper said. The RA transferred to Evergreen College and died on an ice-climbing trip to Peru two years later. He was twenty-two. Nearly every bone in his body was shattered. His fully intact face shifted to the left, and his arms and legs twisted oddly beneath him. He was killed on impact, or very closely thereafter. All this we know from his climbing partner, who wrote a piece about the accident for Outside Magazine.

Students' eyes travel the length of my walls to my apex, and toward the sky, as they tell the story. I hear wonder in their voices, quiet and searching, over the strange fates of the two young men. They ask what might have been different if the first kid had never tried to kill himself, or if neither had left Baines. They wonder if the absence of that one night may have changed everything that was to follow. I've come to think their words are like wishful thoughts, like they hope that if they suggest a different, better outcome to the universe, there's a possibility those boys will be spared.

Sometimes, a different conversation will develop, and one or two of the students will say the boys were lucky to die young and quickly. At first I thought the kids who said these kinds of things were posturing. They were the punk kids, the Goths, or just nihilistic without benefit of a clique. But I've changed my mind about that after years of listening to the sounds of their voices in the dark. It's as if they're speaking to themselves, or to no one, reaching out from their small and private worlds, and under my cover without having to meet another's eye or imagine what they see. I think some people, from pretty early on, contain kernels of world-weariness that will probably grow rather than diminish as they get older. It's like they know this on some level, and an early demise looks less tragic to them, easier, than the prospect of becoming themselves. People do know themselves, I think, if they care to.

Almost every weekend during the fall there's a lot of drumming and dancing, usually fueled by mushrooms or X, or at least these have been the drugs of choice during the last twenty years. The kids begin to gather firewood and drag coolers through the woods at around six or seven at night. They yawn and smile coming onto the mushrooms, and smile 'til it aches and hug coming up on X. Everything is slowed down, the sound of the bongos or drums rhythmically pounding as the kids sway like trees and grasses.

In the 1970s and early 1980s it was PCP, Quaaludes, and blotter that everyone did. The energy was wild, like it wasn't of and couldn't be contained in the world. Kids pretty routinely charred their palms holding them over the fire. The smell of scorched flesh stuck in the air for two hours, even with the flaps open. One time a girl rubbed her eyebrows off in one night; another girl set her hair on fire by mistake. These kids smiled too, at first, but later looked like they were drowning.

Weed has been the one constant. Its sweet and earthy smell and layers upon layers of smoke gently unfurl in the air, settling there, like ghostly sediment.

Mask making, indigenous peoples, black politics, women in cross-cultural perspectives, Birkenstock repair, experimental theater, numerology, meteorology, and astrology are just a few of the courses that have been taught here in the last thirty-five years. In addition to Stella Stiles, Allen Ginsberg, Ken Kesey, Timothy Leary (who was Stile's godfather), Jean Seberg, members of the Grateful Dead, Jefferson Starship, Phish, and Captain Beefheart have all passed through at one time or another. Baines, in the early years anyway, was a reason for a certain kind of person or celebrity to visit Vermont, and the Bread and Puppet Theater famously came and stayed. People who were certain they could help end poverty, sexism, racism flocked here to hang out for a few days or months to talk about what the new world would feel like, how it would work. Of course this movement never got that far. What once seemed like a permanent shift in the collective consciousness, now only seems like a passing fad.

It occurs to me that Baines, like the time in which it flourished, could die someday, that financial mismanagement or one or another scandal could kill the place. One thing is for sure, it will never be what it was when I first arrived. There's no longer even a community garden. What is saddest to me is that individually and collectively, innocence is finite and unknowingly spent, and that in the moment you don't know that it ends.

Ally and Sarah had taken a hit of X each and together had drunk half a bottle of tequila at about eight o'clock the night before. It was now a little after six-thirty in the morning. They were crying, holding on to each other for dear life and rocking, as if at sea. The sunrise had been beautiful. Together, they'd watched slips of brilliant pink fissuring the lemony sky. Ally thought the small ripples off in the distance looked like a lot of things: like steps leading nowhere, or gentle waves in windswept dunes, or even the pearly undersides of shells. She often wondered what it meant that so many things resembled so many other things in nature. It was weird. And beautiful. How everything had the ability to morph into everything else.

At about three in the morning they'd left their dorm and had followed the trail behind campus to an old, abandoned tipi named X. Coming on to Ecstasy during the full moon and while peering up at the crisscrossing poles was something of a freshman initiation at Baines. Ally and Sarah had planned to make it to the tipi for the beginning of their roll, but they'd become stuck in Sarah's room, literally, it seemed, listening to music on the computer and watching the amorphous splotch that puddled from the monitor, its shapes and colors a pleasing combination of octopus and kaleidoscope, all the while talking nonstop. At two in the morning they'd begun to stuff oranges and bananas into their mouths and drink orange juice and water in preparation for coming down. By three, the air in the room seemed to be suffocating them.

"We forgot to go to the tipi," Sarah said. "What time is it anyway?"

A stack of papers and books crashed from the desk on to the floor as Ally reached for the clock radio. "Two forty-eight."

"Aw, man, we should go. It's awesome up there."

The earlier, livid helplessness was absent from Sarah's voice and even her eyes. She stood and reached for Ally, pulling her by the arms. Ally felt her body stretch like elastic. She laughed and let herself free fall, holding on to Sarah's hands. They teeter-tottered for a moment. Sarah's tall frame blotted out the dull overhead light so that she appeared in faint silhouette.

"You're so tiny." Sarah pulled Ally toward her. Ally could feel her warm breath on her skin, smell the sharp perfumey tequila and Sarah's familiar earthy body odor, spiked with garlic. People had always called Ally tiny. Men especially, like she was a small jewel that had caught their eye and they had to say so.

"Let's blow this joint!" Sarah said, letting go of her hands.

"Okay." Ally looked at herself in the mirror on her way out the door.

Her flushed skin and wide eyes made her look so alive. She smiled at herself, her rubbery-feeling lips inching from cheek to cheek.

A six foot bear carving, so old its face was almost smooth, stood just inside the front tipi flap, its paws extended like it had once held a tray. It was a Baines legend, the story of how one night in 1974 all of Shelley Dorm, high on weed and shrooms, had snuck into town and stolen the bear from the front lawn of the perpetual-yard-sale family. The students had carried it over a mile down Route 2 and then another quarter of a mile or so into the woods, coffin-style.

There was a small fire pit at the back of the tipi, and a once colorful Mexican rug and ugly carpet remnants covered parts of the floor. A futon, its Asian-inspired cover a filthy gray color from years of accumulated grime, lay haphazardly on a pallet. It was here that Ally and Sarah first kissed. Ally felt herself momentarily disappear in the warm and dark sensation of their mouths touching. It was after the kiss that Sarah started to formulate her plan. Ally had watched her and listened, wondering when they would kiss again. Sarah's feet hung off the end of the mattress. Her shirt inched up, exposing her round, unapologetic belly. Ally was obsessed with women's stomachs, with her own flat and tyrannical belly, always accusing her after a breakfast of pancakes or too much beer with its repellent bloat. Looking down at her little booze, juice and water paunch, Ally turned her head to study the inside-of-a-skull, gauzy, Tipi material. She hated a lot of her thoughts, which were more like irritating habits than important things to think about. It was like being weighed down by garbage.

"We gotta figure out a way to get them to fire the Dean of fucking Emissions. You know, like direct action. Some concrete thing that would break through all the Community Meeting BULLSHIT and get them to cut his fat ass loose," Sarah said.

Ally raised herself on her one elbow, and touched Sarah's arm, ran a finger over her convex tummy, with her other hand. She hadn't thought she wanted to be kissed by Sarah. But she'd been waiting for Sarah to touch her, willing her to make the first move. It was obvious to her, now anyway. Falling beside Sarah again, Ally laughed, feeling as if at this particular moment there was nowhere else in the entire world she would rather be.

"It's a great idea. It has to be really big, though. Something that would get the media's attention." Ally didn't have a clear idea of what she meant by big. But she could envision crowds of Baines's students hollering, their fists in the air.

Sarah said, "Gross old men. I fuckin' hate them. They love jailbait. It's like stealing innocence. Or not even stealing it. They just fuckin' destroy it. When my grandfather was rubbing his dick against my ass in the basement he used to whisper: 'You're not a little girl anymore, are you? Your mother's jealous of you, you know.' I was like nine years old. I didn't even have boobs."

Fury built in Ally's muscles. She sat up and turned to look down at Sarah. She thought of touching her, but didn't. Instead she drew her knees to her chest and shook her head. "How did you not kill him?"

"I don't know. Just think, if every little girl who was ever incested or molested killed their perp, males might become extinct, or at least we'd be left with the ones that aren't rapists."

"Unnatural selection. The perfect world." It was quiet. No wind rustled what was left of the leaves in the trees and no birds were yet calling.

Try as she might, Ally still didn't remember being molested, even after the extra therapy sessions to try to unearth buried memories, and her rebirthing, which Kayla performed early one Saturday morning at her post-and-beam condominium. Oddly, Ally didn't recall her rebirth, either. Kayla told her that she'd hyperventilated and fainted, which she explained was part of the painful rebirthing process. When Ally came to only a few minutes later she felt not reborn but as if she'd been spit from a disgusting lagoon. When she regained consciousness she smelled shit so strong she was engulfed in motion sickness while lying motionless. She hadn't told Kayla about the awful smell because initially she feared she'd shit herself, and was relieved to the point almost of crying when she realized that she hadn't.

Kayla had brushed her hair from her forehead and said they'd try it again when Ally was in a better position to integrate the experience. She wasn't ready. That was okay. Afterwards, Kayla had driven her back to campus. As they'd passed a diner in town she asked Ally if she wanted to stop for breakfast, but the shit smell was in her nose by then. "I'm not really hungry," she said, shaking her head.

Since then nothing had changed for Ally. In fact, her symptoms had become worse. In addition to her dissociative episodes, she experienced such forceful waves of revulsion when she thought about men abusing children that she couldn't help but wonder if her body was telling her about its secret history. And there were days when she thought about men abusing children a lot. Sometimes all she needed was to see a man of a certain age and it triggered her. Maybe she'd been sexually abused when she was a baby by a man somewhere in his mid-thirties to forties, and like with aversion therapy, the sight of a man in this range repelled her. If that were the case, it wouldn't be latent memory, but a primitive, physical memory, which would explain the rage she almost always felt high in her throat and neck, like she might splutter, explode.

"We could take over the cafeteria, or the dean's office. Lock ourselves in until they fire Dean Leppert." Sarah sat up.

"I feel so bad for her." Ally shook her head.

Since she'd first heard the story of Dean Leppert and Candy Johnson, she couldn't think of Candy without envisioning her in that Native American costume that had gone viral, with feathers, beads, and sequins, and her mocha brown midriff exposed. Rumor, based on emails and letters between the two that a friend of Candy's said she'd read, had it that he'd made her dress as a squaw to blow him and fucked her in the ass only.

Sarah also brought her knees up under her chin. She looked over at Ally from the mantle of her arms and shook her head. "You just know he's done it before, believe me."

"Yeah. Something should be done. It's not right." Ally felt for the roach, the matches, in her back jeans' pocket. Pinching it between her fingers she tried to light it with a series of old, flaky matches. On her third try a tiny flame spit to life. Quickly, she inhaled. The cigarette paper turned tar brown, crackling like cellophane. The back of her throat burned and she coughed, handing the joint nub to Sarah, who squinted at it. Realizing the roach had gone out Sarah flicked it into her mouth.

"Have you ever seen Dean Leppert's wife? She's younger than him, by like a lot. And she seems like a really nice cashier or something,"

Ally shook her head. "My mother would die if it were her. Not because like she'd be jealous or hurt. It'd be about the neighbors knowing. That's all she really cares about."

"My mom would just pretend it hadn't happened." Sarah paused. Ally thought to ask her if her mother knew about her grandfather, the successive basements, but she did not. History repeats itself. Everyone knows that, but no one seems to care.

"You know maybe what we should do is take over the Manor," Ally said. "It's been done before, in the 80s. It would be more disruptive than the cafeteria. They'd have to cancel classes.

"And none of the faculty could get to their offices, Sarah said. "We could get chains and locks and barricade the doors."

Ally excitedly turned to her. "There's that big emergency meeting tomorrow, or today, I guess it is now. We could do it then. Now!"

"We have to get to the hardware store; we could do it around lunch, when no one would be in the Manor. The meeting is at one, isn't it?"

"Yep. It is." Ally stood up. She had no idea how long they'd been out here, if it was four or closer to six in the morning. Tree branches had begun to vein the tipi canvas, a faint brocade patterning that told her it was getting light. "We should get back." Her brain or soul—something—was released into the new light. Empty, she plopped back onto the couch, next to Sarah.

"What's up? You all right?"

"I just…I could cry." She swayed into Sarah. In the surprising warmth of her body she was reminded of the sun, how it would come from behind a cloud just as she was about to abandon her lawn chair, poolside, during those never-ending summers in eleventh and twelfth grade. How was it that those summers seemed so long ago now?

"You're coming down." Sarah put her arm around her and squeezed her shoulder. "Let's get you back. We should eat more vitamin C. A lot more. And my brother gave me some seaweed stuff that really helps keep your immune system up when you trip."

"Yeah, sure. Jeez, I hope I can walk."

Sarah rose. Turning, she took Ally's hand, pulling her up.

"Wait, can we lie down? Not on the futon, not in here. I need to put my head in the dirt, next to the earth. I've wanted to do that . . . for a long time."

Sarah laughed. "Okay then."

Together they crouched through the flaps and lay down in the clearing surrounding the tipi, facing one another. The dirt was rugged against Ally's skin, with little stones and rough, faded yellow clumps of grass.

"I hate my parents. I wish we could not have parents. This is the first time I've ever felt good, ever. Here, at Baines." Before she knew it hot tears streamed down her face.

"I think a lot of people feel that way. You get to be yourself here."

"So you feel that way, too?" Ally ventured.

"I do. I was like a Barbie before I came here. Really skinny, and I went to modeling school. Isn't that whacked? Now I'm me." Sarah sat up. Ally wondered if she was about to cry again. In general, Sarah was too on track to cry, too determined not to. Tonight, she'd let Ally see this whole other side of herself.

Ally rose and put her arm around Sarah. Not looking directly at her, she listened for the sounds that would tell her whether Sarah was crying or not: the subtle change in breathing, and finally, the running nose. Nerves built in her throat when she realized that Sarah's entire body heaved, without sound or tears or a running nose. Taking her in her arms, gently, she rocked her. Sarah began to moan, rhythmic and chant-like. Ally, too, began to wail. Together, they sounded like what she imagined the inside of the universe would sound like, the diffuse hurt and anger at its core. She'd always hated it when therapists told her that she needed to sit with her anger. But for the first time she understood that she could sit with it in power, not in helplessness. She could use it somehow.

Dialogue

From where the narrow blade of light falls, at the crack under my door, I hear a performance which definitely sounds desperate, like the characters have hit the wall. A woman and a man yell to be heard. Their voices are raw. Raw is my favorite kind of performance. Truth telling, which is tough,when you haven't been paying attention, just might kill you a little. Or a lot, maybe, depending.

Now I hear a woman singing. Not a song with words or a melody. More like a call, like with birds. Repetitive, keening. The words "cunt daughter" are also repeated. They slip from the space under my door and fill me with dread. I hear cars pulling in. Too fast. A siren, too. The crows' sharp cries. None of the sound effects come from the direction of the sound and light board on the second floor. Save that gnawing slit of light coming from under my door and my red "Exit Signs," my air is black and undisturbed.

There's a lull. A full stop to all sound that almost makes me think I've been imagining that I hear a performance, it is so complete.

I started out as a hay barn. I was one of the largest barns in Central Vermont during the late 1860s. From 1938 on I've been a theater, and that's my passion, though there has always been something transcendent about my large, often empty space, even as a hay barn. A vibe that catches people's breath when they first enter the room that has them look around wonderingly, in the moments before my overhead lights snap on. The click of my light switch is final sounding in either direction, on and off, and its sound carries. It is a signal that someone has arrived or is about to depart from a different world.

My interest in theater grew slowly at first, as I got the hang of what it was all about from sensing what was happening in my seats, the audience. It's a dialogue and each night of a performance is a little different depending on who is in the house, and how tuned in they are with the performers and vice versa. It may sound obvious, but theater and life are about living in the moment. About listening in the moment. What is obvious is also profound.

In the 1960s and 1970s I hosted King Crimson and Savoy Brown. Tawny Simon's Pulitzer Prize winning play, "Death Call" had its first run on my boards. The birth of the band Phish, Jon Fishman, the drummer, in a dress or naked, depending on the night, was right here, my stage lights, the colored gels, reflecting the electromagnetic waves of the universe in their eyes.

The high of being a theater never hummed more sweetly than when the Bread and Puppet Theater was my resident troupe. The giant, mythically-faced puppets reached halfway to my forty-foot ceiling. The

performers' joyous calls for peace and justice, their ragged pronounce-
ments of evil, rained against my walls, the sound bending and traveling
forever.

What I don't get is why the students would choose to have an outdoor
performance now. Just doesn't make sense. Springfest and the Bread and
Puppet Theater pageant happen when the audience can dance around out-
side without wanting to cry. Now it's cold; the air flows in a constant, freez-
ing stream from under my door. This is the time for a stage performance,
under the proscenium arch, for the thick stage curtains, which smell like
dust, earthy, sort of, slowly withdrawing to either inside of the stage, the
lights coming up, also slowly, on the scene, the characters, and the action.

Regards, Society

Reduced to hiding in a bathroom stall (not using it, mind you), Dean Myers stares down at the tile, dingy and stinking of bleach, on which his feet rest. Since he was a small boy, he's hated that almost all bathrooms smell like sewers. Which is what they are. But couldn't they, whoever they were, have developed a system that didn't so viscerally remind you of where you were and what you, or, as in the case of a public bathroom, like this one, what countless people had done there? A reeking scene of a crime, the note of bleach convinces you only of the rottenness of what lies beneath.

This bathroom is next to the Ratskeller, with its pool table and bookcases and old, dirtyish chairs and couches. The Rat and its bathrooms are empty at seven in the morning. The entire campus is usually out cold, save the cafeteria staff, the clanking of their heavy service dishes and pots and pans reassuring to Dean Myers, as each morning he strolls through campus, preparing for the day ahead. That Sarah and Ally were up, walking his way, not yet having seen him, jarred him out of his reverie. He turned and scuttled off. An overhead bulb fluttered to life as he opened the bathroom door. He met his own eye in the bathroom mirror, noticing, invariably, the hereditary overhang of his lids, which since his late twenties had made him appear more tired than he was, before locking the stall door and sitting on the closed toilet seat.

He couldn't face Sarah and Ally at this hour. It would be enough to see and hear from them later. They'd both signed up to speak at Community Meeting today. Their rage at David Leppert, at the college, would shake the cafeteria walls. Already he could feel its force high in his throat, which felt like it was closing, as if he had a tiny fist lodge in his gullet.

They wouldn't care that he'd tried to get Dean Leppert to resign. Had begged his old friend from Harvard to quietly go away. But David, as he used to think of him—now he was just Dean Leppert to Dean Myers' mind—had refused a fat severance package that Baines College could barely afford, on the advice of his attorney. It was a poor school, despite its notoriety. There were a surprising number of rich and famous former students, especially for a school so small, not to mention the fact that Baines had invented off-campus and low-residency study— something that almost all colleges and universities now offered. This last point was something Dean Myers thought of bitterly, on a weekly if not daily basis. If only someone had thought to monetize Baines' many innovations, rather than set the scene for this hand-to-mouth, poorly understood existence, where much of the public not only didn't appreciate its contribution to the local community—Two Guys Gelato, the

Nobel Prize-winning playwright Tawny Simon, the band Phish, and the many Big Mac Foundation winners, countless novelists and poets, several area business owners and so on—but to Education with a capital E, tortured him sometimes. How could it not? Something like the failure to lay claim to the invention of off-campus and low-residency study and ride on its coattails forevermore would never happen nowadays, when even hippies and New Agers were skilled capitalists.

And now all this crap with David Leppert, and not nearly long enough after the Matty Feldman drug bust. The Feldman arrest had remained safely on the back pages of a handful of national papers, picked up only by reporters who were old enough to remember Baines's reputation as a hippie haven. But the debacle with David Leppert had gone viral. It had all the ingredients that certain online sites used to make their pages clickable. The minute Dean Myers saw the pictures of the student, Candy Johnson, in a squaw costume, a Cher-like outfit from the 1970s that Dean Leppert had bought the girl on eBay, he knew the story would rise from the ranks of other men-behaving-badly tales and the obscure Baines curiosity pieces.

Now, the story had its own Twitter hashtag, a word that he'd been only vaguely familiar with until less than a month ago, was currently threatening to destroy the Baines Community:

"#triggerwarning."

In the space of a few weeks, Baines had devolved from a college where women thrived, to one that was hostile and unsafe.

Dean Myers shook his head at no one. The plastic seat was cold through his pants. The thin, old skin of his flanks was numb. He thought of getting up. He'd have to leave the bathroom at some point, of course. Get his game face on, such as it would be, on this day. But he did not move.

For no reason, the toilet started to run and Dean Myers looked up, from his large feet and the rancid tile to the new graffiti on the door. It was scrubbed clean, or into a swirled smudge, each week; and weekly, new, random scrawls appeared. "Be Proud of Who You Are Unless You Are a Douche," and "I like Writing on Walls. Fuck you society. Ben." And a reply: "Ben, This is actually a door, not a wall. Regards, Society."

He smiled at that. In his head, anyway. No actual smiles would come today. He wondered if Sarah and Ally had seen him. Were they at this moment leaning against the pool table, knowing that he'd run away from them? Waiting for him? He'd be humiliated. Intimidated by their frank stares. They hid little of their scorn for him and other adults, lumped together in their minds no doubt and presumably all disappointing, or worse, as was the case with Sarah.

Dean Myers had been on Sarah's admissions committee, had voted in favor of her powerful writing. Poems that brought you places you'd never been, or would want to go. Baines was the perfect fit for her, he'd thought. A safe place, where women's voices dominated the public discussion. And why not? Didn't they deserve one institution where this was true?

He didn't know much about the Ally girl's background, or of her time at Baines. All he did know was that she'd come under the spell of the therapist Kayla Freeman, and that she and Sarah had become fast friends, or lovers. He wasn't sure which. Try as he might, he could never quite remember what Ally looked like. She was small. That was the extent of what he remembered of her, even after having just seen her. It was curious. He was usually very good at summoning faces.

The running water reduced to a trickle, then came to an abrupt stop. His gaze moved from the stall door to his hands, his eyes drawn to a small scar below his index finger. He'd sliced through a part of it at a restaurant where he'd worked in Cambridge in the 1960s for a few months, so long ago it was funny to think that his time there had marked him for life. Each time he found himself looking at the scar, its significance loomed much larger than its small, Nike-like whoosh. He had been that person. He was still that, but also this person, presently, his life passing before him: from bloodied-finger boy to an old man hiding in a public toilet.

Dean Myers stood, finally. What he wanted to say at the meeting today, before opening up the floor to Sarah and Ally and all the others, was that he understood that Dean Leppert's transgressions were like awful puzzle pieces, clicking into place to depict an all-too-common picture that he understood was triggering to the young women on campus, and the young men, too.

Last night, his wife had helped him articulate this, as he cried beside her in bed, frightened of losing everything the college had worked for and that he had helped build.

"The women have every reason to be angry, remember that and you will be okay. Don't get defensive," she said, squeezing his shoulder. "Include the men, too. Of course you know it happens to them as well."

Dean Myers pushed the stall door. It creaked open and again he stood face-to-face with his mirror image, his eyes looking smaller and smaller as his lids thickened with age, though still searching. Yes, he did know that little boys were sexually abused. That children, who adults the world over claimed to love and value above all else, were destroyed with a sort of casualness that belied the party line of their preciousness.

Stepping from the stall into another day he wished were over, or would never begin, Dean Myers washed his hands. He craned his head and looked out through a small rectangular window above the sink. The pale gray and pink shades of the sky delineated in a way that had always reminded him of sand dunes, something you could climb, gentle rises taking you nowhere in particular.

Outside he heard tires driving over the gravel in the upper parking lot, a car door slamming, and down the hall pots and heavy trays landing on surfaces, as the door to the bathroom quietly sealed after him.

The Fork

The tiny fan from inside the ceramic heater sounded funny. Clyde Drewry figured that must be what woke him up, sort of like a fire alarm. From his bed he saw that the heater had fallen off the stack of books that he used as a platform, and lay on its side. Its coils were a dull orange that had passed through a much brighter phase, the color lethal-looking. Sitting up, he reached for the cord and yanked it from the outlet. A couple of sparks flew, dying on contact with the thin linoleum that covered the cement floor. His feet, up to the ankles, stuck out from the twisted covers. The cold rang through his bones.

"Five forty-two" the clock radio said. Pulling the covers over his head Clyde tried to feel the warmth of his body. He punched the flat, cold pillow and turned on his side, bringing his knees up under his chin. He'd be lucky if he got back to sleep by six-thirty. His alarm was set for 7.

Closing his eyes, he did his visualization. It was the same scene he'd used since he was eleven? Twelve? Before he knew what a visualization was. A sandy beach, empty. He watched as the sun danced on the ocean, a luminous, continuously moving bed of diamonds. He felt himself fall, but shook himself awake. For a moment he wasn't sure where he was. Then, slowly he made out the general outline of his dorm room.

The beach was gone. Instead, he saw his best friend Tristan's face: very round, pale and freckled, with large blue eyes. He looked angelic, but only until he opened his mouth. He had the deep and impatient voice of arrogance undisguised, and Clyde had been flattered, in the beginning, that he had chosen him as his only friend.

Lately Clyde was frightened of Tristan, though he'd never admit this to anyone. To everyone else, they were a pair. They had the same build and were exactly the same height. Clyde had blond hair, Tristan dark brown, but that didn't seem to matter. People still mixed them up all the time, especially in the one course they took together, Pippen West's Creative Self class. Pippen genuinely couldn't keep them straight, shook his head when he substituted one of their names for the other, trying to clear his brain. But Clyde suspected the other students used their names interchangeably on purpose. From the first class on, they were palpably hated by the others, after Tristan told a girl that her poem about losing her virginity was pure *shitr*, a term he'd discovered in Jarry's play *King Ubu*. Clyde had audibly agreed. And Tristan and Clyde had vowed to be brutally honest in class and to invite the same, which of course was forthcoming in steaming heaps. Clyde's academic advisor had told him there was a move to vote them off the Creative Self Island, led by Cassie Knowlton. She was fond of telling Clyde and Tristan how unsafe they made the class, like they were driving fifty in a twenty-five-mile-per-hour zone. "Fuck Safety," Clyde had replied the first time she complained.

"That's enough, people," Pippen West had said, raising his arms like a referee. Cassie's eyes had bulged, and the rest of the class had silently fell in step behind her. Once, he'd overheard her call Tristan Beelzebub. "Beelzebub and his friend," she'd said. Clyde had waited outside the French doors to see if anyone laughed. He thought it was kind of funny. But no one had laughed.

*****

Clyde and Tristan had met at one of Baines's Saturday orientations. It was the first Saturday in June, over a year ago now. Neither of them had committed to Baines yet, and both were also considering Bard and Evergreen. They had spent the day mentally murdering everyone they came into contact with, so that by the end of orientation, they were the only people left standing. The dean of students, the photography and video instructor, the director of the cafeteria, and all of the current students who'd been drafted to regale them with stories that were supposed to describe the unique Baines experience—they'd all been blown to smithereens—stabbed to death, or crushed by the giant chandelier in the Manor by the end of the day, rendered that way by a pencil sketch they handed back and forth in relay. Clyde and Tristan had pretty much decided on Baines by the time all the others lay dead, in a heap on the page. Baines was appealingly remote. More like a strange and isolated location that a bunch of people would flock to drink poison Kool-Aid or hole up against the feds, than a college, and the perfect setting to imagine the post-mad-cow or avian-flu or apocalyptic world that Clyde had written about since he was seven years old.

Pretending was fine with Clyde. Drawing was fine. But over the past summer Tristan had changed, the way he talked about shit sounding less like a jokey game. Tristan's mother had made him work at his stepfather's law firm as a gofer during the month of July, and whenever he and Clyde had talked on the phone all he could say was how he wanted to drown Burt, his stepfather, in his infinity pool or bludgeon him to death in the driver's seat of his eggplant-colored Jag. And then two weeks ago, a couple of days before Halloween, he'd come up with a plan to kidnap the old receptionist's basset hound, Charlie, and hold him for ransom. "We could threaten to kill him if she doesn't cough up six hundred bucks. Trick or treat?!" he'd said.

Clyde looked at him out of the side of his eye and tried to gauge whether or not Tristan was kidding. Not only was he not kidding, but he noticed that the corners of Tristan's mouth curled slightly, the closest thing to a smile that Clyde had seen on his face since the fall semester had begun.

"I like dogs. I like that dog," Clyde said. "It's people who're fucked up. Not that I want to kidnap a person," he was quick to add. "Then, you're like stuck with them—especially if we nabbed anyone from this place—I bet like half their parents would refuse to pay to get them back."

This made Tristan laugh, and for the moment anyway, he'd dropped the idea of kidnapping the receptionist's dog. But Clyde knew that on some level he was waiting for Tristan to return to the idea or to hatch a new, equally nut-job plan, and while he wasn't a sheep who would go along with someone just because, whenever he tried to seriously think about what he would say, his mind went blank.

*****

Clyde woke again at seven. He pulled on his thick, once-white tube socks, filthy with dust and debris from the great outdoors, which made it into his room whether or not he took his boots off in the mud room. Swaddled in blankets, he dragged himself from his room and set off for the lounge kitchenette, putting the kettle on. As he waited for the water to boil, he sat in the living room area, which was a few steps from the kitchenette. Tristan's sketchbook was open on the coffee table. Glancing through it he noticed the sketches from when they'd first met during orientation, his favorite being the one in the Manor Lounge where tiny limbs stuck out from under the giant chandelier. Farther on in the book there was a series of flipbook sketches of a woman dressed in an old-fashioned nurse's uniform, down to the little cap that he doubted any nurse had worn since the 1950s, and a red cross emblazoned on her chest. She wore orthopedic-looking shoes and gray-colored panty hose. The nurse was of indeterminate age and without a proper face. By the final sketch she hung from a spindly tree in the middle of the woods. For some reason Clyde's eyes were drawn to her dangling, very ugly shoes.

"Water's ready." Tristan said. Clyde hadn't heard him coming down the stairs or into the lounge. He stopped himself from closing the book, not wanting to look or feel as if he'd been caught doing something. And he wasn't sure he had been. Tristan had left it out here after all. But there was something about the way the nurse sketches were drawn that felt private. They were skillfully thought out and painstakingly composed. He'd added color for one thing; ghostly whites and grays that alongside the bare trees and the frozen ground bespoke complete silence.

Tristan lifted the kettle from the burner just as it began to whistle. He walked over to the bay window. Already the sky was overcast, the pretty colors faded. The lounge had grown dark. He turned and looked down at the book in Clyde's lap.

"Whaddya think?"

"They're great. Really. There's something about those shoes, man. Props on them."

"I loved when the nurse came to me," he said. He turned again to look out the window, his back to Clyde, who closed the book and returned to the kitchenette. He didn't offer Tristan coffee. Another change in Tristan over the summer was that he went straight edge. No alcohol, caffeine, meat, sugar, or drugs.

"She came from out of nowhere," he said, smiling down at his proud discovery.

"Yeah?" Clyde rose, handing the sketchbook to Tristan. "Great stuff."

Over his shoulder and stepping into the kitchenette, he asked, "Do you want anything? I take it no coffee?"

Tristan smirked. He shook his head. Warming to his subject he continued as Clyde poured the hot water into his cup, hot steam moistening his wrist and the coffee smell momentarily giving his heart a lift.

"I started out wanting to do a flipbook of a hanging. But I didn't even have the woods at first or the nurse. Initially, I thought I'd use the center of town—like the traffic light or by the river next to the diner—where everyone could see. But then the woods definitely seemed weirder."

Back in the lounge, Clyde sat down with his coffee. He watched as two figures emerged from the trail just beyond the dorms, their arms draped around one another. At first he thought it was a girl and a guy, but as they drew closer he saw that it was two girls, Sarah and Ally. Their faces looked loose, their mouths slack and frowning. They didn't appear to be talking but making their way back to Handke Dorm as if from a great distance and journey, like Civil War returnees. He assumed that they would take the stage with Cassie Knowlton at Community Meeting. They would each take turns spitting out Dean Leppert's unfortunate-sounding name.

"A lezzie party, I bet," Tristan said, noticing the pair.

"Speaking of parties."

"Yeah, I know. Maybe they'll enter her squaw costume into evidence at Community Meeting."

"Are you going?" Clyde asked.

"You don't seriously think I'd miss it?" he asked, smiling.

Tristan sat down in the chair closest to the window, a 1950s throwaway with fake chrome legs that had rusted out and mustard-colored plastic upholstery with its filling sprouting out of two large holes.

Sarah and Ally continued to move in slow motion on the footpath to the dorms. Reaching the fork, they veered off in the direction of the cafeteria.

"Train wreck central," Tristan said. He shook his head. "There's not one fuckable girl on this campus. No one would believe that was possible in a college milieu and yet here we are at Baines, breaking the mold in more ways than one."

Clyde laughed, though he understood that he was considered unfuckable by most girls. Though he was tall and reasonably well built, he had a lantern jaw that pushed him from average-looking to some sort of genetic case. Tristan, despite his cruelty, was considered handsome. Girls didn't like him, either, but it took them longer to figure it out.

Sarah and Ally rounded a bend, walking out of sight. Clyde thought of the brain-damaged girl that Tristan visited a few times a week, a townie who had collided with a logging truck while drunk out of her mind, who gave Tristan blow jobs. She was nineteen years old and lived in her father's attic in a rambling home by the river that everyone called the blue house, along with his second family, none of whom seemed to mind that some Baines boy trekked up to her room to get blown on a regular basis.

"Did they ever decide where they were holding it?"

"The Haybarn" Tristan said. "I'm definitely going. Not only am I going, but I'm speaking. I'm part of this community, too."

"I see." Clyde smiled and nodded his head.

"It's natural that old guys when faced with youth, even of the average variety, will bang it. It's happened since forever. That's my position."

"You might be torn limb from limb, saying that."

"Of course. And that would be just the sort of thing that would show how fucked this campus is, if actual physical violence was to befall me for speaking my opinion. And you have to be there because I need you to capture my persecution on film. We can post it all over the fucking Internet. I'd like to see their shitty little faces then."

"What if they don't attack you, though? They might just heckle you and like the film teacher might escort you offstage."

"If nothing happens, so be it," Tristan said, getting up. "But I seriously doubt they'll be able to take that lying down." Tristan laughed.

Clyde listened as the other residents started to move around on the second and third floors. Doors opened and closed, toilets flushed, the noise carrying down the wide, linoleum covered stairs.

Tristan grabbed his sketchbook while the two who roomed on the third floor pretended not to see Clyde and Tristan in the lounge, as they pounded down the stairs and out the door. Everyone else would follow suit, Clyde knew. It was like they were invisible to the other boys, though he knew this was not actually true. They tried too hard, for one. It wasn't natural for people to walk with their heads straight on, without a flicker of recognition, and out the door. They didn't want to see Tristan and Clyde, was more like it.

He motioned at Clyde with the book in his right hand. "My grandmother was a nurse," he said. "So I guess the nurse didn't come from nowhere. But it's not what I sat down to draw, and it's not my grandmother....I lived with her the summer my mother and father got divorced."

"I remember you saying that."

"She was retired, but she still wore her white shoes every day, and she had a shoe rack inside her closet filled with rows and rows of them and packets of hose she'd never even opened."

Clyde didn't know what to say to this, so he nodded his head sympathetically. He had visited his own grandparents enough as a child to know that he never would have wanted to spend a whole summer with their smells and the vacuum-like silence that seemed to envelop their large home since their children had all moved away.

"I'll bring the video camera to lunch," Tristan said. "Borrow one from the film department. I'm heading over there now, before anyone else is around. I have a busy morning ahead," Tristan said. A smile that had nothing to do with Clyde or anyone else, a secret smile, almost, just to himself, appeared.

"Okay, see you later," Clyde replied. A small lump of apprehension knotted in the pit of his belly as Tristan turned to go. Today would be about community meeting, not the dog. He felt sure of that. Tristan would want to speechify about how women attacked men at every chance, not the other way around. How they'd made and ruined the world for men, who couldn't talk about anything. Still, Clyde almost asked abut the dog, just to make sure. He almost said something. But did not.

Small groups of students had begun to wend their way to the cafeteria. A few of the girls still wore their pajamas, and one carried a teddy bear. As much as Clyde hated Baines and its pretentious student body, he knew that he would probably hate it anywhere he was. Plus the amount of energy it would require to leave Baines, not to mention the hope implicit in leaving, in thinking there was a better place, was energy he knew he did not have. Clyde was only nineteen and his body looked much younger, even, like he was fifteen, sixteen, but inside he felt brittle, old and spent. At his core he had always felt just this old, which was why, he felt certain, neither adults nor children had ever known how to talk to him or had liked him much. In turn, he'd stopped hoping for different outcomes with people. Tristan was the first person he'd met in a long time who he could talk to. Sometimes, anyway. And Tristan was not really normal.

Before leaving the dorm for his first class, Clyde returned to his room and wrote for a few minutes. Almost from the outset of his novel, *The End of Water*, he had wanted to describe a quiet end to the world and go against the literary expectation of an end time that depicted the earth being consumed by fire, floods, and earthquakes.

Crow glanced at his watch. Through streaks of blood: 4:52. The high-way looked like an empty soundstage with no characters or props. He realized that it was his ultimate fantasy, to be alone in the world. To walk down empty roads and through vacant houses. The early morning most closely resembled this scenario he envisioned and secretly coveted: emptiness, uncluttered by need—his or other people's, the whole circle circumvented, and he always felt its passing with a certain amount of genuine regret.

Clyde read it over a few times before closing his notebook. He kept thinking about it as the heavy front door of the dorm closed with something between a thud and a whoosh and the crows ascended, blackening the sky in the few moments before they blanketed the tree branches, so silently, it was unnerving. As he passed the chokecherry trees, smaller birds burst into the sky. Hundreds of berries had fallen to the ground in the past few weeks, their crushed skins frozen in patches of ice that had formed under the tree's shade, a mix of a rust-color and splashes of bright red, stained the ground.

As Clyde reached the fork, he heard shouting. The cafeteria, which also had offices on the second floor, and the Manor, were contained in what was called the lower gardens; the dorms, the upper gardens. The way sound traveled up and back was eerie almost. The actual words were not yet totally clear to Clyde, but they were no less sharp and beseeching in their intent.

Community meeting had been preempted.

The day had begun.

Cunt Daughters

Buffy slowed her car and pulled onto the shoulder of Route 14. Since getting her license roughly sixteen years ago, she'd been dreading the day when she would drive past a deer or a dog that she couldn't be sure was dead. This deer wasn't moving, but it was not splattered from one side of the road to another, telltale bits of fur and large pools of blood reassuring motorists like her who thought about such things that it had been a quick, if gruesome, death. It was perfectly intact and very young, with faint spots and a bushy white tail. Turning the car off, she looked in the rear-view mirror and felt around in her purse to make sure she had her cell phone with her. If the animal wasn't dead she'd call the game warden. She assumed, but wasn't entirely sure, that they handled things like this.

The deer's eyes were wild and glassy. It reared its torso and snorted as she neared the spot where it lay. "I won't hurt you." Buffy tried to communicate the full force of her good intention. She stayed back five feet or so, not wanting to scare the deer but trying to see where it had been hit.

The pink of the early morning and the intimacy she'd shared with Ash only a half-hour ago fell away completely. In this moment, there was nothing left in the world but Buffy and the deer's tiny rib cage, expanding and deflating so rapidly she wondered if it was about to have a heart attack. It snorted again. As if taking a last stand it rose on its thin legs and looked directly at her. In the next moment she heard its hooves thundering over the nearly frozen ground, surprisingly loud without competing sounds to deflect and absorb the rhythmic thump. Its tail, straight up, went bouncing off into the woods. The spot where the deer had lain was clean. If the animal was bleeding it was doing so internally, and there was nothing she could do about that except imagine it dying somewhere alone in the woods.

Leaden, she climbed back inside the car, hating that it was overcast, and already wishing that she could skip Baines today. Fuck. But she was nudged forward by a feeling that calling in sick and being pregnant would be associated in people's minds. She cared not only for her own reputation, but that of pregnant women, everywhere. Part of her thought that no one would notice or care. But another part recalled the zero population people, with that Ally girl in the lead, whispering about the privileges granted to "breeders." And so she turned the ignition and slowly pulled back onto the road.

Along with Buffy's interminable morning sickness, she was moody, her feelings more scattered and intense than usual. Already, only an hour later, she looked back to her early morning uncertainty about Ash, and the experience with the deer without the acute weakness she'd experienced.

Now, at eight in the morning, she felt sturdier, more herself as she turned on her computer. A total of twelve new emails. The list of people copied on each of the emails was as long as the messages themselves, and a majority of the mail pertained to additional meetings for which the faculty was asked to make time. The very last of the bunch was an email from Dean Myers and included a two-page agenda for the emergency session this afternoon. He ended the missive by respectfully asking that people be brief during the open forum. Buffy knew that people would speak for as long as they felt like, one after the other, sputtering and bleary-eyed, until seven or eight o'clock at night. As she closed her email screen, she resolved to leave at five-thirty, six at the very latest.

Wednesday between eight and ten was one of three office hours' allotments that Buffy was required to post. So far, six weeks into the semester, only two students had signed or showed up for any of the Wednesday morning slots, most of them preferring the afternoon hours, just at the time she would have preferred to go home. At eight-thirty, just as she was about to run over to the cafeteria for a cup of tea, a student stuck her head in.

"Do you remember me?" she asked.

"Yes, I do. But could you tell me your name again?" Buffy asked, looking up at the girl.

"Cassandra Knowlton. I wanted to ask your advice about something."

Cassie hovered at the door's threshold. A small, three-dimensional heart appeared suspended in the hollow just below her Adam's apple, strung from a length of nylon fishing thread. She was one of the few consistently clean clothed and showered students.

"Do you have a minute?" Cassandra asked, taking a step into the office.

Cassie offered that she needed to talk about her writing class, and asked if Buffy knew who Clyde and Tristan were. Buffy did know of the boys. They looked like cherubs, what with the baby fat still wadding up into their rosy cheeks, but you knew they weren't cherubic. Buffy suspected that they felt superior to everyone and also locked out from the various groups on campus. They walked around the cafeteria, the halls, with a discernible force field around them, like the wiry boy gangsters whose high school resentments were on the verge of flowering or withering, depending. It was hard to miss them. Buffy sighed. It wasn't appropriate for her to talk about students to other students, and she had to choose her words carefully.

"If you're having a problem, it's something you should really take up with the instructor."

"I've already spoken to Pippen. A few times. We all have."

"Have you spoken to Dean Myers?" Buffy asked.

Cassie laughed at this. "No. I won't be doing that."

"Well..." Buffy paused, not knowing what came next. Well. Well what, exactly?

She looked past Cassie to the stalk of lavender thumb-tacked to the front door by the person who'd last occupied her office. Presuming it was some sort of flower essence call for protection and glad tidings, she'd left it there. A talisman seemed like an apt symbol for a prolonged journey into the guts of Baines College. Cassie followed her stare, then sat down in the chair next to the desk, where students were theoretically supposed to sit during fruitful discussions about their academic progress, but more often than not, a chair that remained thoroughly empty—so much so that the absence of a student had taken on its own familiar bulk and depth. The air in the office shifted. Cassie looked at her head-on.

"I came to you because you're new, and you're in the English department. I thought maybe—I dunno." She shrugged. "Most of the faculty here, or the ones who stay anyway, are brainwashed or they just ignore everything. Dean Myers is a total Baines head. He'd make me meet with Clyde and Tristan. The whole class already did that with Pippen facilitating. We had to go around the room to process what was going on, and that changed absolutely nothing. If anything, it encouraged them. They thought it was a joke, and they were right. I don't think I should have to do that again."

Pippen, the Creative Writing teacher, had what Buffy considered the thankless task of two, first year "Creative Self" classes. The course, as developed by the students themselves, involved "unleashing one's creativity using writing, improv, and psychodrama exercises."

Before she'd read the class description, Buffy had thought psychodrama had gone out with the 1970s, along with encounter groups and ponchos.

"Might it help if someone who wasn't faculty offered a fresh perspective, like Dean Meyers?" Buffy asked, leaning in.

"No. It would not help." Cassie shook her head definitively. "I want someone to do something about them. I'm here to go to school, not to take on total whack jobs."

Buffy nodded her head. Having taught for the past four years she was accustomed to this generation of students and their tendency to think of college as a product for which they were paying good money, and of which they had specific expectations. It wasn't the first time that a student had so forthrightly implied that they each had roles, and that one of them was paid to perform certain tasks at the other's behest. It wasn't an attitude she would have ever considered as a student herself, only a few years before.

"Tristan's the worst. He wrote this story at the beginning of the semester where this homely office temp who lives with her obese mother is hacked to pieces by the summer intern. It's set in this busy Manhattan law firm and the intern buries her body parts around the office. As the days go by the secretaries and attorneys are all gagging at the smell of her, until finally, the manager hires an exterminator to come in and look for dead rodents. Instead he finds the temp's decomposing head and feet in the vents. That's not normal. And it's totally triggering, right? Couldn't we at least get rid of them on those grounds? Classes are supposed to be safe spaces. Women shouldn't have to listen to shit like that without a warning."

She met Cassie's eye and then glanced at the small picture of Ash on her desk. Its frame was encrusted with red, blue, and green stone chips that glistened under the desk lamp.

"Horror is genre writing. As much as you or I might find the content disturbing, especially where women are concerned, it's popular fiction. But I do understand that it's offensive to you, Cassie."

"It's not about writing. It's about a feeling," she continued. "You would have to be there to know what I mean." Cassie rested her arm on a pile of student papers and leaned back in the chair.

"Tristan is not the guy who all the neighbors will say seemed normal. He's far from it. Clyde is mostly just an asshole. But they're definitely simpatico." Slumping against the chair back now, she gave Buffy a long, frank look.

Buffy understood that she could be the sort of faculty member who took up student causes and vocalized their often-exaggerated concerns. There had been one such instructor at each school she'd taught at, and they invariably came across to the rest of the faculty and even some of the students as pathetic adults trying to cotton onto their lost youth, or anyone's, for that matter. And because she was new here she wanted to be careful. Neither of the boys were in any of her three Expository Writing classes, and she hadn't been here long enough to gauge whether they were actual threats, or if Cassie saw murderers and rapists in all men. It happened. Buffy understood why it happened. It wasn't easy being a girl, with gym teachers and uncles after you from the age of eleven. Cassie might be out for revenge. Or not. She still thought that the job of trying to answer such a complicated question was the dean's.

"What if you laid it all out for Dean Myers just like you did for me? Tell him that the class has tried meeting with them . . . and . . ."

Cassie shook her head.

"You haven't been here long enough to know how useless he is. I wouldn't be surprised if they went on a school shooting spree. You've heard of those?"

The left side of Cassie's lips curled in a sneer. Buffy looked to the photo of Ash, then down at the desktop. She felt the heat rise in her face. When she next spoke, she knew that her voice would quiver and so she remained silent. Why was she being dragged into this? Cassie wasn't even one of her students.

"A lot of us believe that they're a step away from going postal. Afterward schools are always figuring out what they could have done differently. Doesn't that strike you as supremely stupid?"

Cassie pushed herself flush against the seatback and stared at her. The formerly frank expression in her eyes had turned sharp, cutting. Erring on the side of caution now seemed the only reasonable way to respond. If she decided to take Cassie's part in any way, it was tantamount to stepping onto a high wire. It was one of those kinds of decisions. Eventually people would find out that she'd voiced the accusation, and they would judge her for it. Simply, she wished Cassie had not thought to come to her. She would have liked to remain wrapped in the anonymity afforded new faculty for a little while longer, as long as she could realistically manage. But pictures from *Time* and *Newsweek* and images from *CNN*, the familiar pictorial geography of students ducking behind bushes and of pot-bellied local police officers arriving on the scene while shots rang through the air, were as easily accessible to her as the picture of Ash a few inches away.

Buffy rose from her seat to signal that they were done now. "I'll try to talk to Dean Myers today, although with that special session, I don't know how much time he'll have. But if not today, tomorrow. I'll make sure he gets it, okay?"

Cassie glanced at her, and then rose. Buffy stood to see her out.

"Thanks." Cassie's eyes rested on her beginning pooch, which Buffy always took to be the huge, alien-shaped head of her child.

"I got pregnant last year," Cassie said. "I've never been so sick in my life. I thought I was just going to puke it out. No such luck." As an afterthought, she said, "I think it's a myth that everyone feels so bad when they have an abortion. Not like I loved it, but I didn't feel guilty. I felt relieved."

For a moment, Buffy had an impulse to tell her how much she'd vomited, how often, feeling, as Cassie said, like her body might eject the baby.

Instead, Buffy nodded her head as if she understood, but only theoretically.

"It's like there's a world where everyone tells you what you're supposed to feel about things, and then another world where we feel what we really feel," Cassie continued.

Buffy heard the distinctive whoosh then slap of the downstairs door as someone came in. They each took a tentative step forward, into a murky part of the hallway where the faint light from the 1950s-era globe that hung in the center of stairwell did not reach. Buffy hadn't thought to turn on the ugly fluorescent strip light that illuminated the nether parts of the hallway earlier. She did so now and it fluttered to life, momentarily buzzing like one of those Insect-O-Cutor lamps of which her parents were fond, and one of which, oddly, they'd given to her and her brothers for Christmas two years ago, smiling widely as they each tore into the same-shaped and wrapped box .

"I'm sorry, Cassie, about what you're feeling," Buffy said to the back of her head. She felt visceral shame, a small and crippling regret that her first impulse hadn't been to say she'd talk to the dean immediately. Still, she couldn't be certain if her present misgiving was genuine, or if it had spontaneously arisen from being called out, exposed. "It's hard to know, sometimes. . . . You have to be careful . . . ," she almost said when you're a grown up, but caught herself. "When you're a teacher . . . I will help in any way I can." As she pulled her office door closed the delicate, lavender door talisman seesawed and the hallway went completely black for a moment, subway-tunnel-style, as the fluorescent light momentarily died.

"Women have to stick together. Men don't get it," Cassie said, turning, her long brown hair moving like a glorious, slow-moving creature.

Buffy's phone rang. If it weren't for Ash and his inability to find the reset button on the boiler without her walking him through it, she'd let the answering machine get it.

"I should grab this." Buffy's hand still rested against the porcelain doorknob. It was smooth and cool to the touch.

"Okay. I'll see you at the meeting later, I'm sure. Thanks for talking to me." Cassie waved to her over her shoulder and disappeared into the diffuse gray-black light. So far, only one bar of the overhead lamp had managed to ignite. Briefly Cassie became fully visible again, once she reached the top of the stairs, which she took two or three at a time by the sound of it. The door slammed. The phone stopped ringing and it was utterly quiet. Buffy wondered if she was the only person in the building in the few moments before she heard the familiar sound of furniture scraping against the wooden floors. There were so many meetings that no one room ever looked quite the same. Someone was forever arriving early to rearrange rooms and drag out the folding chairs that were kept in a closet under the stairs. The phone rang again, and she nudged the door closed with her foot. She realized how much she was counting on it being Ash when it was not. It was Dean Myers calling about Community Meeting.

"A nice little reminder," he said, with a small laugh. "We all need to be there. This has the potential to get very intense. Have you seen today's paper?" Buffy heard glass shattering downstairs. She looked at the closed door.

"I must admit I've only looked at the local paper a couple of times. I mostly listen to NPR."

It occurred to her that he must be calling from home if he hadn't also heard the ruckus downstairs. She was about to say something about the sound of glass breaking when he replied.

"Well, don't admit that to anyone, especially not the natives," he said jovially. "Um, I wanted to warn all the faculty that the Montpelier Times is running a front page story about David Leppert today. They know about our special session Community Meeting. Evidently one of the cast in the play the theater department is rehearsing is married to the editor of the paper. They are printing the few emails between David and Ms. Johnson that the online sites missed, I'm told. I haven't the faintest idea how they got those or what they say. And now there's an alumna in the picture making similar allegations against the Dean Leppert," he said.

More glass broke, falling from some height. It might be the antique bowl and pitcher that Dean Myer's wife had proudly displayed in the Manor foyer. She could imagine the strange little maintenance man, the one with gray, papery skin and brown-yellow fingers from chain smoking, as he knocked into the armoire with a chair, and the silent frown that would follow. She'd never heard him speak. He had a special talent for pretending none of them were there, as if he roamed the halls alone. Buffy envied him, and she followed his example now. She didn't mention the crashing noises rising up from the first floor, knowing the antiques had sentimental value for the Dean Myers and his wife. He had enough to worry about, with the emergency Community Meeting looming and the local and online press blowing up.

"That's horrible," she said, remembering Cassandra's angry face, her implicit condemnation of, well, grown-ups, and the particular grown-up on the phone with her. Their meeting, boiled down to its essentials, now seemed to be about Cassie pointing out that, much to her surprise,

Buffy was an adult, and as such, had certain powers and obligations to the young, and to young women in particular.

"This other woman, she's a filmmaker of some notoriety. It means this story has the potential, well, who knows how long this has been going on? That another woman has come forward probably means there are others," the dean continued. "That I missed it is, that none of them came to talk to me, or to someone…well, it will bury Baines."

Buffy hung her head, looking down at the grain on her desktop. Today seemed an inauspicious time to raise the issue of potentially dangerous boys, with everyone focused on Dean Leppert.

For what she took to be obvious reasons Buffy had decided she'd never throw her lot in with a teacher. Okay, she granted that not all males who went into teaching (or school administration, whatever, places with lots of young, impressionable females barely in or out of their teens) always did so to avail themselves of nubile young women, but enough of them did. At most colleges there were one or two males on the faculty who were known to have student affairs, and another one or two who did so quietly, but still everyone knew. And Buffy had her own experience of the teacher-student trespass, though not firsthand. Still, it was close enough to her general orbit to have made an impression. Her friend Annie from high school had slept with their 9th grade Art teacher, Mr. Prescott, after babysitting for his kids for a couple of years."

"How fucked up was that?" Annie demanded, by the time she was a freshman at the University of Mary Washington, when she was Buffy's suitemate in Virginia Hall. By then, her titillation over being chosen by an older, clever man had worn off altogether.

"I feel like calling his wife sometimes. Just blurting out that her husband had sex with me in the public bathrooms at the Blue Ridge Mountain campsite, when they took me along on vacation to watch the kids. It's so gross, right?"

Dean Leppert had a wife and two grown children, older than Candy Johnson by a few years, Buffy remembered. There had probably been other girls, reaching back to when his kids were toddlers themselves. There had been his first foray into the forbidden, Dean Leppert's Annie.

"So do you expect reporters to show up today?" Buffy sat back down, exhausted. How was she going to make it to six or six-thirty tonight? How was she to deal with this place, its furious children and all their inept stewards?

"I do," he said, sighing. "We've set up a perimeter, and they know the rules. They're not allowed on campus, it's considered trespassing. But there's nothing to stop them from parking all over Route 2 and harassing everyone who turns in."

"Oh, that's unfortunate." After years of watching celebrities or big shot embezzlers shield their faces from flashing bulbs, and seeing the anonymous men in dirty jeans and windbreakers who snapped their pictures lurking behind bushes, she'd never once anticipated that she might find herself raising her hand in just that way and for the same reason.

Dean Myers laughed. "Yes, that's a good word for it. They've done it before, camped out near the entrance and down around the intersection. Baines still has enough of a name to pique the interest of national outlets from time to time, so it wouldn't be unheard of if one or two showed up. The Boston Globe, maybe even the New York Times, now that it's becoming something other than just a salacious story. The pattern of abuse has more legs, of course." The dean sounded tired, his voice trailing off for a moment.

"The Community Meeting starts right after lunch, at one, in the Haybarn," he continued. "I'll do all that I can to get folks out of there at five, but you know how these things go."

She did. "I have something to talk to you about, too. Maybe during a break, or after the meeting? Before?" Buffy said. If she didn't say something today, she might not.

Cassandra Knowlton came to talk to me this morning, she imagined starting out.

"Let's have lunch together then. Sometime this week," he said distractedly. There were beeps on the line. "I should get that," the dean said.

In ancient mythology, Cassandra was a seer, a prophetess. No one actually listened to her, because she'd spurned the conceited Apollo. He cursed her after that.

Buffy would not reference the Greeks when she met with the dean. That might seem, well, odd. But Cassie's name, her message, seemed portentous now that she thought about it, her being one of the only normal-seeming Baines students. Or clean, at least. Christ.

After a period of quiet, the dragging of something or a bunch of things over the hardwood floors wafted up the stairs from the first floor, and she heard a woman's voice. The phone rang. Pablo asked her if she'd seen the local headlines. Without waiting for an answer, he continued.

"The article in the Montpelier Times quotes a Sri Lankan filmmaker and former Baines student who claims she had a year-long affair with Dean Leppert in 2002 that involved a lot of 'I'll pay for your camera repair if you meet me at the park and ride at ten o'clock.' "

Tears pooled in Buffy's eyes. She laughed, not meaning to, or not out loud anyway. It was nerves, her mother would say, which covered all manner of poor behavior as far as she was concerned. NERVES, Buffy spelled out on the old, scarred desktop with her pointer finger. Laughing and crying both, she blurted, "It's not funny, I know."

"Well, 'park and ride'—you won't be the only one guffawing at that. But you're pregnant. I recognize that hysterical cackle."

"Are you in yet?"

"Ye-ah. I've been here since seven this morning. I had to come in and inventory all our equipment. It keeps walking off."

Pablo's office was in the library basement, a plum spot on the other side of the campus. Location, location, location, he often said, happy in his exile from the rest of the faculty. He spent his office hours repairing the film and video equipment and avoiding the librarian who eschewed talking, and her assistant, who was himself exiled in a glorified broom closet behind the stacks. Whenever Buffy visited the library, she felt as if she'd entered a remote chamber of Baines's heart, were that possible. It wasn't. But the building had a quiet yet vivid, life-giving hum to it. It seemed to breathe, however raspy.

"God, Pablo. I don't know if I can take all the screaming and crying today. Or it might be me doing the screaming and crying by the end of this thing."

Buffy sighed. Her chest slumped disappointedly. She looked straight ahead past Ash's picture, at the wall. Another thing left over from the former occupant of the office was a small sketch of a woman being blown sideways in the rain. Leaves, her umbrella, even her spine, S- curved in heavy winds. It looked as if it had been tacked up as an afterthought, and it swayed when the door opened or closed so that it was either arcing in the same direction as the small woman or in the opposite one. Today, it was askance. Buffy righted it, like you might remove a piece of hair or food from a loved one's face.

"I hate to be the one to tell you this, but we're in for five, six hours of lurid testimonials and we'll be expected to sit stone-faced through the entire proceeding, no matter how absurd it becomes."

"That sounds painful. Do you feel actual physical pain thinking about sitting there all that time?" Buffy asked.

"I used to, but—I can't tell you how many of these I've endured. You get used to it, believe it or not. Last year there was this faculty member accused of dealing X and mushrooms. Lucky for us he left before it got too ugly. Like in the middle of the night. And then two years ago—this might be the worst, or at least the most public—there was a dance teacher who starred in these weird erotic performances with her students. They'd invite the entire school to whichever piece they'd been working on that week, over lunch on Fridays. Casual Fridays," he said liltingly. "Casual my butt. It was creepy as hell, all of us sitting there in the dark with all these bodies writhing around onstage, rubbing up against their teacher. Contact improvisation, she called it. She was caught having sex with a student in the Haybarn, early one Saturday morning. By a born-again janitor. It was a huge mess."

"So to speak." Buffy now wrote the word MESS on the tabletop. The image of a janitor as he entered the Bowl to sweep and empty the trash surfaced in the front of her brain, along with the look on his face when he heard the unmistakable grunting-moaning sounds of sex. She saw the faded green uniform he would have worn move in and out of the shadows of the empty amphitheater with excellent acoustics, until, well, you know.

"Dirty," she thought. Or she thought she'd thought, but it turned out she'd gone ahead and said it as well.

"Right. He wrote letters to the editors of every paper within a hundred miles of Baines about how Baines wasn't a college but a pagan cult. And he did this for a really long time, like six months. God, I almost forgot that. So many scandals ago." Pablo laughed.

"None of this hit when I googled the place." Buffy shook her head as if she could be seen.

"I don't think Google turns up letters to the editor unless it's like the *Wall Street Journal* and the letter is from Stephen Hawking. But I'm surprised you didn't find the story about the drug-dealing teacher. That story made it beyond *Jezebel* and *Gawker* and into *Times* and the *Globe*. They'll write about this, too. The filmmaker claims that they started out meeting at the park and ride at exit six, but later moved their scene into more comfortable accommodations once he began taking her on business trips the college paid for."

"Jesus. Why don't they just suspend Dean Leppert while they conduct a quiet investigation? Doesn't that seem like it would be less public and upsetting for everyone involved?" Buffy asked.

"Yeah, that won't happen. The administration likes to be transparent. After the airing of all this dirty laundry we'll all be expected to "process", even you. I'm just saying, be prepared. This sort of thing supposedly keeps our community spirit alive, along with Meal Team and Work Program. It's not an awful idea, if it didn't involve actual people . . . talking."

"Yeah, that's the pain I was referring to earlier."

"I think initially Dean Myers thought he could keep it all in the family, but Candy Johnson or someone called the press, leaked the emails and photo everyone is so fond of, with her in that costume."

Buffy heard the stairs moan then fall silent, as if someone had stopped at the sound of her voice, on the second floor landing. She looked at the dusty clock radio: nine-eighteen it read.

"Oh, I should really go. I didn't realize the time. I forgot to mention that Cassie Knowlton stopped by for a visit. Unexpectedly. I'll tell you about it later."

"Ohhhh, a surprise visit. Good times."

"Yeah, it feels like a long day already." Tracing the word SURPRISE, she agreed to look for Pablo at lunch and grabbed her day planner and the play the students were supposed to have read for her Script Analysis class, Shepard's *Buried Child*. It was the one class whose curriculum she had designed, the one class she truly enjoyed teaching, Shepard's bleak vision the only bright spot in the day ahead. Ha, ha, she thought to herself. Ha, ha, ha.

*****

The fluorescent strip outside of Buffy's office had died entirely. The familiar popping and humming, extinguished. The air in the hallway was unusually dark and quiet. Two figures stood at the top of the stairs, with their backs to her, appearing joined in lumpish silhouette. They'd yet to see her, but the heads turned in tandem when the floor beneath Buffy creaked. Ally and Sarah: another odd twosome, the female counterparts to Clyde and Tristan.

Say hello and smile. Act like they are just average, friendly people and not angry young women, opposed to procreation, Buffy managed to tell herself with the few short steps it took her to reach the seemingly paired girls.

The faces that she met on the landing were blank. So much so that she wondered if they knew who she was.

"Hi," Buffy said, as she stepped from the darkness of the burned-out fluorescent bulb. She led with her chest and chin forward. She did not want to appear lumbering and pregnant.

"Hi," Ally and Sarah chimed in unison, with a cheery emphasis on the "i." They turned more fully toward Buffy. Huge smiles broke across their faces. Without looking at Sarah, Ally said, "Improv is beautiful."

Sarah replied, "And synchronicity." She also looked straight ahead at Buffy and nowhere else.

Buffy tried to look past the girls and down the stairs without being obvious. All the chairs from the Manor Lounge were piled high in the front foyer, obstructing the entrance. At first she thought the vacant-seeming janitor, the one who smartly ignored them all, must be about to mop and vacuum. It would explain the ruckus while she'd been on the phone. But she'd never seen him pile furniture in a jumble like that. The way the chairs were stacked was not normal; haphazard, rather than neatly stacked one on top of the other, they looked thrown against the door and strewn across the hall. No janitor, especially an old, lame one with discolored fingers, would have done this. Buffy started to ask the girls if they knew what was going on when they began to laugh. She noticed a couple of bags of groceries on the landing. Next to one of the bags lay a large bullhorn like the kind lifeguards use to clear the water before a storm or to call someone in from the depths. Buffy heard her office phone ring. It rang and rang and she saw it sitting in her empty office, behind the closed and locked door.

Sarah's large thumbs tapped the numeric cell phone pad, the electronic clicks adding their own sense of urgency to the proceedings. Finishing up she snapped the phone shut definitively. She grabbed the bullhorn and walked from the third to the second floor landing. She kneeled on the alcove loveseat, looked out the window.

"I spy with my little eye Dean Myers. Right up front and center. And about ten other people. More coming from the direction of the cafeteria. Not a bad start," Sarah said.

"What's going on here?" Buffy asked. She rooted herself just out of reach of Ally, but too far from the stairwell to try to casually step by her.

Buffy heard people at each of the three entrances, banging on the doors and trying the handles.

She looked at the bullhorn again, the grocery bags.

"A revolution," Ally said. She stepped forward, her face pushed into Buffy's. "That's what's going on here." Ally smiled and tried to grab Buffy's hands.

Buffy ducked past her and ran. She slipped sideways on a stair tread and her feet gained momentum for the remaining five steps, taking her within a couple of inches of the loveseat and Sarah. Almost airborne, or about to be, Buffy grabbed the banister, saving herself and the baby from falling. Flying around the stairwell curve, she took the steps two at a time, as she had watched Cassie do not that long ago.

Within a couple of steps, Sarah was close enough to Buffy for the pungent smell of Sarah's flower from beneath her dress. The empty building seemed to thunder with the force of the two of them running.

Low voices of a crowd gathering, some calling to each other, and not very far. The front door rattled and shook.

"I'm here, help me! I'm in here!" Buffy yelled. Her body sailed around the final hairpin turn.

An elongated "Fuuuuck," streamed from Sarah. So close, Buffy could feel the sound of Sarah's cry in her own body.

Buffy reached to gain better purchase on the banister just as her body slammed against something hard as stone, and her front teeth sliced through her bottom lip. Shocked, the wind knocked right out of her chest, Buffy's hand came away with blood, so slick and red, the sight of it made her dizzy.

Behind her, "You're the shit," Sarah said, laughing and out of breath.

Ally stood in front of Buffy, out of breath herself, having run around and come up the back stairs. Buffy's blood dotted Ally's forehead, form where Buffy's teeth had dug into her skull.

A slackness entered Buffy's limbs and her eyes blinked, slow, doll-like. She seemed to leave her body. Watching herself and the girls from slightly above, she saw herself collapse. Ally stepped toward her, hands outstretched. From behind, Sarah caught her. Together, all three women sunk. Gently, Sarah eased her down, her upper back arching, uncomfortable, against the step.

When Buffy fully came to, they girls stood on each of the two steps below her, Sarah nearest. Balled in her fist, was a coarse square of paper towel, its sandpaper color and texture streaked red. Buffy's blood, the slime of which filled her mouth.

"You fainted," Sarah said. Buffy glanced at her towering silhouette as the cool light from the window framed her uncombed hair.

All the way up, through the gloom, like a culmination of some sort, the chandelier glinted. As if a radio had been turned on or up, she heard the people outside the front door. Clearly, she heard Sarah and Ally's names. Dean Myers voice. The words "open communication."

"You're okay," Sarah said.

"You got a small cut on your lip, you hit my head," Ally added, taking a step toward her.

It occurred to Buffy that no one knew she was in here, that outside, they thought it was a rouge Community Meeting. More of Sarah and Ally spilling over, into the world.

Buffy shivered. She was covered in sweat.

Sarah's cell phone rang from her front dress pocket. She hurried around Buffy and started up the stairs, looking into her cupped hand.

"We don't want to hurt you," Sarah said over her shoulder, sounding impatient.

"I'm going to help you up now." Ally took Buffy's arms. She was surprisingly strong for such a small woman.

Without thinking or seeing, Buffy took off again. Or tried to. Her legs weak under her, barely cooperating.

Ally yelled, "I got her."

At the shock of Ally's touch, Buffy's heard dropped. Like they were dancing, Ally spun her around, cradling her tightly in her arms so that she couldn't move, Ally's small, wiry arms like a vice grip. Head down, eyes bulging, Buffy stared at the filthy stair tread. She could feel Ally's breath on her neck. A brash sugary smell predominated the cramped air between them. Donuts, maybe? Sticky buns? Briefly and unhappily, she remembered the Twinkie defense.

"I can't breathe," she whispered. Coughing, she started to panic, her breaths coming faster, shallower.

"You couldn't talk if you couldn't breathe. Or cough," Ally said matter-of-factly, but she loosened her hold.

"Wow, look at you go!" Sarah said.

"I learned this move when I summered at Menninger's. It's called a basket," she said calmly, addressing Sarah.

To Buffy, she said, "If you don't struggle, you won't hurt yourself. Those are the rules."

Buffy's chest and stomach heaved and along with it, Ally's left arm. Her right arm, up under her chin, acted as a barrier. Buffy could not turn or raise her head.

"Please," she got out. "Let me go." Upside down, her nose blocked up. It felt like drowning.

"No running, okay? Or screaming," Ally asked. You have to promise?"

"Promise," Buffy said, meaning it.

She remembered looking into deer's lifeless eyes. Sad and empty both.

"I promise," she repeated.

"Just hold onto her," Sarah directed.

"We're going to sit down together on the step, now."

Ally lowered her onto the step, falling down next to her, one of her small hands gripping Buffy's arm.

Sweat turned clammy against her skin. She blew through her nostrils, trying to clear her airway. She felt like a sack of something, inanimate for the moment, or just barely animated, by guilt mostly. Or regret? Her small, mean thoughts about Ash, the baby, even, made her wonder if the last thing Ash would remember about her was her irritated voice and expression.

"Just be cool," Ally said. "You're okay." She turned on the step, looking up, toward Sarah. She was nervous, Buffy thought. In Buffy's cool wet hand, Ally's hot, wet one held on. Buffy felt her pulse beneath her bony wrist. Her own blood rushed to her head, pounded along with the fists on the front door.

Outside, the sound of the growing crowd was palpable, like it was at the theater or at a concert, in the moment when you close your eyes and just listen. Buffy swallowed her own spit, coughed and started to hiccup. Of all things.

"You sound like a dying frog," Sarah said as she rummaged through the grocery bags. She threw a bottle of water to Ally. Her free hand fumbled but caught it. "Ow," she said, shaking her hand out.

She twisted the bottle top open with her teeth, and handed the water to Buffy.

"Here you go," she said. "This should help. You should rinse your mouth out."

Buffy wiped her bloody lip on her lime green fleece jacket, an uncharacteristically thoughtful, bright gift from her mother. Along with her first sip, a raw pain lodged to one side of Buffy's throat. Another hiccup produced a rivulet of watery blood that dribbled down her chin. Ally's eyes were on her, waiting for a move. Buffy's limbs were too heavy to lift. She had no impulses at present. No spark to help her run or think of feel. It actually felt good, in the most limited way and in this particular moment. It was Maslow's hierarchy of needs. People, even she, were malleable, relative to their situation. Adaptable.

Buffy's hiccups slowed then stopped and she gulped the water. She admitted she'd have to be more careful on her next escape attempt. It would have to be a sure thing, not an impulse. She'd need to think it through.

"Glad that cleared up," Ally said, laughing. "I hate the hiccups."

"Sarah, Ally please unlock the doors. Come out and talk to us. Kayla Freeman is here with us." Dean Myers again

"That was him on the phone, too. He left a message," Sarah said.

"What'd he say?"

"He begged us to leave the building. He said nothing will happen to us if we leave now. And he thinks we took Charlie, you know the dog?"

"That's so weird. They think you're Nellie's dog," Ally said.

Buffy half-expected a nudge, like they were friends sharing a joke.

Sharp, cold air rushed at her. Her back and neck tightened as Sarah threw open the window and began to sing through the loudspeaker. Not a song as we've come to think of song. She was chanting—clear, low, and extraordinary moans. Ash would never believe this. No one would. You couldn't make shit like this up, as they say; and in fact the chanting had the effect of stunning the people who'd gathered outside. The door banging abruptly stopped, and Sarah's moans were unleashed over the crowd like heady omens

The vocalizations grew louder and less clear, more like actual wails at a designated wailing wall, where, Buffy had always imagined, you just let loose. Where did this girl learn to produce such sounds? Her ease with the bullhorn was similarly impressive, the way she held it a few inches from her mouth as if she was giving a performance. The door banging had resumed. Buffy could hear Dean Myers again, his voice straining over the general uproar at the various doors and Sarah's chilling cries. He kept asking, "Sarah, is anyone in there besides you and Ally? Please answer me."

A familiar voice that Buffy couldn't quite place asked, "Is Charlie in there with you? Did you take Charlie?"

Unbelievable. Buffy had been so sure that the earlier phone call to her empty office was someone who knew, or would figure out, that she was caught in here with the cast of *Girl Interrupted*. She'd thought it was Pablo. But it seemed just as likely no one knew she was in here, that the call had been to ask if she'd seen a lumbering basset hound stranded in the center of the stairwell.

Sarah kept on with her chanting. She didn't answer Dean Myers until the sound of chain saws began to scream right along with her. Then she stuck her head out the window, and, Buffy sensed, looked right into Dean Myers's eyes.

Ally was very still. She confidently kept hold of Buffy's hand while never taking her eyes off Sarah.

"I am a cunt daughter," Sarah said neutrally. "My grandfather had two girls to his name. His name, his name, his name. And guess what peoples? What did Grand-Daddy-O do, do you think, with his daughter and her daughter and all the others? All cunt daughters. And guess what again? We do have a hostage, so put the fucking saws away. When you fire Dean Pervert, we'll come out and no one will get hurt. That's the dealie-o. Where are you with that?" she asked.

"Sarah, listen carefully. You must tell me who is in there with you. This is very serious. You must know that?"

Buffy started to yell, but Ally's hand shot up and cupped her Adam's apple. All that made its way from her throat and between her lips was a strained, balled up and twisted yelp.

"Come on. Remember your promise." Ally whispered. "No yelling.

No running. Bugging her eyes at Buffy, she smiled. "Be cool. That's your mantra today."

Be cool. Buffy's vision and Ally's face blurred through her hot, angry tears.

"Don't cry," Ally said. Her hand slackened, but did not move, ready to tighten, like a choke chain, should Buffy try to scream or run.

"Without the benefit of the bullhorn, Sarah called down to Dean Myers. "WE are serious. Dean Leppert screwing a student is serious. We're fucking sick of men getting away with putting their dicks where they don't belong. Fuck Dean Leppert" she spat.

"Fuck Dean Leppert," a woman called from the crowd.

Buffy closed her eyes; sore, like she'd been up all night and into the day, their rims were livid. And so it began, a chant, a syncopated clap. Had the crowd been inside, the building would have roared and trembled, with the sound of "Fuck Dean Leppert," carrying all the way up, to the crystal chandelier, and back.

"Sarah, please. You say you have a hostage in there with you. Is that true? This isn't a game, you know. If there is someone in there, you need to tell me who, and let them go, unharmed. Immediately."

Leaning out the window, Sarah continued to yell down to him.

"What about firing Dean Leppert immediately? Based on evidence, instead of having a moronic meeting about it? I know it's all so UNIM-PORTANT, really, what men do to daughters. Isn't that because it's every male's fantasy? Who wants to punish some old man for getting lucky, right? But this is your chance Dean Myers to put all that Baines money where your mouth is and DO THE RIGHT THING," Sarah said.

Next to her Ally nodded, and the start of a grin, the corners of her lips, upturned. "Right on," she said. Looking at Buffy she continued, "that's it, you know? They'll never punish each other. It's up to us," she said.

Why hadn't they cut to the chase and taken Dean Leppert? Why her?

"Fuck Dean Leppert." The chant and the clapping continued, the women's voices blank and scary, rather than angry. Determined.

Dean Myers, sounding weary, said, "Folks, please."

Buffy imagined him throwing his arms up in exasperation. Surely he'd called the police by now?

Her mind swam, or, rather, various images in her mind did. From above herself, she watched the scene on the stairs. Maybe her life wouldn't flash before her eyes before she died, like a ticker tape of highlights, but just a moment. This moment.

"Sarah, listen to me. We were about to take the steps required to address the…" here he paused, not knowing what to call it. Changing gears he continued. "There needs to be a process, or…"

"Or what? You'll be sued? By that bag of shit? Big fucking deal. You've been sued before. We should sue him. And we don't have Charlie, Nellie. It's that new faculty chick. The one with child. What's your name again," Sarah asked over her shoulder.

"Buffy Campbell," Ally yelled to her.

"Buffy Campbell. Let us know when Dean Pervert has been eradicated. Oh, and, yeah, we have a gun," said Sarah. "We don't want to or plan to use it, but we have one."

Buffy stopped breathing, frozen now in Ally's embrace.

The chanting and clapping had stopped. Buffy heard Pablo asking Sarah if they would let Buffy talk. To please let her talk to them.

"Let the healing begin," Sarah cried.

The rest of what Pablo said was lost to the slamming window.

Turning to face Ally and Buffy, Sarah towered over them. Lit from behind, the window framing her in shadow then illumination and back again, she loped toward them.

"We won't hurt you. You look worried. Don't be," Sarah said, her face zooming in for a close-up, at wide angle. She started to turn away, but stopped. Leaning against the wall just next to the banister she crossed her arms under her breasts so that her tunic-dress, the only thing she ever wore, bunched up, revealing her dirty bare feet.

"So, we have a gun, but it's a nail gun, which, if pressed—that's pretty good, huh? A pun without even trying. Anyway, we didn't even know we'd be running into you, so there were no real plans to use the nail gun as, well, a gun. It was an impulse buy in our friendly, downtown hardware store, and of course finding you here, just dumb luck. People go bat shit over pregnant women. Isn't it funny that they don't really give a shit about the kid after it's born? What is that, anyway? A royally fucked-up disconnect, wouldn't you agree?"

Sarah walked past the two of them in the direction of the administrative offices on the third floor. The hem of her dress swept against the hardwood floors, her funky smell pooling in her wake.

Ally's grip had tightened slightly, as Sarah walked by. Buffy realized she wasn't taking full breaths.

No one outside knew it was a nail gun, and no one would try to save her now that the notion of a weapon had been introduced. The police, the school, everyone would have a high stake in negotiating.

Plus. And. Buffy, probably most people, had seen enough movies to know that bank robbers, thieves, and assorted insane people like Sarah and Ally often didn't intend to hurt anyone, but then things always got out of hand, didn't they? And they did hurt people, didn't they?

"We need to find something to tie her up with," Ally said.

Letting go of Buffy's throat, she yanked her up.

"No screaming or trying to get away, right?"

Ally cuffed Buffy's hands behind her back with her own wiry ones. Her shoulder wings flared and her arms felt like they might snap off. Ally followed Sarah up the short flight of stairs and into the narrow hallway.

"Where are you going, anyway? I can't just hold her like this the whole time," Ally said.

Sarah's monk's robes and profile were briefly spotlighted as she opened Pippen West's office door, at the end of the hallway.

"Pippen has that ginormous mobile in his office that's made out of rope and string and like shells or something. That'll work, we can tie her up with all that string and shit" Sarah said, disappearing into the room.

"I love it!" Ally paused about halfway down the hallway, in the dark.

This particular spot in the passage had something of a sound barrier quality to it, and any noise from outside fell off. Buffy hated not knowing anything about what was going on with the dean and Pablo. Did Ash know? Would the dean call the police, or would it end up being one of those huge scandals that piggybacked on the first scandal, where the administration chose not to act and she ended up dead?

As if she'd read her thoughts, Ally said, "We really won't hurt you, you know?"

A sweat tear ran down Buffy's spine. There would be no running downstairs or even to the secret room the dean and his wife had shown her on that long-ago day if they managed to tie her up.

Tinkling sounds and then the crash of hundreds of tinkling sounds together, as the giant mobile pounded onto the wood floor from its spot under the ceiling.

Ally chuckled into her ear. "We hadn't planned on you being here. That was a bonus!"

Did she really just laugh? Like this was a happy coincidence? She did. Absolutely, she did. Buffy tugged at Ally's hands, struggling. She wanted to rip her little face off.

Ally jerked her arms back so hard and fast Buffy yelped in pain.

"What did you expect?" Ally asked, looking at her quizzically.

"Mobile down," Sarah yelled. "Jesus, it only took a nanosecond for it to get all snarled and shit. How is that possible?"

"Just get the string at the top of the thing, like where it hangs from?" Ally yelled to her.

Ally let up on her, and said conversationally, "We thought everyone was out of the building. Our idea was to barricade ourselves in here for the day, or until they fired that rapist they call a dean. But when we saw you it seemed fated."

"Ta da." Sarah marched from Pippen's office with what looked like a net draped over her palms, offering it up like some lady from the sea.

"Where do we want to do this?" Ally asked, moving awkwardly and backward to the landing again, with Buffy as her appendage.

"Well, if we use the lounge they can watch us through the windows, like on TV. Or, if we want to be mysterious, we can stay up here, or move even further, to the third floor, totally out of sight. Whaddya think, Al?" Sarah asked. The tinkling shells were dulled in her arms. The whites of her eyes shined in the dingy corridor.

"You know, I think mysterious is better," Ally said. "What about Dean Myer's office?"

Buffy heard the sirens first, or so it seemed to her. The girls appeared to be caught up in their decision making about the optimum location for a Baines hostage crisis. She assumed they would be scared shitless when they realized how far they'd gone, that the police were now involved. Maybe even the FBI. Didn't they get in on kidnappings?

But the sound pleased them.

"It's showtime," Ally said.

"Man, this is excellent. I bet the *Globe* knows by now, maybe even the *Times*," Sarah said. "They are going to have to take us seriously."

Buffy started to cry, at first quietly, and then noisily, with roiling tears, and a loose web of phlegm deep in her throat, puffing in, out, as she breathed.

Sarah shook her head.

"Aw, don't cry. You're part of something really amazing. And we won't hurt you at all. You're like a gift in a way. A beautiful, pregnant gift," she continued. The small iridescent shells shone through her arms.

Sirens wailed, growing louder and more insistent as they pulled onto campus, car after car until they all arrived and their alarms fell silent. Next, car doors opened, closed. People's voices rang out.

Ally and Buffy followed Sarah toward Dean's Meyer's office. At a dark spot in the hallway, their legs became entwined and Ally lost her balance, tumbling backward.

"Fuck," Ally spat.

"Help, help me. Help!" Buffy screamed. The steps disappeared three at a time under her new earth shoes, which Ash had bought for her to comfortably amble around the world pregnant.

When she reached the first floor and the pile of furniture obstructing the door, her wild eyes caught those first of a young policeman, then Dean Myers, and finally Pablo, all gathered in a tight semicircle around the front stoop. The superhuman strength she'd read about for years and years and that could visit you in emergency situations arrived, as if queued up, adrenaline pumping into her veins and carrying messages to her limbs. She swung two chairs, a small table, and a laptop over her shoulder. A second or two later Ally and Sarah scudded down the staircase after her. Ally wrenched her right arm up into her scapula.

"You fucking little shit," Buffy screamed into the air as Ally dragged her away. The policeman, the dean, and Pablo all clamored at the door, screaming her name at the sight of her, the dark of their mouths endless and remote, growing ever smaller.

She felt Sarah's touch for the first time, a rude tug on her free arm. Buffy spewed obscenities as together the girls dragged and pushed her up the stairs and into Dean Myers's office. Yelling until she was hoarse: "fucking awful shitheads asshole shits."

Sarah and Ally worked quickly, laboring over her with bits of string, bone, shells, and driftwood from Pippen West's mobile, tying each of her arms, surprisingly well and tightly, to the legs of Dean Myers's bulkhead of a desk. Sarah pulled the earth shoes off her slightly swollen feet and, starting with the toes and ending at the ankles, bound them in duct tape.

"If you can't be quiet, we'll have to gag you too," Ally said, stepping back a few inches to consider their handiwork. Looking at Buffy, she squatted. "We made an early morning trip to the hardware store. The

Duck tape was another impulse buy. We weren't really sure what we would use it for, but they had this huge display of the stuff in the shape of a pyramid. It was cool!"

Buffy stared right into Ally's eyes, which had turned brown. They didn't look cold or crazy. They were pretty enough. It was her mouth, the way it curled up on one side, like Dick Cheney's, that told you she could be uncaring, dismissive and dangerous, even. Maybe not willfully, but ignorantly. Did it matter, ultimately, the origins of the danger?

"Why did you do this? Are you stupid? Do you know how much trouble you're in? What gives you the right to be that fucking stupid?" Buffy asked.

"You're sick! The two of you are sick little stupid fucking stupid shits," she said. Still tossing herself around violently, Buffy's head banged against the back of the dean's desk. Spit flew from between her teeth. Ally, her voice still soft but not without a certain menace, said, "All right, then. I really don't want to tape your mouth shut, but I will," Ally said. Out of the two, she seemed to enjoy Buffy's capture the most. Sarah liked dealing with the bullhorn. She was the so-called negotiator.

Buffy shut up for a split-second before a more poisonous volley of "stupid fucks" hurled from her mouth like clanging pots and pans, old furniture and books, sailing from a third floor apartment and crashing in an angry heap on the ground below. Before this day, Buffy mostly swore at inanimate objects and sparingly, like when a glass broke, or the car wouldn't start. Things like that. She enjoyed this growling, "fuck"-screaming self better. Plus, she could tell the rat-tat-tat of expletives made Ally jangly inside . She fumbled to locate the start of the tape roll, whispering her own "fucks" as she repeatedly failed to find the seam..

The silver-colored tape didn't make much of a sound as Ally finally unwound it from its spool. It wasn't crinkly like the brown moving tape she and Ash had recently used to pack up their few worldly belongings. Instead, it was soft, pliant, and largely silent. Like a kid glove the cushiony second skin blotted out Buffy's mouth mid-expletive and Ally's smirk bloomed into a full-on smile.

____

Falling

David Leppert steps from the shower. He stares at his naked, somewhat sagging skin, in the mostly full-length bathroom mirror in the master bath. He grabs one of his thick belly folds in his hand, jiggles it. Looking down at his stomach instead of at his reflection, he can't see his cock for his fat-ish belly. Or not fat really, but drooping. It swings sometimes, if he gets up too fast from lying prone, like a discolored appendage.

David's home is uncharacteristically quiet. Every day, he wakes and does not expect such silence. It holds high pitched screams, like high-summer cicadas, sawing into the air.

David's wife, Melanie, moved in with a friend four weeks ago, when she found out about the affair with Candy from the local paper.

Melanie, he now understands, had brought life to their home, with the sound of the radio and the dishwasher, the washing machine and vacuum, and her funny way of talking to their terrier, Rory, all through her housework.

The dog is with Melanie, of course. Tucked under her arm on her way out the door, and with him the clicks of his nails and heavy breathing and yaps of joy and frustration over seeing chipmunks and birds and cats out the living room window, not to mention any time Mary, their youngest daughter, arrived home from Boston to visit. He has two daughters. Mary and Claire, twenty-three and twenty-eight, respectively. Claire lives in Philly. They also found out through the media, or because of it. They were called, approached, and badgered by the world, which was now capable of screaming at you from near and far. Predictably, they've sided with Melanie. Her pain referred, like a rotten tooth emanating distress waves. They are all women scorned.

His wife had been a young student of his once, too. Long ago. His teaching assistant or TA for short, as such pliable students are referred to on university campuses, without any sense of irony. At least publicly. Privately, he'd thought of more than one TA as his tits and ass.

Sadly, he is no longer attracted to his younger wife, who is not young any more. Fifty years old, Melanie has an above average body for her age, her gym membership keeping the outright fat at bay. But from certain angles, she still manages to look like an old hen, her large-ish breasts and loose belly lump together a bit, unkindly. There are ripples and stretch marks on her stomach and the back of her legs that he did not want to look at or to touch. This had been true for many years. It was sad and it wasn't her fault. Or his. He couldn't force himself to desire her. It was a design problem. Men stayed younger looking longer. Everyone knew that.

Also sadly, in the last month, David has been forced to see that he had become old himself. This knowledge is like an object inside of him, hot to the touch, the kind of pain he wished he could die from.

On a ride home from college once, his now deceased father had told him that he wasn't attracted to women over 40, that it was the definitive cut off number for him. David skewed younger than that. By about twenty years. He liked girls. He had always accepted this about himself, assumed other men were lying if they denied wanting to fuck young females exclusively.

David had fallen in love with a few of the students he'd had affairs with in the last three decades. He had even considered leaving Melanie before, but there had been his own daughters to think about. The youngest had been gone a few years when he fell in love again, with Candy. Her beauty was a thing in itself; a natural landmark that you might visit to admire. The Grand Canyon or Niagara Falls. From the beginning, he'd wanted to tell Melanie about her, maybe even to separate this time around.

The affair had ended, was well into its aftermath when the *Montpelier Times* newspaper crashed against their front door. He'd known about the article, but not when it would be published. He'd known and still he'd said nothing to Melanie; had failed to protect even her most basic sense of dignity. The shame of this particular omission eclipsed all others. He lived there, in its shadow, and he would never reside elsewhere in the eyes of his wife, his daughters.

The young, hot-shot female writer they'd recently hired at the *Montpelier Times* had managed to dig up a syllabus from his World Literature class that included "Lolita," and "Death in Venice," along with a com-plaint signed by a number of female and male students, from twenty years ago. Part of the letter was reprinted in the paper: "Professor Leppert not only lauds these books great literature, which is perfectly acceptable, but he appears to delight in reading aloud to the class scenes that depict the repeated rape of a twelve-year-old girl, and an old man's sexual obsession with a fourteen-year old boy."

The old man to which they referred was fifty, in Mann's novella. David had been forty-five at the time. He sees that he should have perceived this as the clarion call that it was. A warning from the chorus about his tragic flaw and his eventual fall. No one at that college had paid much attention to the letter. They'd asked him to rethink reading aloud to a college-level class. It was later, when he was accused of sexual harassment that he'd been asked to resign.

The local reporter unearthed this information as well. Or rather the rumors that weren't really rumors, but formal complaints that the other college had sealed. A former student of David's that had gone on to teach there was her source.

Melanie had read the paper first that morning. He remembers that he noticed a lacy piece of egg white clinging to the side of her mouth, had thought of telling her. But something had stopped him. Instead, his hand involuntarily reached toward his own lips.

He was looking out the window at the flat, gray sky when Melanie pointed at him, her voice evolving from biting, to loud, almost triumphant. Rory stood, trotted over to her. Without looking, she caressed his head.

"You think *you* haven't been having sex with *me* for the last however long it has been—I don't even remember anymore— but *I* haven't been having sex with *you*, either. You're old, too, in case you haven't noticed. I have no idea why these young women would want to have intercourse with an old man. With you. It's gross. I suspect they are not the most mentally stable among us. Including me, back then."

David sat perfectly still and upright, as if erecting an actual wall around himself, trying to prevent her words from reaching him.

Closing his eyes, he prepared himself for more insults and vaguely thought about how long he would let her go on before he rose from the table and said he had to go, that they'd talk about it later.

Instead, Melanie pushed her chair out from the table, and she walked off, up the stairs, Rory following behind her.

"We're done here," he heard her say. "We're leaving now, Rory. We are outta here."

She continued to talk to the dog while she packed, throwing things around the master bedroom by the sound of it, and, after she left, by the looks of it. A few minutes after the front door slammed and her car drove away, David walked up the same stairs Melanie had just hurried down. At the threshold to their bedroom, his eyes had blurred with tears. The dresser drawers hung open, and he came face-to-face with a couple of rows of empty hangers in the closet, that would jangle together whenever he reached in to grab one of his button downs from that day on.

David cried that morning because he knew Melanie was gone for good. A month later, his eldest, Claire, grudgingly spoke to him; Mary not at all. She needed space and time away from him, she said in an email. No speaking to Mary. Or Melanie. Or the dog.

This fateful morning had occurred in late October. Just before the story had broken everywhere, or so it seemed, trending on certain days on websites that specialize in ridicule and witch hunts. They were sites he'd only heard about in passing previous to his personal encounter with them: *Jezebel* and *Gawker*. In this same time period, he'd developed this ritual of looking at his flabby belly or his veiny feet or his age-spotted hands, in the almost full-length bathroom mirror. He was obsessed with his body, now that he'd seen it through the eyes of hundreds of vile comments about his wizened ball sac and fungal toe nails, all imagined. There were no such pictures featuring his naked body online, but the masses surmised, entertainingly and among themselves, about his essential grotesqueness. Sadly, there was a picture of his wife, looking dowdier than she really is and rolling her eyes, lifted from Facebook before she disabled her account, and one of Candy in the costume he'd bought for her on eBay, with its elaborate feathered headdress and Indian patterned mini skirt, the sequined bra-top. The two pictures were often positioned side-by-side on the Internet for quick comparison.

Like stomping on your foot to take your mind of your headache, just when he thought he couldn't bear life without Melanie, his daughters, or Candy, and with all of Baines College and Central Vermont nipping at his heels, his life became even worse. The *Daily Mail* in the UK picked up the story. People the world over delighted at the images of his old Billy goatish looks next to the young, beautiful Native American girl not yet into her twenties. He was a sexist, racist, ageist, old white man, and a virtual piñata. They loved that he'd fallen.

David was crying again. The tears were unbidden, without thought or feeling. They sprang into his eyes and ran down his cheeks on their own accord, it seemed.

Above the small bathroom sink to the left of the shower, David considers himself in the much smaller mirror. He avoids meeting his own eye, reaching over the uncapped toothpaste tube for his newly filled bottle of Xanax. Dirty paste tongues out of the tube's small opening, and damp layers of soap scum have gummed up around the sink fixture. Without maintenance to body and soul and physical surroundings, it does not take much time, none at all, really, for a whole clean, orderly world to disappear and a shit world to take its place.

David hadn't taken any drugs in years, but had made a special trip to the local health clinic to plead his case shortly after Melanie left and Candy had turned him loose. With his face in the local papers and online, that wasn't so hard. His primary care physician, Dr. Alice, quietly asked him if he had a support system. When he said nothing, she said she would make a mental health referral. He should have someone to talk to. He hadn't followed up with the therapist yet. Wasn't sure that he planned to. Dr. Alice had also asked if he owned a gun. He was used to this question appearing on the questionnaire he filled out each year, but not to being asked the question outright. "No, no," he'd replied. Which was true at the time. Call it the power of suggestion. He'd bought a handgun at Walmart one Thursday afternoon. Picked it up that Saturday. He had not even looked at it since.

David pops two 10 mg Xanax. The prescription is for one time-release, 10 mg pill per day. He requires more numbness today, just to leave the house. It might be the worst day of his life, he thinks. Worse than all the other worst days of his life combined.

A special Community Meeting had been scheduled to deal with him. Candy would not be present. When Gretchen Wright, the Human Resources person, mentioned this he was acutely disappointed that Candy would not be there. As ridiculous as it sounded, he missed her, and was looking forward to seeing her again. Gretchen Wright had said it was unsafe for Candy to see him, and that she would have left for the holiday by the time of the meeting. Helen Wallace, her advisor and confidante, would be there. Helen was woman impervious to fashion or caring about others' superficial selves, as she lacked one. She seemed to exist some-where above trivial concerns. Her intrinsic, seeming goodness would not help matters at all. He should have just resigned, when Dean Meyers, an old friend who could no longer quite look him in the eye, offered him this out. But his attorney had said no. To resign was tantamount to ad-mitting fault. And a civil suit might be on its way, Post Traumatic Stress Disorder, something along those lines from the girl, the attorney had said. Such a suit would clean him out; also, clean his wife's, his daughters,' legacies out. There would be nothing left. "You don't admit fault," the attorney reiterated, almost each time he spoke to him. "Ever. There's no fault in a consensual relationship."

After toweling off, David whimpered. Sometimes without thinking of any of the awful things he'd lived through in the past weeks, a small scream escaped from his throat, his tonsils, wherever it was these nov-el utterances emanated from. Other times, it grew from a strong, swift prompt, a terrible image or feeling from the past weeks: watching Mel-anie walk off, the sound of her car door clicking shut and signaling the world falling away, leaving him stranded on a ledge with no purchase; or Dean Meyers calling him to tell him of Candy's sexual harassment com-plaint; or the pings of forwarded articles to his email account, the first day *Gawker* had printed the story, the emails, the now-famous picture of Candy, the picture his wife, and the picture of him from the Baines College website, looking older than he ever thought he would be, with the headline: FUCKED.

Impasse

The bottom-of-the-pond, brown-gray air in my office is disturbed not by the usual sight of the dean resignedly, but with a certain purpose, settling his wide behind into his special Eames chair. Instead, two girls drag a third, their captive, in from the dark hallway whose light had yet to be switched on. If they were all ten, twelve years younger, I would recall when one or the other faculty's children played in the Manor while their parents attended meetings, and the children pretended to tie each other up for a game of cowboys and Indian, sometimes mock-beating or torturing each another. Invariably, they ended up on the third floor and between my walls, where they gave over to their basest impulses and relished their imagined power. Over the years I came to understand that such behavior comes about whether parents liked it or not. It is natural, you might say, and like many such things, nothing to be proud of. Practically all the children dreamed up such scenes had been *reared by PhDs and with little exposure to television, or violent depictions of what people or animals do to each other in the books they read and the cartoons they viewed, and without sugar or caffeinated soda. And still. Through osmosis, or something wicked within, they knew about tying people up, hurting them, or threatening to. But these girls, women actually, are too old to be playacting, and the victim is at a high boil, sputtering "fucking awful shitheads asshole shits." Actual child actor-victims in the past have been resigned, their small bodies pushed through my door without resistance, physical or otherwise; in on the game and titillated.*

I've grown accustomed to bad language over the years, just as I have become used to little children who whip their naked dolls and pluck the eyes from their teddy bears' heads. People often use foul language to assign emphasis. This litany of bad words is new to me however. The captive doesn't seem to be trying to make a point. Instead the ugly, primitive sounds give shape to an unadorned rage, not being used for effect. It is a simple rage, and concerned only with itself.

The taller of the two women turns on my overhead lamp. Its weak light strains through the frosted shade that is more decorative than useful. The dean's wife found the pretty cover at an antique auction, I've heard her say hundreds of times. A faint etching of interconnected spades and diamonds, taken from playing cards, flanks the exterior of the glass, the design visible from certain angles, and from others, hardly at all.

The girls don't think to open the curtains or the blinds, as the dean usually does. Instead they set to work at the bottom of the desk. The tie their captive, each of her slender wrists, to the table legs with a nest of string that doesn't look up to the job of restricting her as she struggles and spits out vitriol.

I listen closely for others to follow, up the three flights of stairs and around the corner, or for a group to gather downstairs to decide what to do, or maybe, finally, for a faculty member in a distant office, on the phone, calling for help. But no. In fact there is an odd sense of nothingness in the rest of the building, as if it has been negated, or has broken off from the third floor, or the third floor from the other two, leaving it suspended in midair. The Persian rug, purchased in the days when the small college was prosperous, which was a long time ago indeed, thirty, forty years, at least, lends me a magisterial sense that I usually enjoy immensely. Today, however, the carpet's deep and various reds, its almost intimidating beauty, cloaks me in a certain feeling of vulnerability, as if something equaling the operatic swells of the carpet's shapes and colors might unfold.

I keep straining to hear far-off, telltale sounds that efforts might be under way to rescue the swearing woman, but there are no sounds to be heard outside of my room, and at my core, only a faint hum that underscores the heightened clinking sounds as the girls pass the jumble of string to and fro, the prisoner yelling and crying. I couldn't tell at first that she was crying, but after listening carefully, I hear the tears. This is often true, when listening to women in particular, whose voices tremble when they don't mean for them to, or break off, as if they've reached an impasse too deep to articulate or cross, or perhaps they suspect that putting certain emotions to words will lay their souls bare, for all to see, or, at least to the dean, who, by proxy, represents practically everyone, in the small world of Baines. Many women have sat across the desk from Dean Myers over the years, almost crying.

I've never really had occasion to think of it before, but now I feel grateful that so far nothing tragic has happened between my walls. I've been proud at the business that goes on in my space, and at my occasional lease to visiting faculty, and with my octagonal window, lightly colored jadeite green and beveled, from which to view the flowering crab apple trees in the spring and the foliage in fall. There's no blind or curtain of course on this window. I consider it an eye of sorts, looking out. None of the current occupants seem to taken notice of it, or have looked out to see the last of the turned leaves, their pale yellows and browns against the clouds.

I feel my own dimness. An acute nostalgia for the wayward little children, the renowned visiting faculty, and the pleasing charm of Dean Myers, which right this minute are painful to think about, past innocences that at the time had simply seemed to be what the world was made of. The poor-intentioned calculation and lack of innocence that now seeps in through my walls, from under the door and from behind the blinds, leaves me feeling bereft.

FIVEFOURTHREETWOONE

Ally felt herself coming down. For most of the kidnapping she'd been high. Not a high high, but a natural one, which she decided was way better than the high you got by ingesting X or acid or even coke. It meant that such joy was inside you, waiting for you to return to how you'd felt when you were a kid, before you'd known anything, but in a way, you'd known all you needed to 'cause you knew this happiness. Strong and powerful, was how Ally felt. Enough that for the first time in a long while she forgot her parents and their shared, depressing past. A world without their eyes on her, defeating her with simple, lingering glances and frowns, was enough to make her feel giddy.

Sarah nodded to her, told her to go ahead, and threw the spool of Duck tape at her. Ally unraveled and tore off a piece of soft tape that seemed more like flimsy, silvery skin than adhesive. The first vowel of the word "stupid" escaped; the second died inside of Buffy's mouth. Touching Buffy's face in the act of taping her mouth shut felt really weird, and once she'd gotten the tape all the way around the back of her head and effectively blotted out her mouth, the complete image of the pregnant Buffy, tied to the gargantuan desk with string remnants from Pippen's mobile, her feet and mouth bound, destroyed Ally's sense of well-being. Just like that, a thick, intransigent fear stiffened her limbs, her body. For the first time she understood they could go to prison for kidnapping. A pregnant woman, no less. They would get in big trouble with the police and judges, bailiffs and lawyers.

Her parents might secretly welcome this sort of end to their relationship, a culmination of her unfortunate, adopted existence, which she knew had been writ large, as far as they were concerned, since about the time she was six, and began to have friends. Early on her parents found ways to imply that she failed to attract normal children as playmates. A plump little girl named Michelle with the cheeks and teeth of a chipmunk had been the first friend of hers to appear on their doorstep, two days into first grade. She was the first in a long line of round faced, bossy girls to stand on the threshold of their home, demanding that Ally come out to play, their clothes stained, their hair unwholesome nests. Her mother was never really able to conceal her disapproval. She hadn't considered the possibility of this type of child climbing the steps to her home to play with her daughter, and she would have preferred a series of astute, thin girls in glasses. No-nonsense and headed to good schools, like she herself had been.

Buffy's eyes bulged out toward Ally. The small swell of her stomach strained against her ribbed turtleneck. Not wanting to look at this particular image of Buffy any longer, Ally stepped behind the back of the desk and sat down in Dean Myers's $2,300 Eames chair. They all knew how much it had cost because the student who'd worked in the post office then, Matty, who'd been busted by the FBI over the summer, had signed for it. The Monday after its arrival, a poster appeared on the Community Center bulletin board with a copy of Dean Myers' stupid smiling face and the word CORRUPTION encircled a ragged copy of the receipt. By Wednesday, smiling magazine images of Bush and Cheney feathered out from the initial photograph. The words power corruption and lies stormed across the board. This happened during Ally's first semester, and it was her introduction to the arc of scandal, protest, and resolution at Baines: rambunctious, over-the-top, and totally effective. Snarky, homemade- poster-making adolescents scared the shit out of the college administration. Dean Myers finally ponied up $1,800 of the total price, even showing anyone who cared to stop by his office a copy of the check he'd written. By Friday the students were one big triumphant being. Ally remembers high-fiving people she didn't know and would never go on to know, hugging cute boys and girls who were no longer around, the smells of patchouli and weed filling her nostrils and clinging to her clothes. It had been so much fun.

Sinking into the chair, which struck her as a combination office chair and chaise lounge, she reminded herself of the power she'd felt during the Eames chair protest and subsequent direct actions. They were fun and scary. Yeah. A little scary in the beginning, like when you fly or something, in that moment when the plane's wheels retract and you soar into the sky. The jitters before the calm. You're okay, Ally thought. Or maybe she said it out loud, low and whispery, to herself. Okay, okay. OK

OK OK OK OK, Onetwothreefourfive. A crazy person at a train stop in Brooklyn once said to her: "I see you counting. I count, too." She'd said it matter-of-factly, as if they shared the same name or eye color. Ally had turned away, ignoring her.

It actually sounded train-station busy outside the Manor right at this minute; a low grumbling sound carried up the three flights of stairs and around the corner, to the very end of the hall and Dean Myers's brown-aired den. Sarah leaned against the window frame, looked out one of the slats in the blinds.

"There are a lot of police out there already," Sarah said.

Ally tried to gauge whether she was worried, but she couldn't tell. Sarah's voice tended toward the flat and uneventful: a long stretch of road in the Midwest, nothing winding about it.

"Two police cars, three ambulances, and a fire truck. And there are a lot of people out there, seventy, eighty maybe, a TV van, and Tristan Walsh has a video camera. That's a dangerous combination." Sarah let the blind clink shut. Ally jumped.

For Baines, with its three hundred students, this was a huge crowd. From under the tape Buffy screamed the little that she could. It sounded worse than the articulated obscenities, as if they were in the room with a feral animal. The murmur from below was like background music, too loud at times. None of the windows were open and the sounds of the crowd still managed to compete with the noisy heating system and Buffy Campbell's muffled swears.

Ally closed her eyes. Sarah came from behind, put her hands on her shoulders, and said: "Breathe."

Ally took a deep, belly breath like they were always talking about in yoga. The three-part breathing or whatever wasn't working though, or not in the way intended. Her inhalations were coming way faster than she meant them to, like she was about to lose her ability to draw air into her lungs.

"Everything's okay. Put your feet on the floor, your hands on the desk. Ground yourself," Sarah's voice continued, sounding vaguely computer-generated. She worked her hands up Ally's neck and onto the top of her head.

Closing her eyes Ally saw small pinpricks of light flickering, at first slowly, then rapid fire. A feeling of dread pulsed, amoeba-like, in among the strange fireworks. She wondered if she were really human at this moment. Was it possible to go from being a human to being a feeling only? A bad, bad feeling? Why wasn't she dissociating, anyway, dangling above herself, numb and merely witnessing the events? She'd rather not feel these particular feelings.

Through a loudspeaker, Dean Myers, or maybe it was one of the police, was speaking. It was the most serious voice she'd ever heard. In the mix of words, the word "surrender," and then a dry cough or a clearing of the throat, it was hard to say.

"Surrender Dorothy!" someone in the crowd yelled.

"This is not funny" came from a slightly accented voice. Bosnian. The cooks were all refugees.

Buffy flung her head into the back of the desk again. From under the small band of tape, she swore, understandably now, as if she'd gotten the hang of enunciating with her mouth totally covered.

"Fucking assholes. Shits." With her eyes still tamped shut, Ally couldn't see Buffy, but she imagined a trapped animal, going for broke, like the foxes and minks who gnaw their limbs off to free themselves from the steel teeth.

Madonna sang Sarah's from Sarah's phone, sounding much like she was standing at the bottom of a toilet bowl.

" 'Surrender'—what do they think, we're at war?"

Well, yes, Ally thought. With the mention of the gun, they will think of war and we'll be fucked. Behind her, Ally could feel Sarah fishing around among the folds of her billowy dress with her right hand. Her left hand continued to rest on the top of Ally's skull, gently doming and then collapsing. By the time Sarah located the phone, Madonna's underwater voice had grown silent. Flipping it open, she said, "Ah, fuck, my battery's about gone. How are we gonna know when we've hit the news. We could have our own Twitter or Reddit feeds by now. Damn. No way the Dean's computer isn't password protected."

Sarah chucked the phone onto the desk, where it skidded into Dean Myers's Rolodex, open to Asa Kachadorian, Premier Saab (789-425-2348). His drab brown Saab was totally old school, had that freaky sloped back and a long nose. It reminded her of an armadillo. The first time Ally had seen the dean he'd been in the upper parking lot and she on her way to the cafeteria. She'd watched as he opened the passenger door of the Saab and a bunch of manila folders had tumbled out and into the snow. Instead of swearing, he'd shaken his fist at himself. She'd thought that was pretty funny. Now, she wished she and the dean could be back in that moment with no inkling of this particular moment. Everything that happened before this morning seemed to have happened in another world. Ally wished herself backward, to then.

Implicit in the notion of surrender, in this context anyway, was arrest.

Ally felt like she'd just woken up.

Ally couldn't help but think of going to prison.

Again with the word "surrender."

Shit. They were totally fucked.

"Sarah?" she started.

"Yeah, sweetie?"

Ally wanted to ask what if Buffy was right. About being in big trouble. Real trouble, not just with the school, but with the police.

Instead she asked, "How long do you think we should stay up here?"

"As long as it takes for them fire Leppert," Sarah replied.

Sarah's strong fingers kneaded the lumps under Ally's scapula and she hummed, somewhat drowning out the din of the gathered crowd, the loudspeaker, and Buffy Campbell's snorts.

Earlier this morning, once they'd gotten back to Ally's room and before they'd gone to the hardware store, they'd made love for the first time, the both of them so unselfconscious that it almost didn't seem real to her, possible that two people could be so close as to not see or care about anything but the way it felt to touch and be touched. Now, Ally knew what it felt like to become someone else, or be consumed or subsumed by them. It was like weight emptying from her limbs.

Sarah's humming subsided. "That little old man who sold us our supplies this morning, 'member?" she asked.

Ally nodded, recalling the hardware store clerk. He'd shuffled toward them on the linoleum with his halo of gray hair and tufts curling from his ears, his nose. They'd mentioned that they'd just gotten mountain bikes and needed good chains, locks. He seemed interested when they told him that you could use mountain bikes during the winter, even in New England.

"He's out there, standing next to one of the sheriffs. I wonder how he even knows? Is he like on his fifteen-minute morning break or something, and decided to come watch the hostage crisis? Weird, huh?"

Their visit to Brown's Hardware already seemed like something out of the distant past. It was roughly two and a half hours ago. In her mind's eye, Ally tried to smooth out and make sense of that visit, the occupation, the kidnapping. As if it were all contained on a balled-up piece of paper, she tried to reread any message she may have thought she understood from that near past.

Sarah had trailed behind the old man, with Ally slightly behind her.

"Mountain bikes have awesome treads, they're totally rugged." Smiling over her shoulder at her, Sarah was obviously pleased at her made-up end of the conversation. A natural.

The clerk had indicated a jot of approval with his eyes when Sarah impulsively grabbed the nail gun and the Duck tape. He said something about them always coming in handy. She wondered if he remembered having said this to them, if he stood out there now because he felt responsible, an unknowing yet vital link in the morning's tragic events. Would her parents blame themselves, or just her? Would their total washing of their hands of her include pretending they'd had no role in her life at all?

"What ya' thinkin'?" Sarah leaned down, whispered into her ear. Her breath was warm and had different notes to it, the first almost powdery or something along those lines, like flour; the second was older, not quite bad but unpleasant, like air that had been trapped at the bottom of a pond for a long period.

"Oh, I was thinking about my parents, what they . . . ," Ally said, trailing off. Buffy continued to buck in outrage.

"Fuck. It's hard with her making all that racket? Isn't that driving you crazy?" Ally asked, looking to the side and up, toward Sarah.

Sarah hugged her from behind, still talking into her ear. "We're doing a good thing, no matter what anyone thinks. When people stop listening …that's a problem, right? You need to take action, we need to take action. This is totally personal. I know you get that, Al. What men do is not right and we gotta do something about it. I mean why do we gotta have a fucking meeting about that, like there's something to debate about?"

Voices over the loudspeaker droned on: tinny and imposing, squawky and affecting, she wished she could turn it off like she would a radio.

The tape puckered only slightly against Buffy's breath and lips. Ally was grateful that she seemed to be winding down. Sharply, Ally inhaled, and she tried to catch her breath even though she was sitting still and not at all exerting herself physically. Psychically, she was running a marathon, climbing a ninety-degree mountain face, swimming laps. Her heart rate soared.

As much as Ally loved Sarah, she knew that few people would think that kidnapping a pregnant faculty member was a good thing, whatever the reason. The administration may have been mildly concerned, vaguely entertained, even, if they'd occupied the Manor and read a manifesto about perverted Dean Leppert, or even if they'd taken the dog. But this was different.

"My parents will hate me more than they already do," Ally said, her voice cracking. It wasn't necessarily their hate of her that drove the emotion. It was her hate for herself, which was balled up with theirs in a way that felt permanent and inescapable. During her first session with Kayla, she'd asked Ally to think about positive experiences with her parents. Did she remember any? Ally had shrugged. Not really.

"It's okay, sweetie." Sarah unwound herself from around Ally's neck. Back at the window, Sarah peered through an opening she'd made with her fingers in the blind. Ally could feel her concentrating, trying to figure out what was going on.

"There's a shit ton of police out there,, way more than a few minutes ago even," Sarah said.

Dean Myers had stopped calling to them over the loudspeaker a few minutes before. She imagined the various male authority figures conferring, their focus torn from the Manor momentarily as they huddled, football-style, to decide on a strategy. Even the murmur of the crowd had lessened, now that most had probably been brought up to speed on the hostage situation inside the Manor.

"Parents are bullshit, most of them," Sarah said definitively. "Why do you think most kids can't wait to get away from them?"

"I know, but . . ." But what? They were always with you, like the poor? But she still cared what they thought of her?

Fivefourthreetwoone. Her thumbs gently tapped out each number against her fingertips, her lips probably moved, though she never sensed their moving. But how else would Looney Toon at the train stop have known? The counting had begun the summer before her senior year in high school. Never above ten, and mostly up to five and then back.

In her short life so far, Ally assessed her high school years as being the most miserable ones. Knowing that she would see her parents in another few hours at any random point in time had conjured in her a near-constant low-grade ache in her chest and abdomen that was dulled somewhat by sucking on joints shared with various boys, before and after classes. She zigzagged through the maze of parked school buses doing vodka shots or lines of coke, scavenging whatever drug was plentiful on that particular day, before the first bell rang and then again after lunch. She was loudmouthed, crude. Her only friends, if you could call them that, were boys who wanted to get high with her, have sex with her, and then pretend it hadn't happened and wouldn't happen again. The girls didn't talk to her. They actually left any physical space Ally arrived in, the restroom, the cafeteria line, as if she came with her own ground zero capability, despite her smallness. Evidently being thought a slut transcended your actual physical size.

She winced with pain when she thought back on it. It was interesting to her that people supposedly can't remember past physical pain, but emotional pain had the force to hit you in the fucking gut. Why was that? It sucked. Really.

The parents. Well, either they didn't know she was using, or they pretended not to notice her strangely focused eyes at the dinner table or in front of the TV. Ignoring her worked, for a while anyway. Until it did not. Then they started to take turns confronting her. They argued about whose turn it was. She'd heard them. Many times. She understood without really knowing that they each waited until they were in the right mood and had emotional strength to spare before facing her. In her sophomore year of high school, things really stepped up. Brazen and full of disgust, her father often stood in front of her mother as if to shield her from Ally, his voice a whisper, telling her to shut up. She knocked the two of them into the walls of that same hallway, to get away, and they shoved her back. The fights stopped being about her room or the slovenly way she dressed, like a homeless person, and started to be about where she was all the time, what she did. But really the fights were about hate. To no one's real surprise, her parents, after adopting, had never gone on to delight family and friends with an announcement of a biological pregnancy, the way some adoptive parents did, two to be exact, in her parents' adoption support group.

The metal blind clanged shut. Ally started.

"Pretend your parents don't exist, that's what I do," Sarah said, coming up from behind her.

"I want to do more than pretend. I really wish they didn't exist. I wish…"

Ally wished not her parents, but she herself were dead. At this moment and ever since she could remember, as if there were one continuous line that was her most consistent and persistent feature: the "I wish I were dead" line. And it wasn't that she wanted to kill herself, but just to be dead. Underneath the bloom of self-hatred, the hatred of her parents, the frightening thrill of having taken fucking Buffy Campbell hostage, and this crazy moment with Sarah, whom she loved, at the bottom of all this shit, she would just as soon be dead.

Sarah touched her shoulder. She spun the chair around and leaned in toward Ally, bracing herself on the arms of the chair. Ally closed her eyes, excited by the touch of Sarah's breasts, and the hothouse air their skin and breath generated. The warmth of Sarah's mouth made Ally flush, starting at her clitoris and spreading into her skin and to the farthermost reaches of her limbs.

Opening her eyes, she looked up at Sarah and then over her shoulder toward a small, octagonal window she'd never noticed before. She kissed Sarah back, soaring, her body light as the air. Maybe what she and Kayla had been working toward since the beginning of her therapy was her being able to embrace her sexuality. Perhaps right here and now, this was exactly where she was meant to be. With Sarah. Ally's doubt about what they'd done receded as quickly as the awful shakiness had begun.

She listened. The outside, incidental sounds were still. You wouldn't necessarily know that Buffy was in the room, she was so quiet. She was displaying learned helplessness. It was one of Ally's favorite psychological concepts, or maybe favorite wasn't the word. But she got it. How after trying and trying to change some shitty, self-same outcome and consistently getting absolutely no fucking results, you give up. Or maybe, most of the time you give up, but then there comes a time when you just get pissed off. Coming to Baines was no mistake, Ally realized. It was her catalyst, a way out of learned helplessness and into action. An image of sixty-six-year-old Dean Leppert, with his loose gray skin and scaly bald head, grunting over a multitude of very young women of color, there for the taking on college campuses as far as the eye could see, fired in her brain. He'd fucked Candy Johnson and the Sri Lankan chick exclusively in the ass, or so their emails and letters said. Doggie-style. Of course.

She heard Buffy begin to struggle again, her mumbly yells and screams traveling the length and width of Dean Myers's desk. Ally opened her eyes. Out the little window, the white November sky rose, cold and formidable.

"Let's talk to her," she whispered into Sarah's neck, running her hands down her back. Looking into her eyes she continued, "Maybe we can get her on our side? And then we could untie her?"

Sarah shifted against her and then stood. Still close, she looked down at Ally.

Ally shrugged. "We shouldn't leave her tied up. She's a woman too." Ally wondered why neither of them had thought of simply talking to Buffy about the issues, asking her if she'd play along.

Sarah cupped her face in her hands and leaned in. "I love you, Ally. You're so good. Inside you are so good, and you don't even know it."

"Let's untie her." The Eames chair nodded back and forth as she stood, like one of those bobble heads people affixed to car dashboards. Sarah took a few steps backward and considered her, shaking her head.

"Ally, you heard her. I don't think that would work, do you, really?"

"Well, then maybe we should let her go." For the first time, Ally looked out the window at the crowd, her eye inexorably drawn to the hardware store clerk, his tufts of cotton candy hair and the loose frame of his suspenders, from which his belly spilled.

Sarah came up beside her.

"You know either way, we're screwed, so we might as well keep her. If we go down now and just hand her over . . . they're not just going to say, 'oh thanks ladies.' They'll arrest us. Either way," said Sarah.

"I know. I just, I think women should stick together. I know she's a good way to get their attention, believe me. I hate how people think someone's so special when they're pregnant, you know I do. I'm against all that. I mean give me a break, right? It's not like it's hard or unusual to get knocked up. It's just what people do, all the time. But she *is* a woman. She may have been abused, too. Most are."

Buffy was absolutely silent. Ally could tell she was listening. She saw the old clerk lean in and say something to one of the younger policeman. She watched as he pointed to the various entrances and some of the windows. The cop he was talking to just listened, not even turning his head, but following with his eyes. At one point, the old man looked right up to the third floor. She could have sworn he met her eyes, though it didn't seem possible that he could see her from the narrow opening in the blinds. Ally let go like she'd been burned and the blind snapped shut.

Sarah leaned close to Ally, her breath warm against her face. Her hands and arms shot through the air, waved at her.

"I don't get what's going on with you, Al. You can't back out now. We're about to make the national news. This is huge. People in the sixties got arrested all the time for causes. They weren't scared, or maybe they were, but they didn't let that get in the way."

"But most of them weren't kidnapping people. They were like blowing up empty buildings or defacing property. That's different."

Ally stepped back from the window and around to the front of the desk. Buffy looked up at her. Her eyes were clear and steady, not begging. It was unnerving, how firm her gaze was.

"I won't hurt her. You won't. There's no problem. But she won't just stay if we untie her. It's like with a dog. I mean, it's a nice idea, but it won't work. Even if she agreed to be part of our protest, she'd just do it long enough to have us untie her, then she'd bolt. You have to know that."

"I guess. But this could be bad. It is bad. We should've made sure the building was empty, that was the original idea. You know it was. We should've stuck with that plan instead."

"Well, we didn't, did we?"

It was the first time that day that Ally detected a shift in Sarah's inflection. Ever so slight, but still. She could tell Sarah was impatient with her lack of confidence. It was true that a big part of what had drawn Ally to her in the first place was how out there Sarah was, how entitled she felt to say what she was thinking. But this was different. Obviously. Her talk had ended up somewhere dangerous.

"Is there a radio in here?" Sarah said, looking at the shelves. "I don't know why I didn't think of that earlier. We might have made the news by now."

Ally dreaded listening to a news report, but she knew there must be a radio somewhere. Baines faculty were nothing if not totally devoted to Vermont Public Radio, obsessively talking about the same stories they'd all heard on their way in that morning, or their way home the afternoon before. She could see Dean Myers sitting in his fancy chair, who pays that kind of money for a chair, anyway? At six, seven o'clock at night, looking at files and writing bullshit memos, while listening to another story about deforestation in Haiti or Brazil.

"Voila!" Sarah said, pulling a clock radio out from under a pile of books. Plugging it in, one of the NPR talk show hosts' voice filled the room, smoothly discussing consumer debt.

It was almost noon when the news headlines came on. These broadcasters' voices weren't soothing as much as grave. She could almost see Korva Coleman or Ann Taylor reading her name from a dark room in Washington, D. C. She blinked at the vision of her parents in New Jersey, at a stoplight or the dentist's, as her name, their names, were carried over the radio waves, part of a new batch of information about the world that only a handful of hours before, did not exist.

Hidden

Sarah and Ally cozied up together behind Dean Myers's desk, the same desk whose bottom left leg she was tied. Buffy couldn't tell who was sitting on whose lap, but from what she could gather that was the general arrangement. Canoodling, the girls were, like they weren't in the beginning or the middle of a kidnapping, whichever, and Buffy was not a few feet away, gagged and bound, on the other side of the desk, the alarming image of her obscured by the desk's bulk and her position on the floor. The Duck tape glue had undergone some sort of sickly chemical change that reduced it to a candy-apple-like mess around her lips. The cloying feeling and taste made her panic. Her accelerated heart beat thumped like footsteps filling a vast, empty gymnasium. Enraged, Buffy rolled her eyes heavenward. Not in a pleading manner, but a threatening one—a glare heavenward. Not that she'd ever believed in heaven or God for that matter, but like all foxhole inhabitants she needed a dialogue with someone or something at this precise moment. Seeing that the two other humans in the room were totally whacked and she had a fucking gluey gag on, there was no one else, save God. Straining against the desk, Buffy yelped again; her words were totally indecipherable, but her sentiment clear. Rage was like that. A pure thing. A salve, applying itself from within. Intent on escape, Buffy again remembered stories she'd heard over the years about people winning out under the most unwinnable of circumstances: the mother who'd lifted a burning car off her toddler, and the man who'd sawed off his rotting arm from under a fallen tree with a blunt pocketknife.

Resolved to win, Buffy arched her pelvis from the floor in an attempt to superhumanly stand. She hoped to flip the huge wooden desk so that it pinned the murmuring, heavy-breathing lovebirds. But out of the side of her eye she noticed the desk's squat legs, how they gave absolutely nothing, while she knocked herself out, her hips and torso tightly bowed. The Dean had once announced that the desk was made of a hardwood Maine ash. He'd slapped its rich, swirling grain on the word "ash," like some men might slap their wife's sturdy behind. Proudly. Also, Buffy was certain it was bloated with manila files and binders that barely contained a riot of meeting agendas and minutes, copies of emails and memos, formal complaints and board decrees. All told, the desk was probably over one hundred pounds and it had the force of gravity on its side. Deflated, Buffy's arched body fell.

"My parents will never forgive me for this," Ally said.

"You're so beautiful. You don't even know how beautiful you are," Sarah replied.

It was like she wasn't there, tied to the bottom of the desk like an animal.

The girls wondered if they'd made the national news. It hadn't actually occurred to Buffy that enough time had passed for her story to filter into the world. But with the advent of Twitter and Facebook, filtering wasn't much of a thing anymore. Information was dumped and disseminated. Like the emails between Candy Johnson and Dean Leppert, the picture of Candy, all of it stoking Ally and Sarah.

Had it been more than two hours? Really, she had no idea.

The word "surrender" was borne up the three flights of stairs. Its faint sound managed to hit its mark. Buffy thought she felt the girls bristle. She pushed her ribs and chest into the shape of a basket, seeing if she'd have any more luck with these body parts, with their higher center of gravity.

However long it had been, she felt pretty sure that Pablo would have called Ash by now. With only the VW between them, someone would have to go get him.

He would feel crazy, having to wait like that. But it would also give him time to call her parents and his. Had he had his own vehicle he may not have immediately let their family in on how his morning and hers had changed from a mundane one to a mythic and unreal one. Buffy imagined that after the phone calls he would begin to float above this particular morning rather than in it. As he stood in the dark hallway waiting for this particular ride, he would enter the relatively safe protective bubble of shock. An almost tangible scrim would grow up between him and all the strangers who would be talking to him about his wife's kidnapping, and the baby. He'd nod at them, like he understood what they were saying. Only later, would he really hear the words spoken by whoever had come to get him, and the events they described.

The lovebirds whispered suggestively. The sweaty tape adhesive tasted like palmed coins smelled. Within a couple of seconds, she was blubbering behind the gag. Flapping like a gill, the tape made little gasping sounds as she breathed in and out.

She relaxed her pelvis, and at the same time her heart dropped into a dark well. Losing hope of any rescue or escape, Buffy stared at the office door. Slightly ajar, it let in some of the buzz from the crowd that had gathered outside the Manor. Someone out there must have a plan. But why wouldn't they just fire Dean Leppert? Suspend him? Demand that the girls let her go? Why was she still up here? Buffy couldn't figure it out. She didn't know anything about hostage negotiations. But neither did the Montpelier Police, she'd bet. FUCK. Had they called in the FBI or some law enforcement that dealt with more than drunk drivers? Jesus, who was in charge outside? Surely not Dean Myers? Or worse, even, the sheriff with the face of a clown? His too-large mouth and sad eyes she'd met at various intersections on her way to Baines during the past two months as road crews raced to finish up summer repairs, before the ground froze and the snow fell. Sometimes, she was lucky and he waved her by. Other days she ended up being the first in line at a full stop. Even with her sunglasses on she felt as if he was trying to look deep into her eyes, lonely or bored out of his mind. Buffy always looked above and around him, not wanting to see whatever it was. Her life and that of the baby's, a baby that didn't seem quite real to her, could not be in the hands of the despondent, rubbery lipped, de facto traffic cop. Instead she imagined a strong, well-dressed federal agent in a rich, FBI-issued topcoat, crisp, handsome, and authoritative in his movement, without the searching gaze. A man success had touched rather than avoided.

"It's okay, sweetie," Sarah said, kindly, soothingly. She was trying to encourage Ally in the ways of kidnapping. Sometimes people just had to be made to listen," she said.

Righto.

Since Buffy could remember—was it first, second grade—she'd been described by everyone as nice. You're so nice (to her face), she's so nice (overheard or repeated to her face), she's a nice young lady (to her parents), she's a genuinely nice person (appeared in various references for jobs). Empirically, she was nice, and so it was said. Consciously considerate, she let people speak and actually listened to them. Or tried to. Asking them about themselves, their lives, she managed to remember the names of their kids and their dogs, and people truly loved that attention was being paid, regardless of the fact that it was from a peripheral character in their lives, as was usually the case. Those who knew her well understood that her extreme care had its origins in a fear of offending people, rather than interest in them. But the fact that she wanted to be thought of as nice meant that she cared somewhat on some level, and for most people this was good enough, close enough, to actual caring. It counted.

Buffy's question to herself, to the universe, to GOD, yes, she was still talking to him, was: What was she being so nice about for all these years? What did it get her?

If she survived Ally and Sarah, Buffy vowed to stop being so fucking nice. Niceness, like insight and a host of other things she was taught would lead somewhere good and true, was overrated.

"I loved touching you this morning. You don't know how much I've fantasized about that moment. It seems like forever ago. I can't believe it finally actually happened."

Sarah's monotone voice floated out from under the desk legs. The rustle of material, along with what she really didn't want to think of as moaning, followed.

I'm here! Buffy thought.

"I knew the first time I saw you that we would be lovers. Do you remember when that was?" Sarah asked.

Twisting her right wrist back and forth, Buffy tried to get some play in the string. It was thin, but there was a lot of it and they'd twined it around and around her wrists, and then to the immovable desk legs.

"Yeah, I was with my parents. I remember. I was soooo tired. My eyes felt like they were bleeding they were so sore. We'd gotten up so early, drove for six hours without barely talking. I think we'd just come from the cafeteria . . . they'd like squinted at everything in the buffet like it was hay and goat kibble or something. My mother kept asking, "What is Satan again?" no matter how many times I told her it was spelled Seitan, and pronounced differently, and a meat substitute. "What? A meat what?"

Sarah laughed.

"And then on the way back to my dorm, first I saw Walsh Pederson up in a tree eating from a can of baked beans with a plastic fork. I kept looking at my parents to see if they noticed him, but either they didn't or they weren't gonna let on. I don't know why, but it made me exceedingly happy to see him up there. And then I saw you coming out of the dorm," Ally said.

"I remember," Sarah said.

"You stopped and introduced yourself like a proper lady, but you had like millions of beads on and they clicked together as you put your hand out, like you were some hippy goddess, and I knew my mother was wincing but I didn't care."

Buffy recalled that Houdini was able to contort his body, his bones, even, to get out of elaborately tied rope and chains, though he'd been able to practice in the comfort of his own home, and not in an actual life-and-death situation. But if she wasn't going to be able to command superhuman strength, she'd have to dream up something else. Along with her knees and her elbows, her wrists were bony, even in her fifth month of pregnancy. Gently and persistently, Buffy pressed her knobby wrist bones against the string, trying to loosen its hold.

"Yeah, your mom looked like she'd smelled something foul when I held out my hand. I almost laughed."

Well, that was almost funny. If Buffy hadn't been sitting there tied up, five months pregnant, with her husband outside, probably on the brink of being slammed with the gravity of her situation, and by extension, their baby's, she would have said, "Bingo! She did smell something foul. You!"

Buffy looked out the slightly open office door. Her eyes fell on the dull blond wood floor in the narrow hallway, then to the lush red Persian carpet that mostly covered the office floor, with its florid drips and swirls. She tried to gauge how fast she could make it out the door. She'd need something to wield. A brass poker set stood next to the fireplace, new and as yet unused. To the left of the fireplace, there was a side table, and a hole-punch acting as a paperweight sat on top of a tall pile of file folders. A battleship gray stapler lay sideways on the floor, knocked there and forgotten. It was probably the closest of any of the improvised weapons, an arm's length away.

The girls had veered away from sweet nothings territory. Buffy listened to Sarah, the smelly thing, refuse to let herself be talked into letting her go by the suddenly reasonable-sounding Ally. Evidently, she was just now, after the whole ordeal of the kidnapping and the tying up, realizing that she would go to prison for this.

Buffy kept at the string, seesawing her wrists until they burned. If she could help it, neither girl would go to jail for this because she would kill them first. Her first deed as a no-longer-nice person would be to kill Ally and Sarah.

She could do that. Of this, she felt sure.

Senior year. Carnegie Mellon. Buffy had played a fury in the play *Agamemnon*. She totally knew how to unleash all the dark bile that lay dormant at the bottom of the blackened part of her heart, which had grown exponentially during the past hour or so. I will fuck you up, she heard herself bellow at them.

Ally's pitch continued. Buffy was a woman, after all. She might not be unsympathetic . . .

Sarah held firm. "Nononono."

The string loosened.

Ally's voice was persuasive, genuine, but no real match for the laconic Sarah. Buffy had met people like Sarah before. They sort of drifted above the level of concern that most people had for others, who primarily served to enhance the image they had of themselves as having a set place in the world. A strong one. Since arriving at Baines, she had begun to think this kind of over-confidence came from having lots of money.

She stopped moving to better listen.

Ally fantasized about convincing Buffy to collude in their hostage-taking of herself, Patty Hearst–style, to avenge Candy Johnson and the other women Dirty Dean Leppert had fucked from behind, over desks and the backend of cars.

"Let's untie her," she implored. "Talk to her."

She laughed. Or at least she was pretty sure it was laughter. Tears, too, flowed down her cheeks, welling at the borders of the tape before seeping underneath to create the ugly tasting slop that made her feel slightly insane. Right alongside the tears and the insanity, running neck and neck with the dismal combo, steely optimism grew. Buffy saw herself tiptoeing across the line from frightened kidnap victim to cunning hostage.

Her right wrist slipped free. In the surprise of the moment, she sat perfectly still, wondering what to do next. Slowly, she leaned over. She tried not to twist or make any noise that would sound like a body movement, while she untied the left wrist. The left wrist free, Buffy quietly undid her bound feet.

She grabbed the stapler at the same time that Sarah came from behind the desk to look for a radio. Bellowing from deep within her heart, she stood, raising the stapler over her head. It was in the standing that she found her superhuman strength, and seemingly many agile arms, for she ripped the duct tape from her mouth, grabbed the poker with her left hand, and threw the stapler back to its forgotten place. Wielding the brass dagger with a tiny barb on the end, she war-cried: "I will fuck you up!"

Buffy slashed through the air in the direction of the girls, screaming. "Fucking little shit heads. I will fuck you up." Her eyes were electrified by the sound of her own voice, by the cowering figures of the girls. Sarah stood absolutely still, considering her. Ally slowly rose from the controversial chair, backing up, toward the window. Her lips parted and she faltered.

Buffy stepped forward. Ally screamed at the dull sound of the poker thudding against Sarah's windpipe. Sarah made not a sound, but continued to look straight into Buffy's eyes, steady as can be. Her small Adam's apple turned purple as a bruise stained her neck. Buffy swung again, this time striking her abdomen. One hand folded around her waist, and the other instinctively shielded her head as Sarah doubled over.

Ally fell backward over a pile of file folders behind the desk; at the same time the smell of shit plumed into the room's little available air in a mushroom cloud of fear. A hot rivulet of vomit rose, then slid backwards down Buffy's throat.

Her adrenaline ebbed long enough for an acute wave of fear to wash in. She backed out of the room, her fingers bent around the poker. Sarah moaned. Hunched over like an old, wounded bull she held her stomach as if it was about to spill out onto the floor. Having shit herself and fallen, Ally simply lay there, too dazed to actually move.

Once in the hallway Buffy could more clearly hear the crowd outside, cars coming and going, and shouts from the upper parking lot and the cafeteria. The sounds buoyed her. In response she yelled: "Help, help, I'm here!" Placing her free hand flush against the wall she walked sideways toward the stairwell, her eyes trained on the office door. The lighting on this floor was a bit bolder than on hers because there were more windows, but still, it was dim.

Behind her, Buffy could hear the girls, "Sarah, Sarah. Are you all right?"

"Ach. I don't know, Al. My stomach hurts like a motherfucker."

"Hold on," Ally said. "I'm coming."

Dropping from the ceiling above the staircase, a frosted globe in the shape of bunched grapes threw a weak, pretty light on the first couple of steps, which quickly tunneled into darkness. On the barely illuminated first step Buffy paused for a second. She looked out of yet another ornate window, arched and crisscrossed with gothic, Victorian woodwork.

Momentary silence from the women. A rustling of clothes, like they were kissing. On the mend, and about to be on their feet again and operational. Instinctively Buffy wanted to run, take the three flights of stairs. To just fly. Just as instinctively, she knew she wouldn't make it. Behind her in no time, Ally and Sarah would drag her up the stairs again. They would furiously grab her by the hair, the arm, and their wrath would focus on her second attempt to escape, not on Dean Leppert. The backward march of her earth shoes as they pulled her up and into the dean's office on rewind would signal her defeat. Nothing good would come of her recapture. Nothing, nothing at all.

The girls would be on their way in a moment. Sarah's voice was fuller, steadier, but still winded.

Buffy had to make a decision, now.

She stood still for a moment and acutely remembered the first time ever that she was in this hallway. This particular and peculiar hallway.

Outside, garbled noise issued from the bullhorn, though distinctly enough she heard the words "FBI," and the name Ashley Campbell. Her heart leapt at the same time shadows of the girls elongated into the hallway.

"You stupid cunt," Sarah roared, now that it was her turn. "You won't get away."

Buffy looked over her shoulder. Eerily, she watched Sarah's shadow walk toward the Dean's door, growing indecipherable in its nearness—no longer cut and distant, but an angry smear.

Scuttling down the opposite side of the hallway Buffy felt for the Braille-like indentation that signaled the hidden passage. In her mind's eye, she was just about to reach it, she could feel it on her fingertips, as Sarah neared the threshold of the door, her voice loud and clear now. All the panels looked and felt exactly the same, though. One after the other.

"Sarah," she heard Ally call out. "Hold on. Be careful near the windows."

A slender, wooden panel that looked so much like all the others, Buffy wondered how the Dean's wife had lead her to it so confidently, opened with a tap not unlike that used on computer screen, rather than a distinct press, and Buffy disappeared, closing the panel on the word "surrender." The brass tip of the poker, its curled and witchy finger, was the last of any evidence of her to slip into the wall. It was black inside, like the Baines itself had vanished, and not Buffy.

Farther back, there was a small room, its ceilings low down, unforgiving. When she'd first seen it on that July afternoon a thin blade of light they'd let in had fallen against its dirt floor, and her heart quickened to think of the people who'd hidden in here. She craned her neck to try and make out the entranceway, but without the cracked door there was no sense of dimension. Bits of plaster and cement came loose against the width of her shoulders. She had no idea about the integrity of old, hidden rooms, doubted that she could actually force herself through the crude archway. Next to the door at least she could get out in time if the walls began to cave in. The baby kicked definitively, three times in succession. She reached for her, stroking what she assumed was her tiny head. It wasn't the first time she'd thought of her baby as a she. Buffy wasn't alone. Not entirely.

The building shook with the combined force of Sarah and Ally running the hallways as they looked for her. Streams of dust hit the ground where she stood.

Buffy felt the way she did sometimes at night when she turned the light out and found she couldn't breathe. Always, during these moments of suffocating darkness, she thought of Marilyn Monroe. It was funny, the things that stuck in your mind forever. Marilyn, she'd read somewhere a long time ago, when she was fourteen, fifteen years old, was terrified to go to sleep. That's where the pills came in. She wanted to obliterate the bridge from wakefulness to sleep—eliminate the potential for falling from such a great height.

The shaking walls had stilled. Buffy listened to Sarah's and Ally's feet as they pounded around the first floor. Soon enough they would figure out that she hadn't gone downstairs, but maybe by then a SWAT team would have stormed the building or her conversation with God would have yielded divine results. And if not? No results whatsoever? She highly doubted that it would ever occur to them that she was in a hidden passage in a wall.

Unless they knew about it too. Why wouldn't they? Baines lore, right? But if they did know, why hadn't they come to find her?

So she was safe, right? They couldn't know. She was safe.

But why didn't she feel that way?

More raucously the baby kicked again, five, six times, and took what felt like a full revolution deep in Buffy's swollen abdomen. The movement within then came to an abrupt halt. Her right hand fisted against the poker until her knuckles felt like they would burst from her skin. There was nothing to see in such complete darkness, no reassuring specks of dust or gray light to weave in and out of the black. She switched from the thought of Marilyn to that of FDR. His famous declaration about fear. Anyone who'd ever had an anxiety attack knew all about the wages of fear: how you were no longer Buffy or Marilyn, for it chewed you up and spat you out. You were nothing; you were abstract, fear itself.

Losing it in here would only defeat the purpose of having one up on Sarah and Ally, but that knowledge did nothing to avert the vision of Buffy had of herself screaming and clawing her way out of the passageway. She had to get out; couldn't breathe. Thump, thump, thump went her heart in her throat, her ear, like footsteps gaining on her.

The smell of the earth totally surrounded her. Being in here was like being buried alive, like being smothered.

Buffy remembered the first time she'd told Ash about the hidden room.

"Can you imagine?" she'd asked.

"Wow, that's really something," he'd said.

"You must like click into another gear to stay hidden in what's basically a small, narrow hole in the wall," she said, yelling into the tiny, plastic cell phone speaker that was an inadequate conduit for conversation.

"Survival mode," Ash said.

"Exactly," Buffy thought.

Sarah and Ally were still on the first floor. Buffy could hear and feel them walking from room to room, opening doors, looking around corners. The building shook. Dully, glass broke, landing on carpeting rather than the wood floor; the sound of breaking glass ended too suddenly for it to mean windows and their panes in the plural. Maybe the antique mirror, with its gilt frame.

"Ally, where are you?" said Sarah.

"In the bathroom," she yelled back. If you didn't know better, they could be making brunch, playing house. "Honey, I'm home. Where are you?"

Buffy squinted at the sound of water trickling then flowing through the pipes inside the wall.

Had one of them cut themselves? Was Ally washing up? Changing her soiled jeans?

The last time Buffy had noticed the free box, there'd been a pair of ruby red stilettos perched on top of the mound of faded corduroy jeans and pilled sweaters. If she was smart, Ally would have traded in her jeans for, if not a clean pair, at least ones that had not been shat in.

The dean spoke. "Sarah, we can see you. What are you doing? Where is Buffy Campbell?"

"Fuck. Ally, hurry up. Are you almost done in there?"

At the sound of her own name the impulse to run was overwhelming. They were out there, waiting for her.

Survival mode meant that you overcame who you thought you were. You had no choice. You did whatever it was, without thinking too much about what lay on the other side of not doing it. And "whatever it was," in this case and as before, over one hundred years ago, happened to be the simple act of waiting in this secret passage and doing absolutely nothing until the right people came for you.

"Sarah, we need you to talk to us. It's imperative that we keep the lines of communication open," Dean Myers said.

Dean Myers was talking to distract Sarah while others who were more adept at hostage negotiations mobilized. Or was that just wishful thinking on her part? Maybe so. The impression was more like a belief, and it may very well have come from the hundreds and thousands of happy endings she'd been witness to over and over, in movies or TV shows, since she was a child. Did it matter where the fuck it came from if it consoled her? Cut me some slack, she hissed at that other self, who wasn't so much behind the scene as on the scene, casting long shadows.

Shut the fuck up, you.

After the clown-faced sheriff, Dean Myers would be her next choice in whose hands she did not want her fate to rest. So optimism it was!

"Come on," Sarah implored. "Nobody cares what you're wearing."

"I care. I care. I CARE," Ally screeched.

"Jesus. FINE. Can you hurry up?"

The water reversed to a trickle.

She heard Sarah and Ally climb to the second floor, Sarah telling her to hurry up. Soon, they would be back with her, on the third floor, searching.

Buffy entered a gentle, internal dialogue with herself that included actual questions, answers, rebukes, and soothing words of encouragement. She took herself in hand, clasping one into the other in prayer position and over her belly. Methodically, she talked herself out of the impulse to run or scratch at the walls with their texture and color of burnt toast. How could they ever guess you were here? They could not. Not without knowing about the room. And if they knew about the room, they'd be here by now. Over the weekends her students got drunk and stoned, and played with Ouija boards. On Mondays they excitedly told her all about sightings of a young student from the 1950s who had jumped to her death from the bridge in town. The Baines ghost. But she'd never heard them allude to the Underground Railroad or the hidden room. If they knew about it, if it was common knowledge among them, she was sure she would know. Looking straight on and not to the periphery, the confines of the dark space, Buffy told herself not to be frightened. She took a deep breath and relaxed at the same time the girls ran back up the stairs.

The third floor floorboards shuddered with the weight of Ally and Sarah. They couldn't have been but a few feet away from where she now stood, to the left of the stairwell.

Closing her eyes to the dark, she refused to let her face prune like a child on the verge of tears.

"Where the fuck could she be?" Sarah asked.

"I dunno. She couldn't have gotten out. What are we gonna do Sarah?" Ally's voice was high-pitched, needling.

Under Buffy's eyelids, floaters drifted by. The smell of old dirt, dust, and spider webs filled her nostrils. She tried not to breathe, but the harder she tried to hold her air, the louder the logistics of drawing breath sounded to her ears, more like a roiling brook thundering through the dark and into the hallway than an invisible stream of air passing through lungs, nostrils, and mouth. Standing here like this, silently, without being able to see what was happening on the other side of the wall, not to mention two inches in front of her face, was the hardest thing she'd ever done. The crumbling walls seemed to close in on her, then in the next moment, fall away, revealing total darkness and nowhere to go, poised to make a single, telling noise.

Air dammed in Buffy's chest. She'd gone from feeling buried alive to drowning, her chest cavity seeming to fill beyond capacity.

Sarah whispered. She sounded so close it was as if she had just leaned over her shoulder, her lips brushing her ear. She couldn't figure out why they were standing in the hallway. Why hadn't they just gone back to the dean's office? Was it happenstance or did they know something? Were they trying to trick her?

"What I need you to do is to stay with me, Al. Okay?" said Sarah kindly. "I want you to go in each room and look in all the closets, behind couches, under desks. She's gotta be somewhere!"

The thread of light, nearly nonexistent to begin with, was now blacked out entirely as one of the girls leaned against the wall.

"Start in Pippen's office. I'm going to—"

"What if she did get out, Sarah? She could have gotten out. They might be trying to trick us," said Ally.

"That's not how they work. They'd be in here by now if she'd escaped," Sarah snapped.

In the quiet that fell, Buffy sensed Sarah regretted her tone. It wouldn't do to trigger Ally, to wing her backward or forward, or wherever she went when she dissociated.

"What do you mean they'd be in here? Like would they shoot us?" Ally began to cry, lips smacking together noisily.

"No, no, no. No one's going to shoot us. You know the game. Shooting two young white female college students wouldn't look good. Think about it."

"But they'll arrest us, Sarah. They'll arrest us and we'll go to prison."

"Ally, I'm gonna work on all that. Trust me. If they want their precious pregnant lady, and they do, they're gonna have to cut a deal. I'm gonna talk to them, and you start searching. Everywhere you can think of. She is here and we need to find her."

The narrow hall seemed to buckle, to sway as the two set off to unearth her. Buffy listened as errant bits of shell and glass from Pippen's mobile crunched under Ally's feet. The dean's office window crashed against the top sill. Behind it, cool air rushed in, seeping through the seam in the wall.

"Sarah, what is going on in there?" Dean Myers asked. "You must speak to us, and let us speak to Buffy Campbell."

"We're willing to work with you toward resolution, but we have conditions."

The voices of Sarah and the dean were surprisingly clear, as if the acoustic design inside the walls was meant to carry and deliver voices from afar. Hidden escaped slaves would have been able to hear their slave catchers in pursuit, questioning people.

Sarah's words drifted through the air. They settled around the ankles of the crowd, the fading and rotten leaves. Would people look at one another when they heard the word "conditions"? It was that sort of word, particularly in this context. A hopeful word, but at the same time, frightening. Conditions might or might not be met; they could fall through. That's why people would meet and lock eyes, over the possibility of the conditions' failure.

Buffy felt slight pressure on her bladder and she knew it wouldn't be slight for very long. Minutes from now she would have to pee like a geyser. Either she would have to try to maneuver her pants down, squat in the dark, as close as possible to the floor to muffle the sound of splashing pee, or remain upright, urine soaking into her pants, socks, and shoes, growing cold as stone. Hopelessly, she looked at the black air. She used to be able to hold it for a couple of hours at a time, but that was before her pregnancy.

From down the hall, Ally whined: "I can't find her anywhere. I don't understand. Sarah?"

Buffy heard footsteps, then, "Could you shut the fuck up?" said Sarah. More footsteps. Now back at the alcove window, she yelled down to Dean Myers.

"We would like Dean Leppert's resignation in writing. And something that tells us it's real."

"Okay," he said. "We can work on that. We will work on that."

Buffy listened for Ally, but the sounds of her opening doors, closing them, and walking the halls in pursuit of a flash of Buffy's clothing, stuck in a closet door, betraying her, that peculiar set of sounds had ceased to be made. It was unnerving to have one of the loose cannons unaccounted for.

"One of your attorneys needs to draw up a contract. And get the cops gone. No one is going anywhere until they've been cleared out, and Ally and I know that no one is going to press charges."

"We can do that. But we need you to work with us, too. We need a guarantee from you that Buffy Campbell is all right. That nothing has happened to her."

"Not so fast. First, we need to see some proof that Dean Leppert is history."

"Sarah, Ms. Campbell's husband is here. This is him. It's only fair that you let him see his wife, or speak to her, whichever."

She'd known Ash must be out there, but it was a relief to actually hear his name.

I'm coming, she said to him, closing her eyes. She repeated it, imagining him standing between the dean and Pablo.

It made Buffy sad to think of him standing there with a bunch of strangers, basically, with so little that was familiar to give him purchase. What was she thinking, moving here? This was her fault. All of it. Her geographical fix like any fix, fleeting. Not to mention punishing. You get what you ask for. Ha, ha.

"I'll guarantee it right now. But I can't let you speak to her."

Liar, liar, liar. She's lying.

"Sarah, that's something we need from you. You need to let us speak to Buffy. Can we call her in my office?"

"Give me proof that he's outta here, and you'll hear from Buffy Campbell." Sarah's voice, normally so blank, was full of edges.

"I'm not understanding why you can't just have her say something to reassure us, so we know that she's okay. That's concerning."

The window slammed shut.

Buffy wondered if she should surrender. Would no condition be met now? Locked in a standoff, it—this—could drag on indefinitely.

Maybe she should have run when she had the chance. She might've made it to her office. She could have grabbed her bag at least, which was tucked away in lower-right-hand desk drawer. Just like a teacher. If she'd made it to her office, even if they'd caught her, she might have her cell phone with her now and at least be able to let Ash know that she was safe. But for the life of her she couldn't remember if she'd brought the cell phone with her today or not. She wasn't one of those people who used her cell phone that often. It was for emergencies. Which of course this was, as evidenced by the rushing, urgent calls of emergency vehicles' alarms and the sound of them pulling over, of people, more and more of them, blanketing the side of the hill, of Ash. Buffy heard his familiar voice, unfamiliarly conveyed through the speaker.

"This is Ash Campbell," he said. "Buffy's husband. I know Buffy understands where you're coming from. She told me you were supposed to have a Community Meeting today. About Dean Leppert. I know it weighed on her mind, as it does on everyone's here. People like him need to be stopped. Absolutely. And he will be. But this is not the way. Buffy has nothing to do with this. She's five months pregnant. It's important that you release her. Please listen to reason. We won't press charges."

With the window now closed, Ash's voice was less clear than the dean's and Sarah's had been. But still, it was a voice she knew and had known for many years. Her throat welled up in recognition, and she felt bad that she'd been finding him so annoying lately. She wondered if her thoughts had been visible to him, sort of—like small movements in a fishbowl—that he could sense out of the corner of his eye.

Ash's voice was drowned out. The walls on either side of the hallway shook with an evenly paced hammering as if someone was hanging a heavy, unwieldy painting. Slowly Buffy moved backward, toward the small, dark grave-like room, her throat closing around a scream. They'd found her. Instinctually, she'd known there was a reason for Ally's sudden quiet. She parted her lips, but instead of a screaming in her own tongue, Ally's screams issued.

Sarah's footsteps again, running this time.

"ALLY STOP IT. STOP IT."

The walls stilled. Ally's screaming devolved into high, airy whimpering.

They were nearby again; she could hear their clothes rustle.

"Ally you're going to hurt yourself someday, if you haven't already. Oh, shit." Sarah's voice was hoarse.

"Don't hate me, okay? Please don't hate me. You hate me now. You hate me, I know you do."

"That's not true. Ally, you were banging your head against the wall, and you're bleeding pretty badly over your eye. Do you feel that?"

"No, no. I never feel it. Don't hate me. I didn't mean it. The walls are just there."

"Stay here." The floorboards wheezed with Sarah's weight. Then there was another trickle followed by a stream of water.

Ally was quiet, though Buffy knew that she was a couple of feet away from her, having slid down the wall perhaps, like something thrown against it, her banged-up head in her hands.

Buffy didn't see how she could stand this much longer. Her bladder smarted. Straining, her eyes tried to make out something in front of or behind her. But there was nothing to see, not even the entranceway to the small enclosure awaiting her was visible in the coal-black air. She tried, unsuccessfully, to feel something other than Ally's close and heavy despair.

Flowing water began to drip, drip, drip, then stopped altogether.

The Manor's foundation creaked at Sarah's return. The steps sounded weary, reflecting generations who'd clomped up and down and into the various rooms and even inside of the walls. It wasn't like Buffy to think of places as haunted. And it wasn't quite how Buffy thought of the Manor. But definitely there was something here. On her first visit to Baines she'd sensed it, even before the revelation of the hidden room. Arriving about fifteen minutes before nine she'd wandered first through the old dormitories that looked military in spirit, utilitarian and without individual bathrooms, wondering about the monks who'd long ago slept here. The squat structures were vaguely Japanese in style and peaceful. But there'd been a marked difference in Buffy's feelings when she got to the Manor. From calmly imagining young devout men rising to a day not unlike this one, their skin turning to gooseflesh as they sprinted from their bedrooms to the showers, the Manor's silent rooms announced themselves to her, boldly, proudly even. Between now and then, the building's posture, its peculiar character, had moved to the background of her comings and goings, the endless array of meetings. The looming sense of meaning now returned.

Slowly, Buffy exhaled a little bit at a time, hyper-aware of the sound her breath might make. Sarah, she realized, scared her more than Ally. Sarah, who wasn't just a kid. No one was just anything, really, meaning innocent. But Ally was so fucked up. Sarah's calculation was there in her footsteps, amplified in the old boards and for Buffy to hear. Her hands moved backward over the rubble walls, gently pulling her into the secret room.

The rush of hot urine surprised Buffy. It didn't drip anywhere, sounding against the dirt floor as she'd imagined, but soaked into the chinos with the expandable belly, a hand-me-down from Pablo's wife. The pee didn't transition to cold as much as turn freezing within seconds. Back here, she heard nothing. Total silence. Buffy lay down on the floor, placing her arms over her belly, the dark gathering in heavy folds around her. She prayed, starting with "Please God." Involuntarily, she looked up. Ash would know where she was. The dean, too, probably. Soon, they would come for her.

Hope buoys the people who've been contained here. They hope that there is an escape from this escape, somewhere less brutal, where they can stop escaping.

I never get to see what becomes of those who've crouched and hidden in my secret passageway, and in the small room at its end, once they've left.

The person here today is in trouble. She is hiding alone. I feel her try not to breathe or move, impossibilities for any living person. A thumping on the exterior walls rains old earth on the floor in the back, pattering in a way that makes the person quickly look toward the shower of dirt and small pebbles. Maybe she thinks the walls might cave, fall in, burying her alive? I wish I could tell her the walls won't come down. They have been made strong with the strength of others. And with memory and the will to be remembered. In the far corner of the small room in the back, a person *once buried a penny paper, which no one has yet found. Blurred pictures of a person who was hung from a tree, taken head-on and from behind. The person's head is covered in a sack, but you can see his hands, and the soles of his bare feet, all dead. Murdered. There's something about the soles of his feet, usually so private, that I never stop seeing.*

The person here today begins to pray, as others before her have begun to pray. She looks upward, as they have also, and there is hope in her line of vision, for how could there not be?

Ally squeezed her eyes shut. Feeling nothing, nothing at all, she had smashed her head into the wall. HARD HARD HARD. SO HARD there was blood. It leaked and dribbled from the soft skin next to her right eye that reminded her of tissue paper. The color of course was perfect: tears as they should be, alarming, red as red can be. Her skull would ache afterward, but right now all she felt was HIGH. SO HIGH! Floating up and away, like a bird in an invisible yet totally powerful current of air, a cylindrical pocket no one else could see or enter, she was now absolutely alone. With the aloneness came the unfeeling, and with that, a high that wasn't about being giddy or feeling joy. It was way better than that. When Ally banged and cut and emptied herself, she felt free. So how to tell the packs of therapists and private school guidance counselors, her parents and teachers, the whole stinking lot of them, looking down at her or sidelong from their own stupid lives that she would never give up this feeling, and they couldn't take it away from her? It was the only time, THE ONLY TIME, she ever felt like anything but total shit.

In the background, at the far end of the corridor, heavy footsteps: Sarah, on her way to rescue her. Sarah, who'd been raped by her grandfather. The cunt daughter of her cunt daughter poems.

And what had happened to Ally to make her so royally fucked up? No one knew. Not even Ally, and she'd thought about it more than anyone else in the world. During high school *Thinking About It* had been her preoccupation. It sucked, was exhausting: *Thinking About It*. Then one day the thoughts flattened out into a long stretch of road, gray asphalt, gray air, and silence, all of it coming at her instead of hateful thoughts. In their place were odd impulses to gouge into unlikely places on her body and ram her head into walls and doors. It was a little like being possessed. And she was. Possessed with absence. A heady fucking absence, it was. Unnameable, unfamiliar, UN-whatever.

Sarah spoke to her in a soothing voice, hovering just over Ally's shoulder, she sounded as if her voice had been left behind, whispering to her from the far end of the hallway.

"Look at you. Oh, Ally."

More footsteps, moving away this time. A trickle then an outright gush of water fell from deep inside the old water pipes. Then silence. The plaster felt cool next to her forehead. Ally touched the bump now erupting over her right eye. Her fingers came away bright red. It was deceiving, she knew, how you bled so much from the face and it usually didn't mean serious injury. Turning, she slid down the wall, placing her elbows on top of her knees. On another day she might be waiting for her faculty advisor to emerge from her office, or for a class to end. Frankly, she wished it were another day, one in the past, or even the future, providing that it was a different future than the one that would unfold from this day.

The footsteps again. Upstairs, around corners, the old building telegraphing Sarah's every move. How did they manage to lose a fucking pregnant hostage in this squawky old place? Not to mention the WHY of the hostage with child. No doubt they'd fucked themselves on that count. Flexing both hands, Ally looked into her palms, at her unbroken lifelines and the faint etchings that resembled the frost patterns beginning to fan across the windowpanes. Really, she couldn't fathom why'd they'd done such a stupid thing. It was like a stupid dream she wanted out of. Only she knew it wasn't a dream and that all the wrongs would stay wrong.

Sarah held out a moist towel that smelled like a bunch of dirty hands. "Here Al, put this over your eye."

Ally reached for the towel as Sarah leaned in. Her distinct odor, an unpleasant amalgam of unwashed hair and skin, garlic, and now the old-facecloth stink, went right up Ally's nose, where it nested long enough to tickle the back of her throat, producing a tiny gag. Skunk-like, it was. Sarah's STAY AWAY stench. An easy metaphor, she supposed, but apt.

In the last few months Ally had thought a lot about how not being wanted by two sets of shit parents simply wasn't as awful as the likes of what happened to Sarah, with her rapist grandfather. Over the years a certain type of counselor had looked across at her soberly, earnestly, and suggested that maybe Ally had repressed the memory of her own rapist father, or some other big male, raping her. And then there was the other sort of therapist, there'd been one or two of them in the past decade, too, who advanced the idea that her literal and figurative abandonment by all of her caretakers had its own valid and wrenching pain. But at heart Ally didn't think her pain should be equivalent to that of Sarah's, or anyone else who'd been incested, molested.

Objectively, if there was such a thing as objectivity, it should be considerably less, smaller. Why wasn't it then? Ally was so royally fucked up, just because, evidently. Just fucking because. Born with an empty space in her heart and her soul, her despair and her anger had no object. It just was, and it was for as long as she could remember and it gnawed at her, right in the lower chest cavity, upper abdominal area, like a burn-hole. Most of the time she wanted to scream and take handfuls of the earth and its people and chuck them all over her shoulders, a King Kong gone nutso. Every fucking day felt like the same one-dimensional, bland, putty-colored, Sunday-afternoon-at-four day, repeated forever and ever. She hated it.

Sarah crouched on the floor and took Ally's hands. Her breathing was labored, like she'd just run the three flights of stairs. Ally remembered the poker, the awful sound of it as it made contact with Sarah's body.

"Are you okay, Sarah?" she asked.

"I'm fine. Just sore. We're just about there, you know?" She looked into Ally's eyes and smiled.

"Yeah?"

"Absolutely. They're about to put it in writing that they're firing Leppert. Do you know how great that is? And I have one other thing I want them to include in the conditions. I was just thinking, there needs to be zero tolerance for this shit. Old man bangs an eighteen-year-old, they're fired," she said, her breath hot against Ally's cheek.

"But we don't even know where Buffy Campbell is." Ally shook her head.

"Yeah," Sarah said, standing. "I realize that. But she ain't out there or they wouldn't be asking me if they could speak to her."

"What if something happened to her?"

"Nothing's happened to her. She's here," Sarah said, motioning with her hands and looking at the ceiling, the walls.

"We need to think harder and smarter. You know those built-in benches, the ones in the alcoves? All these old places have storage spaces. She's hiding somewhere. We'll find her. Can you get up?"

Ally detected a certain irritation in Sarah's voice. She doubted that Sarah was even aware she was irritated. This particular sound in another person's voice was as familiar to Ally as her own. Naturally, on some level, Sarah thought she was pathetic. Self-destruction was a whole lot less alluring to most people in the flesh than it was when they could read about it in memoirs, or watch it depicted by young, pretty actresses.

Ally's gaze followed Sarah down the hall. The back of her head looked imperious and the way her weight shifted from one haunch to the other, assured. Ally started to get up. Feeling something prick her butt she reached around: a lone silver earring. Dangling it from between her fingers she considered the small oval. It could be anyone's, though its smallness suggested otherwise. Baines students, the female faculty, wore long beaded earrings that they'd designed themselves or picked up at craft fairs. Stylistically, this was much more along the lines of what Buffy Campbell would wear; the glint of silver would catch people's eyes, just barely and on the sly. Ally looked up and down the hallway, then at the ceiling. Standing, she palmed the earring. She was willing to bet that Buffy hadn't run downstairs as they'd first thought but was up here, hiding, as Sarah had said.

"I'll be a sec. I'm gonna look around this part of the hall again. I might've missed something," Ally yelled to Sarah.

Sarah's head popped from the dean's office door, leaning into the hallway, "Good," she said. "We need to be able to produce the goods for this to work." A big smile spread across her face. Raising her eyebrows, she added: "I'm going to chant some more. It'll buy us a little more time and freak people out."

"Cool," Ally said, nodding.

The window clapped open in prelude to Sarah's vocalizations, both guttural, and you thought, at first, vaguely recognizable, but you thought wrong. Actually, she sounded like a deep, resonant bell, intoning over and over again.

Ally decided on the direct approach. It was still possible, she thought, to win Buffy over, or at least convince her that cooperating with them was in her interest. Which it was.

Chanting herself, she sang as if to a child: "Come out, come out, wherever you are. I know, I know, you're not very far. Buffy Campbell?"

At timed intervals, every three beats or thereabouts, Sarah pounded her fist against the wall or the desk, something deep and ominous-sounding that lent her chant an inspired and primitive stroke.

Falling into the rhythm, Ally repeated the line until she was dizzy with it.

"Come out, come out wherever you are. I know, I know, you're not very far."

She closed her eyes, losing herself in the various sounds, and especially that of her voice, which was timeless, not entirely her own. This is much bigger than you, she thought. You're part of something. A movement. Be grateful. Namaste, Namaste.

Swaying, she pictured the tiny earring cupped in the small depression of her hand, like a pearl resting in the folds of her skin. Counting backwards she advanced through the hallway: ten, nine, eight, seven, six, five, four, three, two, one, and opened her eyes. She remembered something she'd mostly forgotten about—how the Manor was supposedly haunted by monks and freed slaves, their spirits swirling around like the many strains of music now pitched in the air. Two semesters ago there was this Wiccan student named Maxine, and she'd held séances and played around with an Ouija board in a crawlspace or a closet. The escaped slaves had hidden somewhere. Ally didn't know the story really, had just overheard things that sounded mythic and made-up but might be neither. It would explain where Buffy Campbell had gone. She stopped singing and slipped the earring into her jeans pocket. To her knowledge, she'd already checked all the closets. They were obvious hiding places anyway, so where the slaves had hidden wouldn't look like closets. They'd look like nothing at all, or something else. An expanse of plaster. A large mirror hiding an entranceway, like in old movies. Placing her palms against the wall, slowly Ally began to walk its length, feeling for indentations, a plank of wood different from the others, something irregular.

"I know, I know, you're not very far. Come out, come out, wherever you are."

Amongst Women

So creepy. For a moment, Buffy had to wonder if she was having au-
ditory hallucinations. Could she be? Was that even possible? A high-
pitched, girly singsong snaked in through the walls.

"I know, I know, you're not very far. Come out, come out, wherever
you are."

It was Ally's thin, needling twang. Sarah had commenced moaning,
chanting in a heady Esperanto. Together, they formed a macabre two-
part song.

Buffy reached for the poker, making sure she knew where it was.

Layers of thick black air continued to surround her. She could be
in a deep, dark wood, on its floor, down below trees thousands of years
old. Could be, but she was not. The room was so small it sewed panic in
her limbs. Its claustrophobically lowered ceiling and the too-close walls

seemed on loan from a dark fairy tale, each segment threatening to advance inward and smother her.

Not having prayed since she was about nine, it was odd, interesting, something, anyhow, how well she remembered the words to the *Hail Mary*.

"Holy Mary Mother of God pray for us sinners now and at the hour of our need."

Or was it the hour of our death? She hoped not, but couldn't recall and stuck with "need."

Turning on her side, Buffy scrunched her knees into her chest, protectively curling herself into the fetal position around the poker and her baby, who hadn't moved in the last forty minutes, since she'd secreted herself away. Or was it even longer? She wondered how long the baby was usually this quiet. Each time she decided that on occasion it was as long as an hour, two, she backtracked. It was never that long, or hadn't been since the fourth month. Along with the terror of her unmoving baby, Buffy's breath kept catching in the back of her throat so that she couldn't draw a full measure of air. Maybe there wasn't enough in this little room? Rationally speaking, she knew this was impossible. But nothing about this morning had been rational. Maybe along with rationality, oxygen had been leached from the air she breathed, siphoned off, and in its place a scratchy wool substance that clogged her throat had been pumped in. The thought of coarse wool led to thoughts of orangey pink waves of fiberglass, which in turn made her itch in addition to making her feel as if she was suffocating. A high, gasping sound escaped from her mouth, like she'd just popped up from many fathoms under the sea. Fortunately for Buffy, at the precise moment the small protest issued from the back of her throat, Sarah began to pound on an available surface, the walls or a table, in between and among her plaintive wails. While the new, ominous banging came in handy, adding a whole other realm of noise and distraction to the proceedings, it also made Buffy want to scream. The drumming intimated that they were coming to get her and tie her to a stake in primitive ritual, she their sacrificial goat, lamb, mother-to-be.

Why was this happening? What had she done to deserve these two? She breathed deep into her belly, the faint whiff of dirt filling her nostrils, and sat up, to the extent that she could. Anger drained from and then deserted her. Regret filled the empty space.

Why hadn't she just gone along with them from the beginning? Looking back, she didn't understand the impulse that had made her run. At the time it had seemed the right thing to do. But now? Not really. What would have been so hard about pretending to throw her lot in with theirs, in female solidarity? Though it had been a while, she'd acted before, and these two wouldn't be hard to fool. Plus, while she hated them, she got it. She was a female. An academic who'd seen firsthand how male professors couldn't keep their hands off their barely legal female students. A mother-to-be, her daughter would eventually be viewed by men as "ripe", there for the picking. Couldn't she feel solidarity, if not with these two, then with the overall shitty way women, girls, were used? In a twisty and angering way, if you followed the girls' rage back to its source, men were responsible for this mess, and Dean Leppert had triggered this particular landslide, this shit-show. The seer, Cassandra, had the wrong man or men. At least this time.

Buffy had never heard Sarah's poems, but she'd heard of them. They were famous campus-wide, even among students and faculty who'd just arrived. She'd produced a final project for her Mixed Media lab in which she read her work naked, images of young girls projected on her skin, and on all four walls of the Haybarn. Not teenage girls, Pablo had said, when he became the first in a long line of faculty to allude to the performance. Young girls would have been bad enough, but her slides were of children, three, four years old, their smiling faces circling around the walls and against her body, while Sarah's poems suggested that they might have been or were being raped by their grandfathers, fathers, stepfathers, their mother's boyfriends, brothers, uncles. The last slide had simply been a large mostly blank screen with the word SCREWED staring at the audience, the white of the projector light fully illuminating Sarah's nude body. Pablo had told her the story with awe in his voice that had momentarily transported both of them to the Haybarn. Once there Buffy was able to envision the darkened room with the diffuse shadows and feel how the audience was frozen in their seats. Real pain was very different from acted pain. People wanted to crawl away from it.

"It was amazing," Pablo said. "Amazing and horrible both."

The performance had made him wonder if so many little girls were actually molested. And he'd learned they were.

"You can look it up on Google, along with everything else," he'd said. "Little boys, too, but more so with girls. Almost twice the incidence. I mean, how couldn't I have known such a thing, or had I just not been paying attention?" He'd shrugged. "Which was what Sarah was accusing everyone of, right?"

Right.

Cunt-Daughter. The title intimated that to men, all females, even three-year-olds, were cunts. Or that's what Buffy took it, like a punch in the gut, to mean. Joined together, the two-word title was perverse and totally disturbing. In a way, it was genius.

Ally's story was less articulated than Sarah's. From the looks of it, Ally herself hadn't a clue what was up, either. She was an odd, floaty girl given to strange spells the entire campus had come to know as her dissociative episodes, because she alluded to them as such whenever she tried to speak and failed, in long and painful committee meetings. Her expression, like a fingerprint smudge, was blurred and unseeing. It occurred to Buffy that it was how you looked when you were in pain.

Dear God. Help us in our hour of need. Was the hour of need metaphorical? she wondered. Not the hour of death, necessarily, but all of life? Why hadn't she just gone along with Sarah and Ally? The path of least resistance? If she recalled, in physics and electricity, this was the natural, the good path. The one that made most sense.

Blessed is the fruit of thy own womb. Never could she forgive herself if something happened to the baby because she'd made the wrong choice.

"Buffy, Buffy?" She heard a man's baritone and sat up. It was a voice she knew but couldn't place, whispering on the heels of Ally's "Come out, come out, wherever you are," Sarah's moans, and finally, the flat thud of the drum beat.

Thankfully, Ally was so involved in her weird duet with Sarah, lost in the middle of the hallway, that she didn't hear the raspy male voice behind her.

"Buffy, Buffy? Can you hear me?"

Buffy's heart fluttered and the baby turned a full revolution like a tiny astronaut grazing her abdominal wall.

"Thank you," she thought. "Thank you, thank you, thank you." Closing her eyes her lips crumpled together and streams of tears fell across the bed of dried sweat, her face a sticky mess.

"Buffy? Are you in there?"

"YES, YES, I'm here," she whispered back. More like a stage whisper, but still. The girls had whipped themselves into some sort of crazy, deafening crescendo. Crouching on all fours and with the poker wrapped in her fist, quickly Buffy crawled from the hidden room and rose, her knees and ankles so stiff and sore that she winced. She blinked against the dark air just as the wood panel smoothly opened, and the starburst of Hal Wentworth's head stood on end and in silhouette. Their eyes met once she reached the beam of light emanating from the hallway; his were electrified along with his hair, but there was something else that she'd always seen in them from the time he'd first visited her in the hospital. It was pain, the real kind that you wanted to look away from.

He raised his right hand, motioning for her to stop and be quiet. Around his left shoulder hung a length of rope and in his hand, a boomerang. He looked to his left, and then waved her out.

About ten feet way Ally stood with her right ear pressed against the wall, eyes closed and her palms flattened, repeating the hide-and-seek song. Taking Buffy's left hand, Hal Wentworth launched the boomerang at the side of Ally's head, hitting her as she sang "wherever," so that the "ever" part of the word abruptly sailed from her mouth like a piece of food given the Heimlich, her head flung forward like a crash test dummy. Just like that, she was down and out.

Hal let go of Buffy's hand and quickly knelt to retrieve the boomerang, which he slipped in his belt loop. He hadn't told Buffy to stand perfectly still, but she froze, watching as he tied Ally's feet and hands together in the most remarkable pattern, his fingers moving over the rope like a magician's. She noticed that there was a length of it left over and assumed from its positioning that this was Sarah's portion.

Glancing over his shoulder at Buffy he nodded his head as if to say you can now move. She saw him notice the poker for the first time as she placed both hands around the handle like it was a baseball bat. He dragged Ally behind him, toward the dean's office. Buffy was a short distance behind the odd scene, not wanting to get too close but also wanting to keep Hal Wentworth near. In even measure, he took one step, two, all very stylized, like she'd seen on cop shows. Her gaze fell to the ruby red stilettos Ally wore. One dangled sadly around her left ankle, bumping against the floor. Her too-large free-box clothing billowed and fell in heavy folds under her arms and between her legs. She looked like a battered doll. A switch of blond hair stuck to her cheek, and a thread of blood leaked from her temple. For some reason it occurred to her that Ally had been a baby once. And now, she was this.

Hal stood at the threshold of the dean's office door, the light from within shining through the tufts of his unruly hair. Again he lifted the boomerang into position, skillfully winging it at the moaning, chanting Sarah, who must have turned just in time to see it. Instead of the second thump in the head that Buffy had anticipated, glass shattered at the same time that Ally came to, her voice straining, hoarse with fear. "Sarah, Sarah. Help me. I don't know where I am."

Hal Wentworth stiffened in the doorway and raised both his arms. Sarah charged, her palm fisted around a piece of broken glass. At first Buffy wasn't certain, as Sarah lurched from the room and toward Hal

Wentworth's face, whose blood rained against the wall when the two fell against each other, stumbling like drunken lovers. Reflexively, he grabbed Sarah's arm, and expertly jerked sideways then up. A cracking sound split across the air and Sarah's arm withered against her side as she began to scream. Blood poured from Hal's split-in-two upper lip, and dripped from Sarah's hand and onto the hardwood floor.

Buffy moved without thinking about it.

"Sarah, watch out, Sarah . . ."

Sarah ignored Ally. Instead she looked directly into Hal Wentworth's eyes and advanced. Her hurt arm dangled at her side. Buffy swiped at her knee caps and at then at the tender, puffy area at the back of her knees, the brass poker flashing in the murky hallway. Sarah fell backward, her head smashed first against the glass door knob, then the door jamb. Ally's cries sounded like high, thin hiccups. She lay thoroughly tangled in the net Hal had made for her, her fight gone. Sarah was out cold.

"Are you okay?" Buffy asked Hal, touching his shoulder with her free hand, the left. In the right she still held the poker. She wasn't putting it down. Not yet.

"I'm fine," Hal said, his voice calm, flat and assured. Buffy wondered if he knew that he was bleeding, his upper lip grotesquely swollen.

"You're hurt. Do you know that?"

Hal reached his hand to his face. The blood had quickly spread to his chin and neck, so that if you didn't know where he'd been cut, you might not guess.

"It's your lip," Buffy said.

Looking down at his blood covered hand, Hal said "I'm sure it looks worse than it is. I'm not in pain, he continued, almost clinically.

"Thank you," she said. "Thank you so much. You saved my life. Come on, let's get out of here."

Holding Hal's hand, together they ran down stairs, toward the furniture haphazardly assembled near the entrance.

"Help us, help us," Buffy yelled through the door, as she and Hal began to disassemble the mess of chairs first. She looked at the various people through the small window until she found Ash.

There were people who lost one another in a thousand, a million arbitrary and brutal ways every day. Buffy could keep it together for now, for the few seconds it would take for the bolt cutters to snap the metal locks, and she'd be okay after that too, but mixed in with her gratitude would be the knowledge that it could have turned out differently. That she, Ash, and their baby could all have just as easily fallen into the unlucky, unblessed column of life. It was when the chains broke, and as she and Hal Wentworth stepped from the door, that her own knees buckled and she fell, crying and laughing both, into Ash's arms. The poker fell to the ground and landed with a clink on the pea stone path. The crowd clapped, as if it were the end of a performance, until they saw Hal, slick with blood, his upper lip two sizes larger than normal, the blood darkening around the wound. Quietly, people moved out of his way and the emergency medical technicians approached Hal, one on each side, leading him off. In the moments before the other EMTs came for Buffy, she hung on to Ash.

Looking over his shoulder, Buffy breathed in the chill fresh air, her eyes drawn up, toward the sinister daisy chain of turkey buzzards directly overhead. To their left, perched high, a single crow somberly looked on before unleashing a volley of caws as she lifted from a tree branch.

Buffy closed her eyes as the first few snowflakes streamed from the sky. Slanting to the right, in only a few seconds' time, the precipitation picked up speed and numbers, the almost weightless flakes pricking her skin.

Sirens

Clyde took the fork away from campus, not wanting to deal with the impromptu Community Meeting that must account for the raised voices traveling up to the dorms from the lower gardens. Faded peace flags that announced the library trail entrance, flapped in the wind. Most of the tree leaves had been taken in a weekend storm, and the few that remained looked beaten. The ground was cold and wet. Shoving his hands in his jean pockets, he ran toward the library, the wind hitting him in the face and back.

Clyde was sure the women on campus had planned a spectacle that would dominate the morning, if not the whole day. Maybe a procession, carrying a white, old man effigy—something Bread and Puppet and third world—despite their existence in the first world. If his mother were here, she'd join in. He smiled at this incongruous—his uptight mom protesting at Baines—but probably true, vision of his mother. His mother, who now organizes and leads walking tours of Europe. His father has a second family, a young wife and two young children who, conveniently enough, live in San Diego. Far away. If it wasn't for Clyde, it would be like his parents had never met and married.

Years ago, his father, over dinner with guests from his office, said: "I think men mellow with age, and women get more neurotic."

General agreement, even one of the three women present said she agreed.

"You're the picture of mental health, *all of you*, his mother had said," raising her wine glass to each man in a toast, her index finger pointing around the table.

She pushed her chair out, like she might get up and leave. Clyde had silently prayed that she would not. There would be something unsolvable about leaving the guests, about leaving Clyde with them, too. It would be too much. She must have thought that, also. While the chair legs screeched against the parquet floors, she remained seated. Wine glass in hand, the pale yellow liquid sloshed. "That's just so *rich*."

His father laughed. Nervously, but also a little meanly.

The third woman present said, "I'd say there's a fair number of women who are driven crazy by men. Look around at all the violence, all the shit. That's you, men," she continued.

His father responded, "blame, blame, blame, yadda yadda, yadda. I'm tired of it, I tell you."

Seamlessly, his mother rose and was at the back of Clyde's chair, hands on his shoulders.

"Let's get you upstairs, sweetie."

Clyde doesn't remember hating his parents fighting. It was another thing they did, like his mom putting away the groceries every week and his father practicing his golf swing in his study at night. He doesn't remember much about his childhood. Mostly, he sees an image of himself as a little boy, four or five, in the backseat of the car, looking out the window and waiting to get somewhere, the silence from the front seat, from the space between his parents, oozing toward him.

✶✶✶✶✶

Clyde runs. He likes the feeling of tearing through the woods unobserved, branches reaching out for him, slapping him in the arms and face, the trees separating in front of his eyes. A dog barks. High pitched, urgent, the yelps evenly spaced, like a call. The dog is calling and Clyde runs faster, slipping a little on the smashed, fallen leaves, toward the sound of the dog, to where the sparse, twiggy, canopy of trees gives way, and the scant light there is in the sky breaks through and the path wends upward, toward the library and the stones and beads of the peace mandala, smeared in places with shit.

Charlie, the receptionist's dog, is on the library roof. Clyde meets his eye and talks to him, saying it will be all right, buddy. Charlie does not seem to see or hear him. Either he is blind and deaf, or he is so scared he's somewhere else. He is not himself.

Clyde recognized the roiling in his chest as his hatred for Tristan. For a moment he hears all the things he would like to say him, things he has tamped down over these past few months. Clyde's jaw sets, like a trap that will soon release.

There is ladder on the ground where Tristan probably left it. Clyde lifts it. It is unwieldy, and the plastic grips don't easily gain purchase on the landscaping pebbles around the building's perimeter. Finally, he balances the cold, heavy rungs against the wall and climbs, to the sound of the dog's rhythmic cries. Clyde talks to Charlie through the noise of his barking, like you would to someone in a coma, hoping you can get through.

He thinks that if the campus were a ship, it would be listing now, everyone else at the Cafeteria and Manor side, while Clyde would be on the whole other end, climbing a ladder to the mast? Isn't that what it is called? The dog flinches at Clyde's reach, then pees all over. The urine smells just like you would think yellow might smell, dull and loamy. It runs into the gutter, where it will freeze in the shape of a vein.

"It's okay, Charlie," Clyde says. He places his hand out flat, for the dog to smell. His mother taught him this. "It's okay, Charlie," he repeats. He climbs onto the roof with the dog and sits near him, thinking how saying "it's okay" goes both ways, from the sayer to the sayee and back again, a reassurance to all, and how it usually means the opposite.

Charlie ambles toward him. Luckily for him, the roof is flat and modern, or he would have skidded down the pitch. He is an old, ungainly basset hound. After a few seconds, he licks Clyde. One tentative slobber, then unabated thanks. Clyde's cold hand stings with the sudden warmth of the dog's tongue. Charlie's tail wags and Clyde looks back toward campus, which even though the trees are bare, he cannot see. It is the sound of sirens that makes him squint in that direction, and the start of the blowing snow, caught in pockets of wind, sent spiraling through the air.

Symbiosis

The EMT on the left-hand side of her stretcher was so young. Buffy kept staring at his clean jawline and long eyelashes. As she held on to Ash's hand she kept her eyes on the boy, grateful for his strength and the certain way he forged through the crowd. He didn't acknowledge individual people or say excuse me, and the invisible wall he seemed to have drawn around the stretcher made her feel as if she could breathe again. Silently he put his free hand into the air in a stop gesture, as the only African American news anchor in the state stepped toward them, her microphone clasped to her heart. She asked if Buffy had known the girls. Underscoring her rich, professionally concerned voice, a photographer snapped one photo after another, and a Baines student she recognized but couldn't quite place, shot video, holding the camera high and facing down, running slightly in front of her. Ash shielded her face.

The other EMT talked to her softly. "Are you in pain?" he asked kindly. "Were you hurt? Are you cold? We're just going to get you to the hospital and check you out. Make sure everything is fine with you and the baby."

There was about an inch of new snow on the ground. As their small procession cut through the throngs of people, Buffy noticed Cassandra toward the back of the crowd, her face sad rather than enraged, as she'd been earlier. The sound of the people and the newly pristine landscape came as a surprise to Buffy. Their existence only a few hundred feet from where she'd buried herself in a wall for the last two hours was something that she'd begun to doubt. Those hours seemed to have occurred in a no-man's land where people and trees and snow had no place.

Coming around the bend in the Manor path, at the spot where the now dead-looking bleeding heart bushes had turned brittle and gray, Buffy squinted at a hunched and hurrying figure she couldn't initially make out. Only when she heard the name "Charlie!" did she realize that someone was trying not to let go of the old Bassett hound's collar as he strained ahead of him.

The ground shook and Buffy lifted her head. Two ambulances idled on the concrete drive that wended its way around the upper gardens and down toward the Manor. Hal Wentworth was in the first ambulance, sitting upright and talking to the EMTs. The snow blew around and the sun came out. Not a warm sun but brilliant and fast moving, like time-lapse photography. She heard what sounded like a gunshot. No one else seemed to notice. People got used to the sound around here. Hunting season ran for a few more days, until November 29. She'd taken note of the end date at the country store near her house, grateful that it was nearly over. During the past month Buffy had occasionally pulled in behind a truck with a deer tied to its tailgate, its glassy eyes not as lifeless as she might like.

Four state police officers hurried by. Buffy imagined they would take over for the town cop she'd recognized from traffic duty. Probably hand-cuff Sarah and Ally as the TV crews filmed their parade from the Manor to waiting cars and people in the crowd snapped pictures with their cell phones. The busy scene fell away as they slid her into the ambulance. Ash sat on one side of her and the young EMT sat on the other. The second EMT closed the doors and went up front with the driver. Inside the cab it was quiet. The light was dim, trapped in a ghostly fluorescent ceiling strip like you'd find in a gas station restroom. It was cramped with the three of them. Four, actually. Buffy felt the baby kick and float around, once again a tiny astronaut in her mind's eye. Softly Ash told her how they'd be at the hospital soon and how her parents and his were on their way. The red light circled the small cab as they pulled out of the Baines College parking lot. For the first time she knew what had happened inside the vehicle, and she didn't have to imagine the worst. Ash leaned over and kissed her forehead and she tried but wasn't successful in smiling. In-stead of being able to smile she thought of Hal Wentworth, of his rescu-ing her and the mess of his face. She wished she didn't have to deal with seeing him again, or anyone. Instead, she wished she could check out from the hospital and disappear. Simply leave Plainfield, never go back to their rented home or to campus. It wasn't just Hal Wentworth that she didn't want to deal with, but everyone connected with this morning and the days to come: the police and doctors and college administrators, her parents, Ash's parents, too. Herself. Now, of all things, her life had been distinguished by a kidnapping. She knew that few of the people she was to encounter in the hours and days to come would be as comforting in their reserve as the EMTs.

The baby kicked and the ambulance came to a stop. The EMT and Ash both stood, hunched over in the cab, preparing to disembark. Ash extended his hand and shook the young man's, thanking him. Buffy felt emotion rise in her chest. It was perverse how good people wouldn't exist without bad. They defined one another.

The doors opened and cold air rustled beneath the heavy hospital blankets in which they'd wrapped her. The second EMT climbed back into the cab and together he and the boy with long eyelashes lifted her out. The sun streamed from the sky, blinding her in a way that she'd never found unpleasant. Buffy had always liked looking into the sun even though it was supposed to be bad for you. In its diamond rays she felt singled out. She loved the way the light rippled the air, and the quiet. To slip into the sun like that and let it fill your eyes, it was as close to disappearing as you could get.

Death Mask

Soaring into the light, he called and the murder of crows silently drifted into the high tree branches, knocking narrow threads of snow onto the ground. For a long moment he was absolutely silent. Landing next to a dead body he carefully stepped around its limbs, then called again. Three abrupt caws. Two other crows landed. Then five others followed by too many to count. The snow turned black with their bodies, the deep purple sheen of their feathers iridescent in the sunlight. He jumped onto the body's chest. His talons stuck to the fabric as if he were walking through mud. He began to peck at the left eye. Another crow landed. She also cawed. Two or three others set down and then flew off, all trying to reach the right eye but acutely aware and observant of the first crow's possession. A couple of others used their beaks like needles, pricking at either side of the body's bloody mouth, then tearing off pieces of deep pink skin. Thirty others loitered around the body's hands and its feet, disappointed that it wasn't covered in eyes. They were easy. They could be extracted in a few deft movements. The crows heard the turkey vultures perched in a nearby tree hiss at the sound of something moving through the woods. All at once the murder lifted into the sky, except for one. He was slightly smaller than the first crow but larger than the rest, and he took this opportunity to linger momentarily and alone, long enough pluck the right eye from its socket. He worked the orb down his gullet like he would the viscera of a small bird or a squirrel, and then roosted in the tree with the others. Quietly they waited. The buzzards began to wheel through the air, preparing to dive at the body. When they were on the ground a few seconds, the crows harassed and pecked at them until they retreated. Returning to the body, or more specifically the face, the crows took what was left of the eyes. Again, the buzzards hissed from the trees. As a large object threw its shadow against the bright snow, the vultures swept up into the sky, circling once before disappearing. As if connected by invisible strings, the crows too ascended, leaving behind the ghostly, eyeless face of the man.

Ugly Song

"SEXUAL HARASSMENT PIGGIES. GET YOUR MOTHER-FUCKING HANDS OFF US, MOTHERFUCKERS."

The hallway was dark and full of people. No one yelled except Sarah. The others spoke in low voices and moved quickly in and out of the bit of light thrown from the lamp above the third floor stairwell.

"MOTHERFUCKERS, SHITHEAD MOTHERFUCKERS."

First the recitation of her rights, then silver handcuffs, each delivered to Ally's back as she lay face down on the floor and inhaled the earthy smell of the carpet. Out of the corner of her eye she saw the cuffs flash in the brown hallway air. Like pincers they fastened onto her narrow wrists, and the young female officer asked her to stand up. She walk-pushed Ally down the stairs, like she was resisting. But she wasn't. Ally was just so tired. She'd seen the stripe on her pressed slacks, the leather holster with a billy club, and a handgun. She knew how easy it was——not as easy as if she were a black man or woman—but still. The cops could shoot you in the time it took your heart to beat. Ally looked up toward the ceiling as they neared the front door at a water stain like a Rorschach splat. On the first floor, the officer leaned down and said, "If you don't get up and walk I'm going to drag you to the car, do you understand that?" Her eyes peered at Ally from under the deep brim of a Smoky the Bear hat, her face a total blank. Ally said nothing.

"Okay then. We're about to leave the building. I need you to stand up. Do you hear me?"

The words washed over Ally, and then away. She stayed dead weight as the cop dragged her from the manor. Chilly fresh air, a few heavy snowflakes whirled around in crazy patterns. Baines students crowded together on the pebble path just outside the entrance and fanned up and out in all directions. They called her name and reached toward her. Some of them cried. They were told to stand back and out of the way by the police officer. Ally's shirt bunched up. The ground was wet against the small of her back and her bare feet. The sun held no warmth. Its white color made her skin livid and hypersensitive.

From behind her the first few lines of Sarah's "Our Grandfather" poem: "Grandfather Rapist. Cunt daughter. Hallowed be thy name. Thy will be done. Thy will be done. Forgive us our trespasses. Amen."

Sarah repeated the lines over and over again so that it became a chant, a song with beats and measures, etc. An odd, ugly song. Sarah's song.

The crowd had also begun to chant, led by Kayla. "Al-ly, Sar-ah. Al-ly, Sar-ah. Al-ly, Sar-ah." Hundreds of feet stomped together like they were at a rock concert. A voice on a loudspeaker asked them to disperse, and a daisy chain of police with their arms outstretched tried to herd them away. The voice from the loudspeaker told them to go back to their dorms and wait there until they were contacted. There would be a meeting. The crowd went wild. A girl from Fisher Dorm that Ally barely knew fell to her knees. Tears streamed down her cheeks; she implored of them: "ARREST THE RAPIST, ARREST DEAN PERVERT."

The Al-ly, Sar-ah chant gave way to the ARREST THE RAPIST one.

A black woman with a microphone yelled questions into the air and a photographer aimed his long lens at Ally as the cop continued to drag her toward one of the waiting police cruisers. Tristan Walsh had joined the press, not shouting, but talking to her like they were buddies.

"Hey, Ally, are you and Sarah fucking or what?" His lips curled knowingly, a sneer rather than a smile.

From behind her, she heard Sarah yell, "Crawl back under your rock, you slithery bastard."

The police officers finally yanked on her arms, and up she went, in time to see the crowd break through the police-arms barricade and rush into the Manor House. Someone threw the disgusting trash can with an ashtray on top, the one that stood just next to the entrance, through a window. Glass from all the windows began to shatter, and you could hear the students stampede up the stairs from where Ally and Sarah and their respective police handlers had just come, crying: "rapists," "fucking rapists," and "motherfucking rapists."

There were things no one else knew about Sarah. Omissions in her poems that were almost like decorum. About getting pregnant by a married neighbor when she was fourteen. The abortion. An ectopic pregnancy at sixteen, when she got pregnant again, by one of the many boys in her neighborhood she'd slept with, and had lost an ovary. It was easier, Ally thought, to shock readers with "Grandfather Rapist, Cuntdaughter" than to write about all that had really happened. Or maybe it was just that words that told Sarah's story in any sort of normal way, like this awful thing happened then this one, would never do. It wasn't that kind of story. It was mythic and dark. It was triggering. It had triggered all this.

When they reached the police car, Ally turned as much as she was able with the lady cop nudging her toward an open door, and she looked back at the cohesive and angry wave of people, students mostly, women and men. The black reporter was run-walking alongside of them, asking Ally if it was true they'd kidnapped Buffy Campbell because they opposed reproducing. Ally's bare feet, totally numb, purply and ringed with gray-blue cold spots, were the last thing in the car as the officer shoved her headfirst into the backseat. Through the tinted windows she stared at the sun. It took her eyes a few seconds to adjust and to be able to see anything but the way the rays penetrated the silvery glass. Once she could see again, it was like looking at a living negative. She saw the reporter thrust her microphone at Sarah as she was folded into another cruiser. Two ambulances pulled out of the lot. There were three vans with local television station logos painted on their sides parked at the Baines entrance, and people and cars everywhere. Even at this distance Ally could hear the riot in the Manor, the dean's now hoarse voice through the megaphone, people swishing here and there. The cruiser pulled out. Ally again concentrated on the sun coming through the window, letting all the rest, the trees and the oncoming traffic, go all blurry and unfocused.

She smiled. For the first time in a long time she felt happy and unafraid. This was it, really. What she'd wanted from life all along. Everyone agreeing and screaming about the shitty way things were, about the fuck-ing rapists. It was like a war, was what she thought, between the kids and the adults and men and women. It was the story that couldn't be told in a normal way, being told. That people didn't want to hear what children and women had to say, regardless of how they said it, was a given. Along with all the other activism stuff she'd learned at Baines, like the how-to-let-them-drag-you-to-the-cruiser-perp-walk, was that finding your voice was only the first step.

———————————————

Blood

All night the wind managed to whistle through the plywood that maintenance had installed in each of my broken windows. The moment Dean Myers stepped back into his office, as if he sought the third eye or a touchstone, his gaze had traveled directly to my small stained-glass piece, hoping it was intact. When he saw it was not he averted his eyes quickly, as if to say that's that, and sat down. He had two space heaters going, the squat silvery one next to his feet and a tall ceramic heater on the other side of his desk, aimed directly at him. Also, on the phone with someone or other, he said how he couldn't believe any of it. All night the dean wept as he spoke to colleagues and old friends, and then at five in the morning he wrote his letter of resignation. To the last person with whom he spoke he stated that he was resigning not because he believed he was to blame. The various scenarios seemed to transcend individual blame. His resignation *was a courtesy, he said sadly. The honorable thing to do. He knew the board would likely ask him to stay on until they found a replacement or at least an interim dean, and that was all well and good, but he wanted to send the message right away to the parents and students and faculty that he understood that he was a scorched-earth dean, and would be leaving.*

Throughout this call the dean squinted to get a closer look at what might be someone's blood as he spoke nonstop about the events of this day. Was it Buffy Campbell's or Ally's or Sarah's or the unfortunate Hal Wentworth's blood in that small, swirly pool that had just caught his eye, or merely the blood red of his ornate Persian and not human blood?

"I must be imagining things," he said, ostensibly to the person on the other end of the line, but more likely, to himself.

He continued, explaining that his new day, like the one that had just passed, would also be full of awful phone calls. Plus, he had to make some kind of public statement about David Leppert, who'd shot and killed himself in the middle of the neighbor's field. The neighbor, an old, silent man, who, for all these years and against all odds, Baines had managed to keep in its good graces. Dean Myers rubbed his eyes. He didn't know why, but he kept seeing the old man's hands holding the phone, his mouth, speaking into the receiver on the sort of phone call you've heard a million times on TV shows, or, more recently, on CNN. The sort of call you hope to never make, involving a dead body and blood everywhere. It wasn't the sound of the gunshot that had brought the land owner out into the field, he'd told the police, but the crows and turkey vultures.

"No classes today," he said into the receiver and laughed. Not because it was funny, but the thought of classes suddenly seemed laughable, that the idea of them could exist in the same world as this new off-the-edge-

of-a-cliff one. There would be lawsuits. The pregnant Buffy Campbell and The exploited Candy Johnson. Some attorney had already contacted Dean Myers, said that he was sending a letter of representation for Ms. Johnson. There might be a class action against Baines for negligence. For triggering. Think of it. Sexual harassment, the Manor house riot, and the suicide of the Dean of Admissions. Emotional suffering all could lay claim to, rolled up in one big florid lawsuit.

"And did I tell you about the dog?" the dean said as an afterthought. "I think I should end on that note, since it's the only high one of the day. Our receptionist Nellie's dog, was saved." He said that the beginning of the day seemed so long ago, that the Community Meeting about Dean Leppert and Candy Johnson had seemed enough for one day, frankly, when the switchboard operator had darkened his doorstep, tears streaking her puffed-up cheeks. Her dog Charlie was missing. Well, like a relatively insignificant parenthesis, now he is found. Albeit on top of the library roof, howling his head off, by weird little Clyde, of all people. One of Baines's most likely active shooters, according to some faculty, had climbed up a ladder to rescue the old dog. The dog and the boy were unharmed, thankfully. Hopefully, Nellie and Charlie won't sue, too. The other member of the Matrix Twins, that horrible Tristan boy, had sold video to TMZ of Buffy Campbell and Hal Mayforth tumbling out the front door of the Manor, and of Ally and Sarah being arrested. Baines had helped him find his calling. Perfect for him, the dean said, almost, but not quite, under his breath.

Pausing, Dean Myers rubbed his eyes and stared at his daily planner, at the meeting times and dates jammed into the too-small Monday, Tuesday, Wednesday, Thursday, Friday squares. He saw that he'd penciled in Buffy Campbell for today at lunch, before Community Meeting. His fingers hovered over the twelve forty-five to one pm sliver. He hadn't remembered this until now, he said into the phone. Just a day ago she'd been a young faculty member who he thought was a bit shy and conventional for Baines. Someone who would last here only as long as it took her to find another teaching job, someone he would have largely forgotten in couple of years. Now, all that had changed. It was funny how things could just change like that, he said. Also funny was how when the world fell apart, things like meetings and classes, the sort of things we generally filled our lives with, how they looked flagrantly absurd. It begged the question of what else we should be doing with our time, didn't it? The dean laughed again. Then he began to cry and hung up the phone.

The sun is up, though not able to penetrate the newly boarded windows on my first floor. The maintenance man installed ugly plywood sometime in the night. This was after my siege and the stomping of the police and firefighters, up and down my old, creaking stairs.

My windows were smashed with rocks thrown by the mob gathered outside, just as the girls who'd been holed up in the Dean Myers's office were dragged off. A flood of sirens and people's yells and blasts of cold air washed over my floors and walls. With all of that, it has been the sound of the night wind buffeting the wooden windows that has exhausted me, finally. I imagine what I must look like from outside. A building on its way to being condemned. It is the only dawn ever that I have not loved. It has always been my favorite time of day, when, before the arrival of the students, the faculty, I pause to consider the silence and in doing so find a measure of comfort.

Baines has never been an easy place for me. The days are long and emotional, the undercurrent-hum in my rooms and in my hallways and stairwells, a lot like the unrelenting wind of the last six hours. But the sense that the ebb and flow of insight and creativity, of anger and sadness, that all of it led somewhere, and by somewhere, I mean to something different and good, an improvement on the present lot of people, that was what the hum was all about, what everyone was straining toward. Or that's what I've thought all these years. I don't know if I've been wrong so much as deluded. If any change in the world might be glacial, not to mention loud and violent and awful, rather than imminent or peaceful. That the 1960s and 1970s are long behind us is something I've not admitted, as if Baines had been able to carve out the place and time to which it was devoted, and had chosen to stay there.

Today for the first time, I wonder if Baines and by extension, if I, will survive to see anything bright or hopeful again. If my windows might not stay boarded up, emitting no light, each room filled only with the quiet of falling snow.

Acknowledgments

I would like to thank Donna Bister and Marc Estrin for their generosity and artistic vision, and to everyone who helped breathe life into these pages: Shelagh Shapiro, Jennifer McMahon, Susan Ritz, Kathryn Guare, Claire Benedict, Tamar Cole, Rebecca Williams, Susannah Noel, Anne de Marcken, Michelle Richter and Dawn Kearon.

Fomite

About Fomite

A fomite is a medium capable of transmitting infectious organisms from one individual to another.

"The activity of art is based on the capacity of people to be infected by the feelings of others." Tolstoy, *What Is Art?*

Writing a review on Amazon, Good Reads, Shelfari, Library Thing or other social media sites for readers will help the progress of independent publishing. To submit a review, go to the book page on any of the sites and follow the links for reviews. Books from independent presses rely on reader to reader communications.

For more information or to order any of our books, visit
http://www.fomitepress.com/FOMITE/Our_Books.html

More Titles from Fomite...

Novels
Joshua Amses — *During This, Our Nadir*
Joshua Amses — *Raven or Crow*
Joshua Amses — *The Moment Before an Injury*
Jaysinh Birjepatel — *The Good Muslim of Jackson Heights*
Jaysinh Birjepatel — *Nothing Beside Remains*
David Brizer — *Victor Rand*
Paula Closson Buck — *Summer on the Cold War Planet*
Roger Coleman — *Skywreck Afternoons*
Marc Estrin — *Hyde*
Marc Estrin — *Kafka's Roach*
Marc Estrin — *Speckled Vanitie*
Zdravka Evtimova — *In the Town of Joy and Peace*
Zdravka Evtimova — *Sinfonia Bulgarica*
Daniel Forbes — *Derail This Train Wreck*
Greg Guma — *Dons of Time*

Fomite

Richard Hawley — *The Three Lives of Jonathan Force*
Lamar Herrin — *Father Figure*
Ron Jacobs — *All the Sinners Saints*
Ron Jacobs — *Short Order Frame Up*
Ron Jacobs — *The Co-conspirator's Tale*
Scott Archer Jones — *A Rising Tide of People Swept Away*
Maggie Kast — *A Free Unsullied Land*
Darrell Kastin — *Shadowboxing with Bukowski*
Coleen Kearon — *Feminist on Fire*
Coleen Kearon — *#triggerwarning*
Jan Englis Leary — *Thicker Than Blood*
Diane Lefer — *Confessions of a Carnivore*
Rob Lenihan — *Born Speaking Lies*
Colin Mitchell — *Roadman*
Ilan Mochari — *Zinsky the Obscure*
Gregory Papadoyiannis — *The Baby Jazz*
Andy Potok — *My Father's Keeper*
Robert Rosenberg — *Isles of the Blind*
Ron Savage — *Voyeur in Tangier*
David Schein — *The Adoption*
Fred Skolnik — *Rafi's World*
Lynn Sloan — *Principles of Navigation*
L.E. Smith — *The Consequence of Gesture*
L.E. Smith — *Travers' Inferno*
Bob Sommer — *A Great Fullness*
Tom Walker — *A Day in the Life*
Susan V. Weiss —*My God, What Have We Done?*
Peter M. Wheelwright — *As It Is On Earth*
Suzie Wizowaty — *The Return of Jason Green*

Poetry

Antonello Borra — *Alfabestiario*
Antonello Borra — *AlphaBetaBestiaro*
James Connolly — *Picking Up the Bodies*
Greg Delanty — *Loosestrife*
Mason Drukman — *Drawing on Life*

J. C. Ellefson — *Foreign Tales of Exemplum and Woe*

Anna Faktorovich — *Improvisational Arguments*

Barry Goldensohn — *Snake in the Spine, Wolf in the Heart*

Barry Goldensohn — *The Hundred Yard Dash Man*

Barry Goldensohn — *The Listener Aspires to the Condition of Music*

R. L. Green When — *You Remember Deir Yassin*

Kate Magill — *Roadworthy Creature, Roadworthy Craft*

Tony Magistrale — *Entanglements*

Sherry Olson — *Four-Way Stop*

Andreas Nolte — *Mascha: The Poems of Mascha Kaléko*

Janice Miller Potter — *Meanwell*

Joseph D. Reich — *Connecting the Dots to Shangrila*

Joseph D. Reich — *The Hole That Runs Through Utopia*

Joseph D. Reich — *The Housing Market*

Joseph D. Reich — *The Derivation of Cowboys and Indians*

Kennet Rosen and Richard Wilson — *Gomorrah*

Fred Rosnblum — *Vietnumb*

David Schein — *My Murder and Other Local News*

Scott T. Starbuck — *Industrial O*

Scott T. Starbuck — *Hawk on Wire*

Seth Steinzor — *Among the Lost*

Seth Steinzor — *To Join the Lost*

Susan Thomas — *The Empty Notebook Interrogates Itself*

Paolo Valesio and Todd Portnowitz — *Midnight in Spoleto*

Sharon Webster — *Everyone Lives Here*

Tony Whedon — *The Tres Riches Heures*

Tony Whedon — *The Falkland Quartet*

Stories

Jay Boyer — *Flight*

Michael Cocchiarale — *Still Time*

Neil Connelly — *In the Wake of Our Vows*

Catherine Zobal Dent — *Unfinished Stories of Girls*

Zdravka Evtimova — *Carts and Other Stories*

John Michael Flynn — *Off to the Next Wherever*

Elizabeth Genovise — *Where There Are Two or More*

Andrei Guriuanu — *Body of Work*
Derek Furr — *Semitones*
Derek Furr — *Suite for Three Voices*
Zeke Jarvis — *In A Family Way*
Marjorie Maddox — *What She Was Saying*
William Marquess — *Boom-shacka-lacka*
Gary Miller — *Museum of the Americas*
Jennifer Anne Moses — *Visiting Hours*
Peter Nash — *Parsimony*
Martin Ott — *Interrogations*
Jack Pulaski — *Love's Labours*
Charles Rafferty — *Saturday Night at Magellan's*
Kathryn Roberts — *Companion Plants*
Ron Savage — *What We Do For Love*
L.E. Smith — *Views Cost Extra*
Caitlin Hamilton Summie — *To Lay To Rest Our Ghosts*
Susan Thomas — *Among Angelic Orders*
Tom Walker — *Signed Confessions*
Silas Dent Zobal — *The Inconvenience of the Wings*

Odd Birds

Micheal Breiner — *the way none of this happened*
David Ross Gunn — *Cautionary Chronicles*
Gail Holst-Warhaft — *The Fall of Athens*
Roger Leboitz — *A Guide to the Western Slopes and the Outlying Area*
dug Nap— *Artsy Fartsy*
Delia Bell Robinson — *A Shirtwaist Story*
Peter Schumann — *Planet Kasper, Volumes One and Two*
Peter Schumann — *Bread & Sentences*
Peter Schumann — *Faust 3*
Peter Schumann — *We*

Plays

Stephen Goldberg — *Screwed and Other Plays*
Michele Markarian — *Unborn Children of America*